MELISSA ADDEY

BENEATH THE WAVES

· THE COLOSSEUM SERIES ·

For Julia Legg
I love how you've built the joy of music and
dance into your everyday life and shared it with
hundreds of children over the years.

Have you read the Moroccan Empire series? Pick up the first in series FREE from my website www.MelissaAddey.com and join my Readers Group, so you always get notified about new releases.

The city of Kairouan in Tunisia, 1020. Hela has powers too strong for a child – both to feel the pain of those around her and to heal them. But when she is given a mysterious cup by a slave woman, its powers overtake her life, forcing her into a vow she cannot hope to keep. So begins a quartet of historical novels set in Morocco as the Almoravid Dynasty sweeps across Northern Africa and Spain, creating a Muslim Empire that endured for generations.

Download your free copy at www.MelissaAddey.com

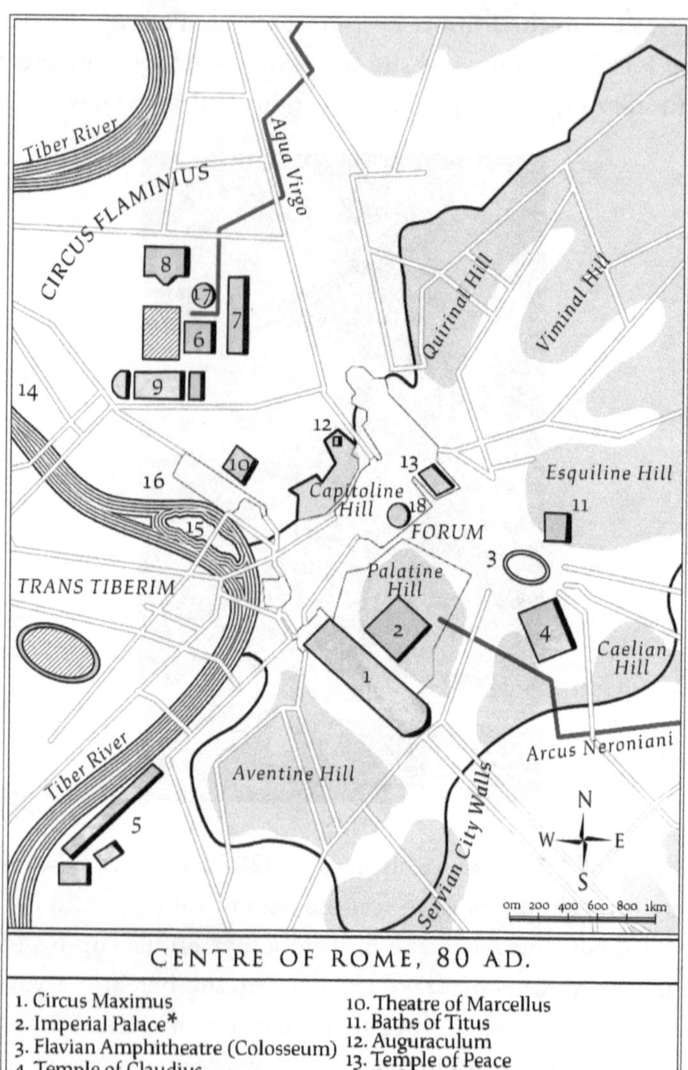

CENTRE OF ROME, 80 AD.

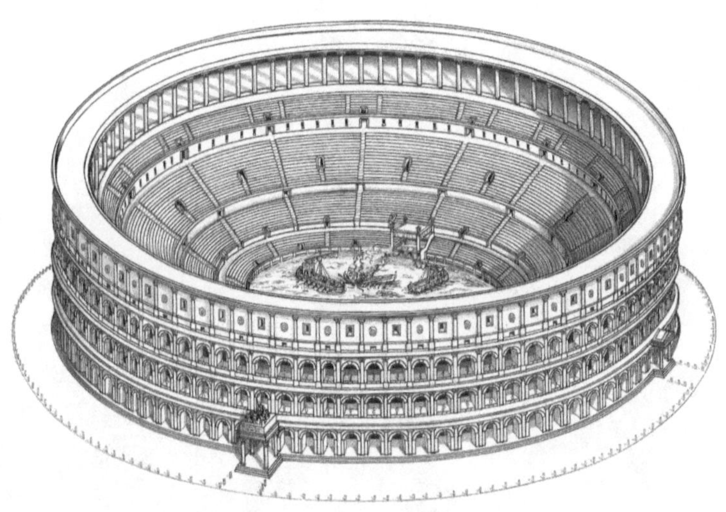

The Flavian Amphitheatre

BRIEF HISTORICAL BACKGROUND TO 80AD

I N 66AD THE ROMAN PROVINCE of Judea rebelled against Roman rule and drove the Romans out. Fearful that this might spark further rebellions in other provinces of the Empire, Emperor Nero recalled General Vespasian from exile (he had fallen asleep during a poetry reading by Nero) and sent Vespasian and his son Titus to quell the rebellion. This took four years, one quarter of the entire Roman army and ended in Titus' troops looting and burning the Temple of Jerusalem in 70AD. Hundreds of thousands of Jews were killed or enslaved during this period.

Emperor Nero died in 68AD, the last emperor of the Julian-Claudian dynasty. His reign was mostly associated with extravagance and cruelty, although he enjoyed popularity among the lower classes. He had a large area of central Rome cleared to create his Golden House, a vast palace complex with a lake. Rumours said the Great Fire of 64AD had been deliberately started by him to enable this project.

Following Nero's death came the Year of the Four Emperors, which culminated in Vespasian taking power in 69AD and founding the Flavian dynasty, which lasted twenty-seven years. He was the first emperor to come from the Equestrian rather than Senatorial rank and he set in motion a large number of building works, including the Flavian Amphitheatre, known to us as the Colosseum, which was located on Nero's now drained lake and largely paid for with loot from the Temple and the sale of Jewish slaves. Vespasian died in June 79AD and was succeeded by his son Titus. In October 79AD, Mount Vesuvius erupted, destroying multiple cities including Pompeii. In spring and summer of 80AD, Rome suffered first a "pestilence" (possibly malaria) in which 10,000 people died, and then a three-day fire. The Flavian Amphitheatre was inaugurated that summer, with 100 days of consecutive Games.

ROME, EARLY
AUGUST 80AD

THE AQUARIUS

I'M SPLASHING WATER ONTO MY face when the hammering starts. Marcus curses under his breath and pulls a pillow over his head, in a futile attempt to go back to sleep. I know better than to try. Once the builders start for the day it's best to get out of the insula as quickly as possible. It's hardly light when they start, even though dawn comes early in August.

Our whole life is filled with dust and the sound of hammers. For the past month the entire area around Virgin's Street, turned into a blackened ruin by the three-day fire at the start of July, has had to be torn down. All the wooden buildings went up in smoke and their remains had to be dragged away. Emperor Titus has pushed for the area to be regenerated as quickly as possible, not wishing for people to dwell too long on the multiple disasters that have taken place so far in his one-year reign. Town planners descended and agreed with local landlords where replacement buildings could and could not be built, aiming for the Ninth Region to join the rest of Rome in having larger streets and fewer buildings made of wood, to reduce the risk of fires in the future. The rubble and ruins largely removed, work has already begun on repairing any buildings, like ours, that are still standing. Important properties will be rebuilt and many new buildings will be created, mostly larger insula with more room for businesses on the ground floors. Every builder in Rome has more work than they can keep up with, plumbers and carpenters too. It's probably why they start so early and work long hours; they know they can get another big job as soon as our insula is finished. Still, at least when it's finished Marcus and I can return to our rebuilt roof hut, rather than sharing a cramped corner of the baker's family apartment.

"I'm going to Cassia's. Shall I order for you?"

Marcus grunts. I think it's a yes. He's not going to go back to sleep anyway, he might as well join me for breakfast.

CASSIA ROLLS HER EYES WHEN she sees me. "We'd barely pulled the shutters open, and the builders were here, wanting their breakfast," she says, yawning. "I'd only just got the fire going. Father's not even up yet, I had to manage by myself." She lifts a large pot of dried beans, soaking in water. She's about to make what she calls her weekly soup, a hearty mix of beans and vegetables to which she adds scraps of this and that as she goes along, including the bones of the meat she gets from the amphitheatre, for flavour. She keeps it simmering away over the week. Anyone who is hungry in our Region knows that they can come and ask Cassia for a bowl of hot soup and she will give them a generous portion, no questions asked. She does it without fanfare, her own small way of sharing plenty.

I lean my elbows on the counter as Karbo joins me. "Don't rush on our behalf, I don't mind waiting. I just had to get away from the worst of the noise. It's not as bad if you're not trying to sleep."

Cassia nods and disappears for a few moments, returning from the bakery next door with two large baskets of fresh bread, fruit rolls and cheese pastries, which she places just under the counter, ready to serve her customers. "The fire's hot enough now. Pancakes?"

"Yes," says Karbo. "Three."

"Three? You'll be sick."

"I'm a growing boy," says Karbo.

"You'll be growing width-ways if you eat three pancakes every day. Althea?"

I shake my head. "Too hot for pancakes. Fruit, please."

Cassia pours batter on the griddle, which hisses pleasantly while she chops up fruit. By the time Marcus joins us, Karbo has demolished two pancakes drenched in date syrup, while I'm slowly making my way through a plate of figs, sliced melon, and a large peach.

"Still got a sweet tooth, whatever the weather," Marcus comments, glancing at my plate.

"Have a fig," I offer as he bites into a cheese pastry. I hold one out, already pulled in half, its vivid green skin contrasting with the jewel-like sweet pink filaments inside.

He bolts it in one mouthful. "Good. Pass me another."

"Get your own," I tell him.

Cassia laughs as he tries to filch one from my plate. She pops two next to his half-eaten pastry. "Hungry work, is it, running the Games? You all eat like you spend your days labouring in the fields."

"I'll bring you two deer later," says Marcus. "Today's theme for the morning hunt is the goddess Diana with her hounds. There's over a hundred deer to kill."

"Are the hounds killing them or the woman?"

"Both. She's vicious with her bow, arrows in all directions, fast as you like. We've had to place extra supplies of arrows all around the arena so she can swap quivers."

"Well, venison will be something to look forward to. I'll tell Father when he gets up. He can spend the afternoon butchering."

Cassia's father was older than most when she was born. Now he's getting on, he is happy to spend his days chopping up meat and vegetables for stews to be served in the popina that evening, or decanting wine into jugs that can be poured by customers. He rises later than Cassia, and retires earlier, although he can be relied on to rise again should Cassia need help fending off unwanted suitors, not that she wouldn't be capable of wielding the stick he keeps for that purpose herself.

"Naumachia," I say to Marcus.

He chokes briefly on a crumb. "Must you repeat that word every single morning? You spoil my appetite."

"I'll keep saying it until you find us an aquarius."

"I don't have the time."

"Titus expects a naumachia on the final day of the inaugural Games," I say. "You promised."

"I regretted it immediately."

"You going to pop by the Palantine and let him know that?" Marcus sighs.

"Time's running out. We've already done thirty days out of the hundred."

"Will you stop nagging?"

"Find us an aquarius, then."

Marcus finishes his glass of cool watered-down wine. "Alright."

"Today."

"I've got Diana's hunt to oversee."

"I can do that."

Marcus' eyebrows go up. "And the execution afterwards?"

I swallow. Thirty days in and I still dislike the executions. "I can manage. There's just one."

"Fine. You manage that, I'll find an aquarius."

"Did you hear about the Jewish queen?" asks Cassia, busy pouring drinks for new customers.

Marcus frowns. "What about her?"

"She's in Rome."

"Titus sent her away when he became emperor last year."

"Well, she's back. Her ship arrived two days ago and yesterday she sailed up the Tiber in a barge. They said it was all covered with flowers and coloured awnings, Berenice was wearing a golden crown and beautiful silk robes."

Marcus shakes his head. "I thought Titus had more sense. The senators won't like it. So far, they're praising Titus to the skies. But none of them want some foreign queen thinking she can claim a place as ruler in Rome if she gives the Emperor a child. Cleopatra was enough trouble back in the day."

"She hasn't given him a child," I point out.

"Tricky to give him a child if she's not by his side," says Marcus. "Hence her visit?"

"She's fifty-two," says Cassia. "Much chance."

"She could adopt some likely child," says Marcus.

I eat the last slice of peach. "Let's go, Karbo. Marcus: stop putting it off. Don't come back without an aquarius."

Marcus sighs. "I don't know why the naumachia couldn't have been held somewhere else."

"Because the amphitheatre is more spectacular than a jumped-up pond."

"Augustus managed to have perfectly good naumachiae in a 'jumped-up pond', if you mean the man-made lake the other side of the Tiber. It worked just fine and it's still there if they cleaned it up a bit."

I shake my head and turn away. "Bye, Cassia."

She waves us off, one hand wiping down the counter, the other pouring wine with practised grace.

THE CROWD HAS BEEN SEATED, gentle pastoral music is playing, and the beast hunt is about to begin. In the gloom of the under-arena, Labeo, owner of the gladiatorial school that has provided our Diana, makes a few last-minute adjustments to her costume before she appears to the crowd. The woman playing the goddess is one of his best gladiatrices, a woman named Alyssa. She's over forty, her face is lined, but she's fearsome. Usually she takes part in the gladiatorial bouts in the afternoons, but her skills with a bow make her an excellent venatore for the hunts, so we sometimes bring her in for those too.

"I'll just pin it in place," Labeo says, briskly pulling her tunic down so that one breast is on show. Alyssa's of a tall and wiry build, her breasts aren't exactly large, but Labeo is now busy tucking the extra fabric tightly under the exposed breast, giving it extra volume and lift.

"Is she supposed to be naked?" I ask.

"Puts a smile on the punters' faces," says Labeo, a brooch held in his mouth while he finishes tucking the tunic into the right place and then fastens it. He tugs at her extremely long and thick hair, large parts of it no doubt bought from slaves and woven into place for these events, checking that it will not come undone. A goddess' hair can never be too long nor lustrous. "Alyssa has followers in that crowd who've lusted after her since she was sixteen and first went into the arena, they've still got a soft spot for her. Or a hard one, eh?" he adds winking. "Plus, it fits your execution story later, doesn't it?"

I grimace. "Yes."

"There you are, then. In you pop, my lovely."

Alyssa shoulders her quiver and steps into the lift. The two lifts either side of her hold twelve panting hounds each, snapping and growling at each other, eager for the hunt to begin.

"You have everything you need?" I ask.

She nods, her face set. I've never yet heard her speak, nor seen her smile in any of the rehearsals, nor on other occasions, but she's a regular headliner, comfortable in both the beast hunts and the afternoon gladiatorial combats, an unusual combination. Today she's wearing a gleaming white tunic, along with the cheaply gilded sandals and jewellery that will indicate her divine status to the audience.

I make my way back upstairs, reaching my designated watching spot, just to one side of the imperial box, today occupied by some distant family connection of Titus'. Watching me through specially designed grating set into the arena wall are Strabo and his team, awaiting the signals that usually come from Marcus. Today, I'm on my own.

The amphitheatre is two-thirds full, I'd guess. It's a hot day to sit in an amphitheatre that doesn't have awnings, the Emperor will not be attending, and the full crowd usually only turns out for the gladiatorial sessions later. Still, there's over thirty-five thousand people and we have a show to put on.

The space itself looks delightfully peaceful. There's a small grassy hill, various trees grouped into small groves and a pretty pool made with an extremely large, though shallow, wooden circular trough we had commissioned specially. It's coated with pitch, like a boat, to make it waterproof, then lined with blue mosaic tiles, to give a more attractive colour to the water. It's a good prop, we've used it on several occasions, and it hasn't leaked yet. Drinking from the pool, eating piles of grass laid out for them, standing in the shade of the trees, are over one hundred head of deer, mostly females with a few stags and a couple of fawns, just to complete the picture. Nervous this morning when we first sent them up in the lifts, they've had two hours to settle down and get used to the crowds as they entered. The music is mostly soft piping, combined with the trilling of the water-organ, in keeping with the forest idyll laid out before us.

I lift my hand and the music changes, dramatic drumming heralding the arrival of the goddess.

Diana rises from the floor of the arena, the lift trapdoor closing behind her, leaving her to stand on the small hill, surveying her domain while the crowd whistles and stamps at the sight of her, especially her partial nudity, which several shouts from the onlookers indicate has gone down well. She lifts her bow and pauses. She has been taught well by Labeo and her years of experience show, she knows how to work the crowd. When she does move, her arrows are so fast the crowd gasps, three deer already struggling on the ground, legs still trying to run, too late. I raise my hand again.

The hounds pour out, Diana raises her own arm in response as trumpets sound, as though commanding the pack. The deer scatter in alarm, but they have nowhere to run to, no woods to hide in, no streams to jump that might erase their scent. The hounds fall upon one animal after another, ripping at their throats, while Diana strides about, her arrows striking in all directions, one quiver after another exhausted.

The crowd love the combination, the glamorous goddess elevating what would otherwise be a simple hunt. Today I have only allowed a brief pause between the hunt and the execution, just enough time for most of the deer carcasses to be removed and the hounds dispatched back under the arena.

Now Diana drops her quiver and her bow. She makes her way to our blue pool and slowly, provocatively, removes first her golden sandals and then her tunic altogether, leaving only her jewellery to indicate her status. I wonder whether it's blasphemous to have a goddess stripping for a baying public like this, but clearly, she's a hit. She steps into the blue pool and stands, washing herself after the exertion of the hunt, turning on the spot so everyone gets a good view. Time for the music to change, which it does at my signal, the loud hunting music fading away to be replaced by an ominous low-pitched drumming, as a door in the wall opens and a man stumbles towards her. Our criminal for the day is a slave who stabbed his master. Now he finds himself re-enacting the story of the unfortunate young hunter, Actaeon, who saw the goddess Diana bathing naked and was cursed by her to be turned into a stag and hunted by her hounds, dying a horrible death for daring to glimpse her divine beauty.

Our Diana looks up and startles, as though the eyes of this one hapless man are suddenly more than she can bear after the gaze of thirty-five thousand lascivious onlookers. She holds out her hand to stop him approaching, then screams an inaudible curse and splashes water in his direction. The man cowers as she strides towards him and rams down onto his head a metal helmet without eye holes, shaped like a stag's head, complete with vast antlers. He tries to remove it, but he is already too slow. A rope swings into sight and Diana seizes it, is quickly lifted to safety over the wall, taking her place beside a startled senator in the front row as a lift trapdoor opens in the floor and a new pack of hounds are released.

These hounds don't care about deer. They have been trained for other purposes. They leap at the man, who screams and tries to run, but, blinded by the helmet, he stumbles and the hounds go about their business, tearing at his throat and belly. It does not take long. His limbs still twitch, but their work is done. The crowd applaud, well satisfied with this extended mythology linking the beast hunt and the execution. Now they hurry off to the toilets before the queues build up, or wave over food vendors, paying scant attention to the various dancers and actors filling in the time with light entertainment until the gladiators arrive in a procession for the afternoon's bouts. The senator who unexpectedly found himself with a naked goddess by his side looks delighted, even as Diana stalks away and back into the space under the arena, where Labeo will be waiting with her clothes and no doubt a warm welcome should the senator care to send a message asking for Alyssa's company one of these days. Labeo's a showman through and through, no better than a pimp, although a successful one, as the many golden rings on his fingers can testify.

The gladiators in the afternoon are a solid range of performers, we have one 'to the death' bout, dispatching a troublemaker the trainer can't be bothered with anymore, the rest put on a reliable and professional show. They come from Patronus' school and have been highly trained, even the newer fighters are never hired out until they've had a decent schooling in combat. The regular audience appreciates their skill and bravery, point out good technique and daring to one another, cheer on their favourites and, as usual, bet incessantly on possible outcomes. There's little to do during this part of the day other than watch the bouts, make notes about the next day's events, and answer any questions the team have.

WHEN I GET HOME THAT evening I see Adah's door ajar and

look in on her. She's busy dipping candles, so I settle myself on a wooden stool, looking about me. It is a sparse place, her silver seven-armed candleholder the only item of any worth. She has managed to polish away the soot that blackened it during the fire, and it takes up a favoured spot on a shelf, much like the Lararium does in my own hut.

The room smells deliciously of honey. Adah stands hunched over a pot of melted beeswax, set over a portable clay stove in which burns a small fire, just enough to keep the wax liquid for dipping. She has twisted strips of papyrus and now is dipping them over and over again into the wax, building up layers. Her candles are in demand for use in temples, and add a little money to her income from the honey her bees make.

I tell Adah about the Jewish queen arriving. "I'm sorry for Titus," I say. "They say he really does love her but had to send her away. She must love him too, to come back when she knows she's not welcome by anyone but him."

Adah tuts in disapproval. "Why would she love a man who desecrated her own place of worship? She only wants to secure her own status." She makes a dismissive sound. "Enough of these people. We should give thanks we have good people in our own lives." She pats my hand with her wrinkled one. "Time for you to marry," she adds, as if this has been an ongoing conversation between us.

"Oh? Who am I supposed to marry?" I ask.

"There are good men in the world," chuckles Adah, showing a rare glimpse of humour. "If you know where to look."

I shake my head. "Then I must not be looking about me enough," I say. "What I need is sleep. It's been a long day."

"Perhaps you will dream of him," says Adah.

"What nonsense," I say.

"Dreams can foretell the future," says Adah.

"My future is already foretold," I say. "One hundred days of Games for the people of Rome. Nothing else is happening in my life until they have been delivered."

THE TABBY CAT WHO HAS taken up residence in the amphitheatre has given birth to kittens. Karbo is curled up next to the rags the cat has settled into, stroking the kittens with the tip of one finger.

"You'd think she'd be scared of the lions and tigers," says Strabo, "but she doesn't seem to care, lies right next to their cages and hisses at them if they so much as glance at her babies. Helps keep the rats down, anyway. She and her kittens are going to be the fattest cats in Rome. Eh, Domina?" he adds, having bestowed this name on her.

"Will you keep them all?" I ask.

"There's enough rats to go round even if she had another litter after this one," says Strabo.

I make my way up a ladder and onto the arena floor. The spectacle is over for the day, the crowds have departed and now there's only the swish-swishing of brooms and gurgling water as the stone terraces are swept and washed by our cleaning team. Below the arena Strabo will be checking the animals' pens for tomorrow. I consider returning to the insula, but the dust today will be awful. Having removed the ruined top storey of the building, the builders have now started to rip off all the plasterwork, inside and out, including the interior stairs and the walls of every apartment. Nothing else will get rid of the stink of smoke. Meanwhile new waterworks are being plumbed in, which will improve the smell of the block's toilets and allow the plumbers to install a fountain in the centre of the courtyard. I'll be grateful not to have to carry water from the public fountains, but the digging required to lay the pipes means the courtyard is barely passable.

I take refuge from both the building works and the unbearable heat of early August in the shade of the cool stone corridors of the amphitheatre, sitting on the floor, my back leaning against a column with my knees pulled up, so that I can rest my tablet on them and write. A pale green dove wanders past, one of the five hundred birds we had dyed for the opening ceremony of the amphitheatre. A month later, they can still be spotted all over Rome, their once-white feathers now faded hues of the original brilliant colours we chose.

I look back down at the wax, which I'm surprised isn't melting in the heat, and re-read my notes, mostly relating to yet more building works. The barracks for the amphitheatre's slaves, located down by the docks, is in need of a lot of renovation. We took over two decrepit warehouses, one for the animals we cannot store beneath the arena floor, one for the slaves. We have over one thousand in all, employed in many roles including cleaners, toilet attendants, ushers, an animal-handling team, and the teams of men who turn each windlass lifts to bring animals and gladiators up to face the crowds. Strictly speaking, the slaves all belong to the imperial household, as we are all paid for from the imperial purse, but as they have been designated fulltime amphitheatre workers, they come under our jurisdiction. Both warehouses were falling apart, but now that the hundred days of inaugural Games have got underway, and we have a steady schedule in place, they are slowly being repaired and better laid out internally. We have built a cooking station and established a routine which means the slaves work in two shifts. The cleaners are not needed till late afternoons when the crowds have gone home, so they work on repairing the warehouses under the direction of a small team of professional builders, looking after the animals next door and cooking for their peers. The slaves working during the spectacles return to the warehouse once the Games conclude, to find food waiting for them and their own domestic tasks to take care of, including fetching water, preparing the sleeping mats for that night and the tools and materials for the next day's work. Marcus raised his eyebrows at the amount of time I spent making these arrangements, but I reminded him that I used to be a slave myself and he nodded and said no more. Besides, it's in our interest to have a smooth operation we can rely on, with this many people to manage. It's just as well we have a large workforce; we'd never have secured enough builders for a low-paying job like warehouses for slaves and animals when there's a whole Region to rebuild for good money. I could go and inspect the works in the warehouses, I suppose, but it's just too hot.

My eyes linger on the note about an aquarius and the thought of water makes me long for the baths to wash away some of the endless dust. My hair is lank with it. I pull myself up off the cool stone floor, walk back down to the arena, kneel on the sand and put my head down through one of the trapdoors.

"Is Fabia there?"

"Althea?"

"Do you want to come to the baths with me?"

She nods, then makes her way awkwardly up the ladder, her short legs struggling with the depth of the rungs.

"I'm sorry," I say. "I never thought about the ladders being difficult for you. Shall I get one of the carpenters to make one you can more easily use?"

She grins up at me, pulling her tunic back down where it

has rucked up during her climb, cheeks flushed pink. "It would help, though I'm used to managing without much in the way of special consideration."

"I need the baths desperately," I tell her as we make our way out. "I stink."

THE BATHS ARE A RELIEF. The hot rooms not so much, although rubbing down with oils and scraping off the dead skin and grime that has collected is satisfying. We help each other. The first time Fabia and I visited the baths together and saw each other naked I found Fabia's little body strange, but I am used to it by now, am more likely to comment on her unruly hair.

"Venus and Juno! How does your hair tangle like this when it's just been oiled? I can't get a comb through it."

Fabia giggles. "I don't know, it's a pain, isn't it? Tell me when your arms get tired, and I'll finish combing it myself."

"How's the work going?"

"Not bad. My father is so happy taking care of wounds again. Stitching away with a smile."

I laugh. "And you?"

She wrinkles her nose in irritation. "I help him, but I'm only an assistant, I never get to treat the wounds alone. The gladiators send for me and then when I arrive at the barracks it turns out they want their women seeing to, there's a baby due or a child with a fever or stomach-ache. They think a dwarf as a midwife is lucky, got the idea from the Egyptians. I want to do the same work as my father, but they insist on having a man to do it."

"Would he let you?"

"Father? Oh yes. I always assist him with the difficult cases, and he sends me on purpose sometimes when he's called for a stab wound or a broken nose, but I can tell they don't want me.

They let me dab them with vinegar if they get some tiny scratch, that's all."

"I suppose all you can do is keep trying."

She nods. "Let's go somewhere else. It's so noisy here." She's right. The baths are an endless source of noise. There are the grunts of men lifting weights and medicine balls too heavy for them, just to show off, as well as those who dive into the pools and then splash about with a lot of huffing and puffing, ignoring those trying to simply relax who end up getting sprayed in the face. There are people lounging in the water who, busy cleaning their ears out with a tiny metal ear scoop, are temporarily deafened and thus speak far too loudly to their friends. That's leaving aside the various cries of people advertising their wares and services, from the hair-pluckers to the cake-vendors. The prostitutes take a quieter but no less active approach, slipping into the water next to potential customers and murmuring in their ears about the delights that are theirs for the asking... and payment, of course.

We walk in the baths' gardens instead, which are cool and shady, then settle under a tree and call over a seller of drinks, sip some well-watered and chilled wine. Out here are mostly people playing board games, a quieter pastime. Fabia is a calm person to spend time with, a thoughtful woman. She tells me about some of the books she reads, educating herself further in medicine, even though the gladiators she would like to care for still doubt her skills.

"I'd better go and find Marcus," I say at last, though with reluctance. "See if he's secured an aquarius for us."

THE INSULA IS LOOKING MOST peculiar. The outer layer of plaster, cracked and chipped as it was, its paintwork fading to nothing and covered with graffiti on the lower walls, has all been chiselled off. The grouting is being refreshed, old mortar chiselled out and replaced with new, strengthening any weak parts. It looks exposed, fragile without its outer layer, even though it's being made stronger.

"Don't even say the word," warns Marcus with a grin when I find him having a drink at Cassia's. He looks fresh and rested, dressed in a clean green linen tunic that shows off golden-brown skin from months in the sun, his hair newly cut, beard trimmed short. "I've found someone suitable, and he'll meet us at the amphitheatre first thing tomorrow morning. Aulus Tuccius Merula's his name."

I make a note. "Strabo will be over soon with the deer," I tell Cassia.

Almost daily we have large quantities of animal carcasses to dispose of. Everything from commonplace hares, sheep and goats, deer, wild boars, and pigs, to the exotic zebra, antelope, rhino and more, all butchered after the day's show is complete. The best cuts and any unusual animals are sent to the Emperor and senators. A selection is regularly sent to the gladiatorial schools, our musicians, and other contacts. Most of the meat is distributed to the poor as a gift from the Emperor, to supplement their grain rations. They queue up outside after the shows. Some of the animals have an odd taste, mostly the carnivores, but the poor aren't fussy about what they receive and the imperial family like to try new flavours. In the past month I've tried bear, wolf, hyena, lion, and tiger. Overall, I prefer regular woodland and farm animals. As Marcus gets first pick, we must be some of the best fed people in Rome. We use the scraps, bones, and poorer cuts to feed the amphitheatre slaves, sending the meat down to the warehouse to add flavour to the thick vegetable and grain stews that make up the bulk of their food. As soon as the Games got properly underway Marcus made a deal with Cassia, he provides her with a generous daily supply of good quality meat, and in return she feeds the insula's inhabitants at a discount. She's a good cook and there's no shortage of meat, at least while the Games are on. Any animals who survive a show stay in pens below the arena overnight or are sent back to the warehouse until the next time they're required. We got through three thousand animals in the past month and no doubt we'll get through the same again for each of the two months to come. The skins end up in the tanneries just across the river from us, we catch whiffs of their working stench from time to time in the insula. Cassia's father has started salting and smoke-curing some of the excess meat we bring back, setting it aside for the leaner times of the year, after the Games finish.

I look down at my tablet. "Also, I need to check the list of animals with you for next week," I tell Marcus.

"No," says Marcus firmly. "I've had enough of work for the day. Tell me tomorrow."

"You work too hard," says Cassia over her shoulder to me.

"Yes," agrees Marcus. "She does. Tell her to ease off, Cassia." He waves as he walks away. "I'm going to see Fabius. See you tomorrow."

"What you need is a bit of fun," says Cassia when he's gone.

"What do you mean?"

Cassia lays down her spoon. "Look," she says, elbows on the counter, her earnest face close to mine. "You were only made a freedwoman less than a year ago. And since then, you've dealt with one disaster after another. But in two months the inaugural Games will end and then you'll have a quiet winter. You've been working so hard you might as well still be a slave. Soon you'll have a chance to have a bit of fun, think about what *you* might want in life."

"Oh, it's that easy? What do *you* want, then?"

Cassia grins, her cheeks a little flushed. "Maybe… maybe a husband?"

I raise my eyebrows. "Oh? Someone we know?"

She giggles. "No, I don't have anyone in mind. But a sorceress could make a charm to bring me one, what do you think? You, Fabia and I, we can go to the sorceress and ask her to bring us what we most desire."

"How do you know where to find a sorceress?"

"*The* sorceress. The one who lives three streets down from here. Just before the fullers'."

"I've never heard of her."

"Well, you haven't been here as long as I have," says Cassia. "But she can help us. She can bring me a husband, make the gladiators accept Fabia as a physician. And…" she gestures towards me "… do whatever you want her to do for you."

"I don't think I have anything I want her to do," I say, uncertain of what I am agreeing to.

"Nonsense," says Cassia firmly. "Everyone has something they want, and the sorceress will help us to get it. I'll get us an appointment, you tell Fabia. But keep it quiet, or we'll get in trouble for using her. She only sees people who are local, in case anyone tells on her for practising magic."

I head into the insula and run into Maria. After the wooden walkway and stairs went in the fire, she took to sitting in a chair looking out of her window, so she can continue to watch any interesting comings and goings in the insula. Occasionally, like today, she brings a chair down into the main courtyard for a better view.

"Sorceress?" she says when I mention Cassia's plans.

"Do you know her?"

"Oh yes."

"And?"

Maria thinks. "She knows things," she says at last. "But it's whether she'll tell you them."

"Meaning?"

"What she says isn't always clear until… later."

"Like most oracles?"

Maria nods. "Better not to know sometimes," she says. "Oracles can make you forget common sense." She folds her arms over her ample bosom with the air of one who can be relied on to keep her wits about her.

THE NEXT MORNING THE AQUARIUS is late.

"If he's not here soon he'll find himself taking part in the beast-hunt," mutters Marcus. "I've got a show to put on, I'm not standing around all morning for someone who can't be bothered to be here on time."

"You're so grumpy," I say.

"I'm fed up with hammers everywhere. They feel like they're in my head."

I nod.

"Marcus Aquillius Scaurus?"

We both turn, then look down. A man's head is sticking out of one of the trapdoors.

I consult my tablet to check I'm getting his name right. "Aulus Tuccius Merula?"

"Yes."

"What are you doing down there?" asks Marcus.

"Checking the drainage."

We walk closer and the man climbs out of the trapdoor to meet us. He has a satchel like the one I carry my writing implements in slung across his chest and once he's standing fully upright is revealed to be taller than Marcus but with a skinny frame and an awkward demeanour. He holds out a hand to Marcus and nods warily to me, as though he finds me frightening, then stands facing us, one foot crossed over the other, a position that looks hard to balance in. His eyes and hair are dark, but his skin is very pale, considering it's August. Marcus and I are already summer-brown and Karbo's black skin has gone even darker since the spring. I wonder if the aquarius spends a lot of his time underground, in drainage tunnels and water tanks.

"When did you get here?"

"Just after dawn. I've been measuring the amphitheatre so that I can calculate filling and drainage speeds. Depending which options we use, of course."

Marcus softens, now that he realises the aquarius wasn't late after all. "And what have you found so far?"

"The building's plumbing is excellent. You're using Nero's extension of the Aqua Claudia, it's a good source, nice water quality. Forty input channels where your water comes in, for the toilets and water fountains. Four drains laid in the base, they're very large, can tackle a huge amount of water. You could have a thunderstorm in here and it would cope, no problem, even on top of the usual drainage."

"Let's worry about filling it before we talk about draining it."

Merula rocks slightly on his crossed feet. "How deep does the water need to be, as a minimum?"

Marcus grimaces. "Somewhere close to the height of a man. Otherwise, the show ships won't have enough water to float, even though they're made specially for us, flat-bottomed, with wheels so we can drag them around in rehearsals. And it will look too shallow. But the problem is that if you only fill it to that kind of depth from the current base under the arena, the sightlines from the seating won't be as good. This wooden floor we're standing on sits at least four times higher than a man above the under-stage area, so the performers are usually much higher up."

Merula nods, his face serious. "But if you filled it from that base enough to have the surface of the water where the wooden floor is now, it would be very deep. It would take four times as long to fill – and drain."

Marcus shakes his head. "It has to fill and drain fast, or it won't be impressive."

There's a silence.

"Leaving that aside," says Merula at last. "The current base isn't waterproofed. It's just a big empty space under the arena floor, in a basic brick."

Marcus sighs. "The architect never got round to it, he died in the run-up to the inauguration and there just wasn't time."

"Well, it will have to be done if you want it flooded to any depth at all."

"The problem is that we have to complete one hundred consecutive days of Games, which means putting on a daily show. There are no gaps in the schedule. The whole area down there gets used every day: lifts for all the performers, props, animals kept in pens, people coming and going."

"I would need three days to have it waterproofed, to allow the mortar to be put on and dry. Can you keep that area empty for three days and still put on the shows?"

"I don't have much choice. And it'll be five days. One to empty the area of everything that's down there now, three days for waterproofing, one to put everything back. But Titus wants a naumachia and none of us is going to tell him he can't have one. Tell me you can fill it easily, at least," he adds, fixing Merula with a direct stare.

Merula opens his tablet. "There are several options," he starts.

Marcus' shoulders slump at the thought of extending this conversation and I give Merula an encouraging smile to make up for Marcus' grumpiness, but the aquarius is consulting the notes he has made and doesn't seem to notice either of us.

"Now, you already have a flow of water for your usual use: the toilets and water fountains within the amphitheatre. How many fountains?"

"One hundred," I say.

"So, with that many, if we used your usual water capacity, we could flood the hypogeum, as discussed, in about five hours."

Marcus, who has been looking bored, suddenly snaps back to attention. "Five hours? That's completely unacceptable. It must be *fast*. If it's slow it's just boring. And our toilets and water fountains can't be out of use during a show."

Merula doesn't seem worried. "Another option is to simply divert, for the occasion, all the water from the Aqua Claudia. That would probably fill it in two hours."

Marcus rolls his eyes. "Still too slow. Plus, the new Baths of Titus are opening the same day as us; they're just across the road and will be using the same water source. We can't shut off their water supply. Not to mention the surrounding homes and businesses that all use the Aqua Claudia, what will they have to say about it?"

Merula nods. "There's another option. Nero had a cistern built on the Caelian Hill to allow for a greater flow of water to his own private baths and fountains, as and when required. It's disused now, but we might be able to press it back into service, if it doesn't leak. It's about three hundred paces from here and the elevation in relation to the amphitheatre is substantial. So, we could fill it before the show and then use it to quickly bring in a large body of water. It could be flooded to the height of a man in half an hour."

"That's more like it," says Marcus.

"But it still doesn't address the problem of the sightlines," says Merula.

I walk to the edge of the arena and stand against the stone wall, looking up at the seating. Marcus watches me with a frown.

"What are you doing?"

"Just thinking."

"Thinking what?"

"This wall is higher than a man."

"And?"

I shake my head.

"I'll take any idea," says Marcus. "Whether you think it's ridiculous or not."

"If the entrances to the arena were sealed…" I start.

"We can do that."

"Could the flood start from this wooden floor, going up to the edge of the seating?"

Marcus looks down at his feet. "It's wooden boards," he says. "There are gaps between them. The water would leak away."

"Boats are made of wooden boards," I say.

"They're waterproofed."

I nod. "With pitch."

Marcus waits.

I raise my eyebrows.

"Are you actually suggesting we seal the entrances, waterproof the whole floor with pitch and then flood it?" he asks.

I shrug. "It would make the water level a perfect height. The senators and Emperor would almost be able to reach out and touch the water, it would be very impressive. So that's the sightlines taken care of. Plus, you can be using the arena and then have it flood. It'll start off shallow but get deeper right in front of them. In half an hour, like Merula says."

"And the waterproofing underneath?"

I shake my head. "You'd still have to do that because the water has to drain down into that space. But the drainage would be equally impressive because we can have a large drainage hole, or multiple holes, maybe even use the trapdoors as our plugs. The water would drain very fast when we open them but the audience wouldn't be able to see how. The floor will reappear."

"So, you're suggesting we seal the whole floor, but we'll only have the time between one show ending in the afternoon and the naumachia taking place the next day to apply the pitch?"

"We have over one thousand slaves in our team to apply it."

"It'll never dry in time."

Merula is listening, his head turning between us as we speak. His dark eyes are bright with interest, reminding me of the blackbird for which he is nicknamed. "Actually," he offers, "my father had a little boat, and a coating of pitch could dry overnight. One coating wouldn't last over time for a boat at sea, but for just one show, if it leaks a little it can be topped up. And," he adds with increasing confidence, "you'd only be filling and emptying the shallower depth. It would take half an hour in each direction if we use the cistern to flood and then the trapdoors to empty."

"The timescale and sightlines are good," says Marcus grudgingly, "But what am I supposed to do with boards coated in pitch after that?"

"It will be the last show of the inaugural hundred days of

Games," I remind him. "We'll have all winter to replace the flooring with clean boards."

"The gods give me strength. I was hoping to have a quiet winter, with absolutely no building works. Now you're saying we'll have to re-lay the entire floor? Jupiter, the hammering will never end!"

We wait.

"Oh, very well," says Marcus at last, tilting his head back and closing his eyes against the bright sun. "Pitch it is. Let's turn the floor of the greatest amphitheatre in the empire into a poorly-made fishing boat and spend our winter with a constant headache. This will teach me not to say yes to emperors and their ridiculous whims."

I DEPART WHEN THE CROWDS do, leaving Marcus the job of overseeing the post-show work, from the building being cleaned to the butchering and distribution of carcasses. The undertakers are just arriving. One gladiator was killed and will be returned to his school, where his companions will mourn him and arrange his funeral. The six criminals who faced execution today receive no such honour. Their bodies will be loaded onto a cart by means of the same hooks we use on the animals, before being dumped into a mass burial pit, denied the usual rites of death.

Merula has gone to search for the disused cistern, hoping he will find it still waterproof, which will give us a better chance of a dramatically quick filling of the arena, turning it from land to sea before the audience's eyes, as Marcus insists.

CASSIA HAS NOT GIVEN UP on the idea of a sorceress. When I return home a few days later with Fabia, she leads us both down the tangle of back streets at the end of Virgin's Street. The smell of the local fullery is very strong here and even from the street we can see the bobbing heads of the workers through its open gates, still stamping down urine-soaked clothes.

"Here," says Cassia, turning one more corner into a tiny courtyard.

The room we are ushered into by a silent slave girl is full of perfumed incense and lit with only two lamps, the window covered over with a red hanging, which both tints and dims the last of the daylight. There is a low bench with cushions and a large carved chair draped in a dark red throw opposite it, but there is no sign of the sorceress. We are all a little nervous, keeping close together, looking around us as though she is about to appear from thin air.

"I'll sit there, then, shall I?" says Fabia, nudging me and grinning at the chair.

"If you already know what you desire and how to achieve it, why not?" says a deep voice.

We startle. A woman appears, stepping out from behind a red screen set against a wall. She stands still, watching us as we scurry to sit on the low bench, Cassia to one side of me, Fabia on the other. We look up at the sorceress. She is tall, and her hair is a silver grey that falls loose around her shoulders, as though she were a bride. Her tunic is an unassuming and undecorated brown, but her palla, which is draped about her head and shoulders, is a vivid green and embroidered all over with leaves, as though she were a tree come to life. There is something about her that reminds me of Julia; the ability to stand entirely still and upright, without shifting from one foot to the other or finding something for her hands to do. They hang at her sides, relaxed. She does not cock her head to one side or change her expression, only looks at us.

Cassia finds her voice. "We have come for a charm," she says, a little too loudly.

The woman's eyes glimmer with what looks like amusement. "A charm," she repeats, as though this is an entirely new idea to her rather than what she makes her living from. "And what should this charm do?"

"We each of us have something we want," says Cassia, her voice quieter.

"And can you not get it by yourself? Three young, free women, with spare money for charms? It must be something very difficult that you each want."

"It is," says Cassia.

The sorceress moves and the three of us all shift closer so that we are now huddled together. I can feel Fabia and Cassia breathing too fast. The woman sits down in her chair, takes her time leaning back. I notice the subtle showmanship of this seating arrangement, the bench her customers must sit on built a little lower than is usual, the chair a little higher, so that she holds the power in this room, merely through her furniture. Marcus would approve.

"You first," says the sorceress, pointing to Fabia.

"I want to be a physician to the gladiators," Fabia says. "But they don't trust a woman, they want a man to stitch their wounds or amputate their limbs. They only send for me when their womenfolk need tending to."

The sorceress looks Fabia over. "They don't want you because you are a woman, or a dwarf?" she asks bluntly.

"Both, I expect," says Fabia sullenly.

"And are you capable of doing the work you wish to do?"

"Yes," Fabia says, lifting her chin.

"You are sure?"

"Yes."

The sorceress nods. "Then await your moment and when it comes, do not hesitate or it will be too late," she says.

"How will I know when my moment comes?"

"If you are truly a physician who can tend to the wounds that gladiators must face, you will know your moment."

"And if they refuse to let me treat them, even though they are wounded?"

"One will not refuse."

"What one?" asks Fabia, confused.

The sorceress smiles. "You ask too many questions," she tells Fabia. "Know this: when you are certain of your desires in this world, when you can speak their name without hesitation, as you have done to me, your moment will come and all that is required is that you recognise it is your time and step forward to claim what is rightfully yours."

Fabia gives an obedient nod, though she still looks a little confused.

"Now you," says the sorceress to Cassia.

"I want a husband," says Cassia.

The sorceress looks as though she is trying not to laugh. "That's not a desire."

"What is a desire, then?" asks Cassia.

"It is something you long for when it is not there. It is the thing the Fates wove for you the day you came into the world, that which will make you whole and certain of yourself. Your little friend there knows what her desire is, she has known it a long time, that is why it comes so readily from her lips, so certain. She has named her desire out loud, and once your desire is named, it is only a matter of time until it comes to you, for you have summoned it by its name and it will begin its journey towards you. Some journeys take longer than others, but once a desire has been summoned, it will make its way to you for sure."

Cassia looks put out. "I want a husband," she insists. "That's a desire. I desire a husband. There."

"You can open your lips and ask for a husband but then what? Will any man do? Was it any man the Fates chose to be your husband? Do you think them so slovenly in their work as to weave only the rough shape of a man and not name him, not single out the very one to whom your spirit will be bound, if it is a man that is your true desire?"

Cassia is growing impatient, scowling. "I want a charm to bring me a husband. You're a sorceress, you can make a charm for that."

"Words can be dangerous. Be careful how you ask for things. Do not ask for an empty shape, for you may not like what fills it."

"I don't like riddles."

The sorceress laughs out loud. "Think on it, girl. Find your true desire, not some vague thought you had in passing. When you know it, name it. Not just to yourself, not secretly and half-whispered, but out loud. When you know your desire with certainty, speak its name and its journey towards you will begin."

There's a silence. Cassia looks as though she would like to argue further but daren't.

"And you?"

The sorceress' eyes appraise me, her gaze unnerving. "I don't – I don't have a desire," I manage. After all, what is there I can ask for? Cassia's romantic notion of seeking a husband has already been dismissed. I have a job, a home, even my freedom, which I would have begged for a year ago, when I was still a slave. As for feeling whole, or seeking something the Fates wove for me… what would that be? Anything I think of would sound foolish, too small, set against such a description.

"A husband?" says Cassia, smirking.

The sorceress laughs again. "Your friend still does not understand," she tells me, nodding to Cassia, who flushes at the jibe.

"I never said a husband," I object quickly.

"She was a slave," Fabia explains. "She was set free less than a year ago, she is still new to life as a freedwoman. She has never made her own choices."

"Then she must learn what it is to be free. One step, one choice at a time. She must learn not to think like a slave. And when the time comes that she knows her own mind, she will name her desire. Out loud," she reminds me, smiling.

"How does one know a true desire then?" asks Cassia, stubbornly questioning.

"Because it will complete you. Because it will not require charms nor curses, only what is in you already. Because you will be certain. Specific. And all those around you will know it is right for you."

"But –"

The sorceress rises, still smiling even as she is clearly dismissing us. "Charms and curses are for those who find themselves powerless and must grasp at that which they do not understand for comfort."

"What do we owe you?" asks Fabia, ever practical, as we shuffle off our bench, keeping a wary distance between ourselves and the sorceress.

"You will pay me when your desire completes its journey. You will know when to come to me and what to bring with you in payment."

"THAT WOMAN IS VERY ODD," complains Cassia, once we are out on the street. It's late, growing dark. "I still think I should have been given a proper charm. Perhaps she's not a real sorceress after all. A *real* sorceress would have taken our money and given us what we wanted, there and then."

"What if I miss my moment?" worries Fabia as we walk back to the insula.

I stay silent. Fabia knows what she wants, even the hard-to-please sorceress seemed to think so. But I cannot name what I want, cannot look ahead into my future and name anything at all, only see what is already in my life: the amphitheatre, the insula, the people I know. I bid my friends goodnight. I think of asking Marcus for advice, but what would I say? And he might laugh at me for consulting a sorceress. Instead, I make my way to the small room I share with Marcus. He is already asleep. I lie down on my sleeping mat and try to recall the exact words of the sorceress, hoping I might suddenly understand her better, but I only confuse myself more and for a moment think I can smell her close to me before I sniff my tunic and realise I smell of the incense that swirled around her room. I fall asleep and dream strange dreams, of perfume and questions to which I have no answers. I try to open my mouth, but nothing comes out. I wake a few times, sweating in the August heat, my tunic clammy, and finally sleep more deeply, though I wake no less confused.

TITUS WILL BE AT THE Games today. We've saved up criminals for the executions for over a week so we can put on a good show at midday. The team all arrived early, and the seating is full. The crowds like to see the Emperor and the senators want to be seen by him.

The trumpets sound and Titus makes his entrance to loud applause, but Marcus' eyes narrow at once.

"What is it?" I ask, under the noise of the cheering.

"Berenice," he answers.

Sure enough, a woman is entering the imperial box and settling herself at Titus' side. She looks well preserved for her age, her dark hair elaborately arranged in towering curls in the latest Flavian fashion, as it's known, with a gold circlet fixed just above her forehead, emphasising her regal status. The crowd is not quite sure what to make of her; the clapping for Titus grows uncertain and fades away.

Marcus quickly signals for the beast hunt to begin. Hyenas chase down unwilling antelope before defending themselves against a team of dark-skinned venatores with spears, dressed in something approximating African dress, a deliberately exotic demonstration of just how far Titus' empire stretches. The criminals are executed in style, forced into fighting lions whom they have no chance whatsoever of beating, since their swords are blunt. The gladiators re-enact some of Titus' most daring military conquests in Judea, although the actual desecration of the Temple has been left out, the painted walls of Jerusalem merely falling in an obliging manner when his "troops" attack them, the inhabitants on the other side putting up a brief but compelling series of bouts and then kneeling in homage to their rightful ruler. Titus generously gives the gladiator playing the part of Titus-as-general his freedom, presenting him with a traditional wooden sword, much to the crowd's pleasure, as he's a well-known headliner with an excellent record of wins, nearing the end of his fighting life. Now set free, he'll be able to earn a comfortable retirement making guest appearances for wealthy patrons to liven up their dinner parties with very little risk to himself. The crowd is happy enough with the day's entertainment that they even give a good-natured small ripple of applause as Queen Berenice rises to leave, then a standing ovation for Titus as he departs.

CASSIUS IS BUSTLING ABOUT THE popina when we go for our evening meal, making small adjustments to just about everything, from where pots and pans are hung to tut-tutting over a chipped jug.

"What's got into your father?" I ask Cassia.

"We've got a cousin of mine coming to stay, name of Rullus. He wrote to say he'd like to visit us for a few weeks, help out in the popina. Father wants to make a good impression, show we're doing well for ourselves."

Fabia has joined us for dinner. "So you asked the sorceress for a husband and now a man is coming to stay with you?" she teases.

Cassia laughs. "He better be good-looking, if he's been sent by her."

WHEN I COME DOWNSTAIRS EARLY a few days later, Julia is standing in the middle of the street looking up at the building. Despite there being plenty of people around, no-one asks her what she's doing blocking everyone's pathway. Instead, they skirt around her, giving her a wide berth, nodding deferentially as they pass. A Vestal Virgin commands respect, even if she is retired.

"The new plaster looks good," she says. "They're going to paint the popina today, so Cassia will get a day off."

"I'll have to get my breakfast elsewhere then," I say. "I can't wait for all the building works to be over."

Julia gives a patient smile. "All in good time. Will you come to mine for dinner, since the popina is closed?"

"No thank you," I sigh. "I need to go down to the warehouses to see some of the repairs that need doing there. I'll be back late. But if you can feed Karbo I'd be grateful."

"Don't walk alone in the dark. Can't Marcus come back with you?"

"I'll be back before it's dark," I say.

"I'll make sure Karbo is fed and goes to bed."

"Thank you."

I DO LEAVE THE WAREHOUSES before dark, but only just, twilight has already fallen and I walk quickly back towards the Ninth. Rome's streets at night are not for the fainthearted, especially down by the docks. I feel better once I am away from them, but by the time I reach the start of Sand Street, it is really quite dark and I am relieved that the safety of Virgin's Street is not far away, although the shutters of Cassia's popina are closed tonight, this being her one night off each week when she does not run an evening service. I hurry towards the dim outline of the insula, grateful to be almost home. I can smell paint in the air and remember that the painters were due today, to start work on the outside of the building, though I can't see their handiwork in the darkness. I can only see the dim flicker of a lamp from Julia's courtyard, she likes to keep one burning till very late at night.

The man's hand is so swift that I do not even open my mouth and already it is sealed shut, his other hand twisting my right arm behind my back, dragging me against the outer wall just on the corner of Sand Street and Virgin's Street, opposite the gateway I was hurrying towards. I can smell him pressed against me, a sour-sweat reek that only seems to intensify as I struggle against him.

"Stay still, pretty, or it'll be the worse for you."

I jerk in his arms, kicking backwards with my right foot, left hand flailing behind me trying to grab at him, mouth still trying hopelessly to open. I feel as if I can't breathe properly and when he tightens his hold against my struggles I claw at his forearm, digging in my short nails as hard as I can.

"Futuo! I'll teach you a lesson for that!" he spits and pulls his arm away for a too-brief moment. I gasp for air, ready to scream but he cuffs my head so hard I stagger and this gives him a chance to grab me around the waist, shoving me hard against the street wall while pulling up my tunic from behind. But to do so he has to let go of one of my hands. I reach behind me and scratch his other arm, as hard as I can and he loosens his grip for one brief second. I turn to flee and he trips over my foot and stumbles, grabbing at my tunic but I kick out and run. The heavy wooden gate is open and I dart through it, not even pausing to shove it shut behind me, running to a corner of the courtyard where Julia is growing a vine and pushing myself against the wall so that I cannot be seen when he comes after me. I am shaking so hard I think he will spot me just from the trembling leaves around me, but he does not come through the gateway after me, as I expected. I wait, still shaking, still panting, but nothing. Nobody. I am alone in the dark courtyard and after a few moments I take one cautious step out from the vine and then another, creeping towards the doorway to the interior stairs and then slowly making my way up, looking behind me so many times in the darkness that I stumble more than once.

In the apartment, everyone is asleep. I tiptoe to the room I share with Marcus and lie down very quietly. The sound of his light snoring, the faint warmth from his body being nearby, is so comforting that I weep, silent tears sliding down my face. I breathe slowly and deeply, trying to calm myself. It is alright. The man did not succeed in raping me and now I am here, with Marcus beside me, safe in our room. I will tell Marcus everything in the morning and he will be on the lookout for the man, whoever he was. If he stays close by we will know him by my scratches on his arms, for I am sure, given his reaction, that I drew blood. At last my tears slow and then stop. When Marcus rolls over and stops snoring I move a little closer to him, to better feel his warmth and listen to his breathing now it is quieter, each breath a protection.

WHEN I WAKE MARCUS HAS already got up and left, so I cannot tell him what happened. But I will see him shortly, at the amphitheatre and I am not so afraid by daylight. Before I go to work, though, I must find Cassia and tell her too, so she can be careful herself and keep an eye out for any strangers she notices loitering nearby. I make my way out of the gate and am about to turn left but find Cassia right in front of me, standing in the middle of the street, arms folded as she inspects the popina, ignoring the traffic trying to get round her.

"Look at it," she crows, beaming.

The painters have finished their work for Cassius and the large counter that encloses the popina has been painted a strong dark red along the top, marked out with a bold yellow trim all around the side, over which have been painted, in bright colours, a crowing rooster and two mallard ducks ready for plucking, rosemary bushes, as well as a scene of a Nereid riding a horse through the waves, surrounded by all types of fish, placed near to where Cassia keeps her barrels of salted fish for the little saltfish fritters of which her customers are so fond as a snack between meals with a glass of wine. There's even a painting of a dog tied with a lead, into which image a couple of metal rings are set where the popina's customers can tie up their own dogs if they wish to take a seat inside and stay for a more leisurely meal.

I try to gather myself and focus on her happiness for a few moments before confiding in her. "It looks wonderful," I say. "When I think of how it was the first time I saw it..."

Cassia nods. "It was so run down," she says. "I used to think we'd have to move one day. But now that the whole building's been strengthened and replastered and painted... this is where I can spend the rest of my days." She beams at the rest of the building's exterior, the bare dried plasterwork ready to be painted in the usual white with a dark red band on the ground floor, against which her cheerful yellow will stand out, drawing new customers her way. "They'll be done in a few days."

"They're working fast," I say.

"They've got work available from now till next year's Saturnalia and beyond if they get each job done quickly, so it's in their interest to work fast."

"I wanted to tell you something," I say.

"What is it?"

"Shall we go inside?" I ask. I don't want to be talking about what happened last night in the middle of the street. I'm still a little jumpy despite the welcome light of daybreak, looking around me in case I should spot some unknown man, recognise my assailant.

"Of course," says Cassia agreeably, still smiling at the paintwork. "And you can meet my cousin."

"Oh, did he arrive this morning?"

"Yesterday afternoon."

I follow her. It's good there will be another man about, I think, especially for Cassia, who after all often has to work evenings and sometimes has trouble with over-familiar customers, who need to be reminded by Cassius that he keeps a big stick inside the popina for just such patrons. The cousin can help keep a lookout for any unwanted men hanging about.

"This is Rullus," says Cassia.

The man behind the counter of the popina is probably in his mid-twenties, of a sturdy build and with a wide smile. "Ah, you must be Althea, I've heard all about you," he says. "I'm very glad to meet you."

His voice sounds familiar, it must be because he's related to Cassius. I nod and smile. "And I you," I say. "Welcome to the insula."

Cassius comes bustling out of the back part of the popina. "Met our new family member, Althea?"

"I have," I say.

"So good to have another man about to help us," says Cassius. "I'm getting on, after all."

"You should be able to take things easy," smiles Rullus. "I can do whatever is required to help. You sit down, tell me what to do and I'll do it."

"Be with you in a minute," Cassia says to me. "Just sorting out the plates." She disappears from sight, ducking down under the counter. I can hear her shifting crockery about, preparing for a busy day ahead. I stand, shifting from foot to foot, still nervous.

"Excuse me," says Rullus, coming towards me. He is carrying a large pail of dirty water from the back of the popina. It's been used for scrubbing down the tables in the back and washing the floor afterwards, which Cassia does first thing every morning and now he is about to throw it out into the street. I step out of his way but as he passes I catch the scent of him and stagger backwards, grabbing at the counter.

The smell of him.

He smells like the man who assaulted me.

Cassius is burbling on about something from his table, but I can't really hear him. I'm staring at Rullus' back as he throws the water. When he turns back I look down at his forearms, where I scratched the man, where I drew blood.

His arms are scratched.

He is the man who assaulted me.

I hold the edge of the counter and watch him as he comes back past me, catch the smell of him again and swallow. He puts the pail away and tends to the fire but my eyes do not leave his forearms, where multiple scratches have freshly scabbed over since last night.

"I need to go," I say, my voice too loud.

"No breakfast?" says Cassius from the back. "Thought you'd come for your breakfast."

"No," I say.

"Unless you wanted something else," Rullus adds, hands on the countertop, smiling sweetly at me, but his eyes are no longer on mine, they have travelled down to my breasts.

"No," I say, backing away. "No, nothing."

"You said you had something you wanted to tell me?" says Cassia, popping her head up from under the counter.

"No," I say again. "Nothing. It was nothing."

I hurry away from the popina, back into the courtyard of the insula, see the open door of a storeroom the bakery uses and slip inside.

I am shaking. What do I do? I try to breathe.

One breath.

What do I do?

Two breaths.

Perhaps I was wrong?

I clutch at this idea. Yes. Perhaps all I smelled was the sweat of any working man, perhaps Rullus' arms were scratched by a stray cat or...

No.

I know it was him.

And he knows. His too-sweet smile, his words, *Unless you wanted something else...?* Bile rises in my throat for a moment, bitterness in my mouth. I force a swallow. Breathe again, forehead pressed to the cold bare plaster. Think. Think. The man who attacked me, who tried to rape me, is Cassia's cousin. How can I – *what* can I say? He arrives here, is a family member to one of my dearest friends and I must accuse him – without any evidence, only a few scratches on his arms and my say-so?

The cold wall is chilling me. Julia, I think. I will confide in Julia first, she will know what to do, she will understand.

"Althea?"

Julia is calling from the courtyard, like an answer to a prayer. I hurry out to her.

"Julia," I say gratefully. "Hello."

"I have to go, but I just wanted to check something quickly with you."

I want to tell her now, but this is not something I can tell quickly. It will have to wait. When she is back from wherever she is going, I will talk to her properly. "Yes?"

"I meant to tell you before: Adah will not take the second roof hut when it's built. She says she would prefer one of the small rooms on the top floor."

I barely understand what she's saying, it's so removed from what is important right now. I try to focus. "Probably for the best," I say at last. "Especially in winter, if you're coming or going when it's cold and wet. She's pretty old."

Julia nods. "So, there will be a spare hut and it seemed more fitting if Marcus lived in one and you in the other. I will put Karbo in with you, he has need of a motherly figure in his life, with Fausta gone."

I blink. "Did Marcus agree?"

"It was his idea."

She's already moving away with a brisk wave over her shoulder to me, through the open gateway and away down the street. For a moment I stand alone, staring after her.

No.

No, no, no.

I need Marcus near me. I need him, after what happened to me I cannot have him sleeping elsewhere. I hurry back out through the gateway after her. "Julia –"

"Get out of the way!" yells a passing trader and I jump aside to avoid being run over by his mule cart. Clearly, I do not have the traffic-stopping status of an ex-Vestal Virgin. I look about me, but Julia has already disappeared. I try to think my way through what Julia said but it only feels worse. Of course, if Adah is not going to take the second roof hut, it is sensible to suggest that Marcus and I should each have one to ourselves, and Julia is right: we are not a couple, so it is hardly proper that we should live together as though we are. I will have more space and the hut will be mine to manage as I wish. But to lose the comforting shape of Marcus after what has happened, and face whatever each night's darkness may hold all alone…

I ARRIVE LATE AT WORK. The familiar darkness under the arena feels uncomfortable, the vast shadowy space closing in on me. I tell Strabo to open up all the trapdoors. He looks puzzled but doesn't ask questions. Gradually the space lightens and my fears subside a little. I will tell my friends and they will protect me. Fabia is standing in the physician's area, preparing the space for her father.

"Morning, sleepyhead," says Marcus when he sees me. "Bet you're looking forward to not hearing me snore anymore," he adds, grinning.

I open my mouth to speak but he is already halfway up a ladder to the arena floor above us.

"What's he talking about?" asks Fabia.

"Julia is giving us a roof hut each. Adah will move into a room instead."

"You don't sound very happy about it."

"I'm... not."

"What's wrong with it?"

"No-nothing," I say. Strabo is standing nearby, checking animals off a list. I will confide in Fabia, but I don't want an audience.

"But you're not happy?"

"I just didn't..."

"Are you in love with Marcus?" asks Fabia, leaning forward and lowering her voice.

"Oh no!" I say, hastily checking over my shoulder that Strabo has not heard this suggestion. "No, no, I just... we... we got along fine there before the fire, sharing one hut..."

Fabia waits for me to finish a coherent sentence and then shrugs. "Well, you'll have more space," she points out. "And you're unmarried, you don't want word getting around you live with a man if he's not *your* man, do you? It would discourage suitors." She continues laying out instruments, each one neatly lined up in a certain order.

I stare at her tiny hands, not seeing anything, feeling again Rullus' hands on my mouth and pulling up my tunic, hurting me. "Suitors?"

"You might want suitors?"

"I don't... I haven't..."

Fabia laughs. "Are you going to finish any of your sentences today?"

"People keep saying things and asking questions I wasn't expecting!"

AND SO THE DAY GOES on. I stumble from one thing to the next, every time I think I might have a moment to speak with Marcus, or Fabia, there is someone else there or the hunt has started or the gladiators are about to begin the pre-battle parade.

When I return to the insula I skirt around the popina, slipping quickly through our gateway, hoping to avoid Cassia and especially Rullus.

"Met Rullus?" asks Maria as I pass through the courtyard. She's in her usual spot, watching everything that goes on in the insula, missing nothing. I wish she had been there last night but it was too late, she goes back to her rooms when darkness draws in.

"Yes," I say tightly.

"Seems all right," she says. "Polite enough. Won't be here long I suppose, just visiting family. Cassia said a few weeks."

My shoulders relax a little. Yes, perhaps he will stay just a couple of weeks or so and I can stay well out of his way, then he will be gone and no-one need be told anything difficult. After all, I escaped, he did not manage to rape me. I let out my breath in a rush. Yes. I need only avoid the popina and he will leave soon. All will be well.

THE NIGHTMARES START ALMOST AS soon as I have fallen asleep that night. *Hands grabbing at me as I try to open a mouth that is sealed shut, the overwhelming smell of sour-sweat and my own fear.* I jolt awake over and over, but each time I do Marcus is there, one arm over his head, peacefully sleeping, and I can listen to his breathing and sleep again, albeit briefly.

I AVOID THE POPINA FOR three days, eating elsewhere, making sure to come and go from the insula only in the full light of day, even though Marcus calls me a lazybones for not rising at dawn like everyone else. I stay at work as long as possible and when I get home each day I go to my room in the baker's apartment and stay there.

THE PLASTERING TEAM WORK FAST. By the fourth day plaster has been applied to all the inner walls of the insula's courtyard and is awaiting a decorative coat of paint to complete the work. Inside, one apartment and room after another has been worked on; most are now finished. The lingering odour of fire damage is slowly being replaced with the smell of wet earth from the plaster.

"The roof huts are complete," says Julia, appearing in the doorway of my room, where I am darning a tunic of Karbo's. "Do you want to go and see them? Marcus and Karbo are ready downstairs."

She leads the way with Marcus, Karbo and I walking behind her up the inside stairs.

"Will you put a wooden staircase back on the inside of the courtyard?" I ask.

"Yes," says Julia ahead of us. "I liked it the way it was and besides, having two staircases was a blessing during the fire. Then I can plant out my herbs and flowers again."

"They're bigger," says Karbo excitedly as we emerge onto the rooftop. He's right, the two huts are now larger, one set into one corner of the rooftop, the other diagonally across from it. Karbo opens the door of our hut and goes inside, exclaiming at something, but I'm distracted by Marcus, who has disappeared into his own hut. It's strange to be separated after everything that has happened over the past year, when we have slept in any tiny space available together, after we had both lost friends and family and faced the devastation of a volcano, of plague and fire. Julia, who has been looking out over the city, turns to me with her eyebrows raised and I make my way inside the hut, away from her gaze. She will be expecting me to be curious, to want to look inside my new home.

The larger space inside should be welcome but it feels too big somehow. The doorway is too wide, there is space to move quietly around without tripping over anything, without disturbing anyone until it is too late… my breath comes short. I put out a hand to touch the wall to give me back a sense of balance, to take away the dizziness that was sweeping over me.

There is room for the two simple wooden beds tightly strung with linen cords that Julia has had the carpenters make for Karbo and me, which will be more comfortable than the simple mats we have slept on thus far. There is additional space to keep clothes and any other possessions as well as shelves on the walls. The plaster is still bare but there is a new lararium on one of the shelves. It's very similar to the one I had Balbus the toymaker make for Marcus and me barely a month back. I recognise his painting style in the bearded serpent and delicate images of household gods set into a decorated wooden frame. In front of it are two tiny dolls, symbolising my dead parents. Marcus must have commissioned this shrine for me and put it here along with my ancestral figures, keeping in his hut the figures of his dead wife Livia and son Amantius, as well as the one of Fausta, his best friend and my mentor. Our odd little household of three, the straggling survivors of the past year, is now split in two, each with its own lararium, clearly indicating that we no longer share a common home.

"Going to need a lot of paint in here," says Karbo, who hasn't noticed that my eyes have welled up. "Are we going to decorate our hut?" he adds eagerly. "Can we have pictures on the walls, like a fancy villa?"

"I think a coat of white paint will do," I say.

Karbo looks disappointed. "I want chariot races on the wall," he says. "And a red trim around each picture."

I raise my hands. "If you know someone who can paint a chariot race on our wall for nothing, you can have what you like," I say. I can't face arguing with anyone, my legs feel shaky. I step out of the hut, only to see Marcus already disappearing into the stairwell.

"Are you happy with the hut?" asks Julia, walking over to join me.

"Yes," I say. I'm thinking about whether I can have a lock put onto the door, whether it would be strong enough to withstand a man, if he were intent on reaching me. Rullus could easily find out where I live, I cannot be too careful.

Julia is looking at me, expecting more. I want to talk to her about Rullus but Karbo is still close by and so I force a delight I do not really feel. "It's a wonderful space, so much more room. Thank you for the beds."

"Are you happy…" she begins again, and Karbo or no Karbo, I want to confess to her about Rullus right now. I want to tell her that no, I do not feel happy. I already feel lonely in this new arrangement, cast off from the only person I have clung to for stability over this past year, as all around me people I loved have died and left me to manage alone. I am scared of Karbo being given to me as though he were only my responsibility when I know nothing of being a mother, let alone to a nine-year-old boy who has spent most of his life on the streets. I am terrified to sleep in this new space alone, without Marcus by my side for protection, when there is a man who has attacked me living in this very insula, unknown to all except me.

I open my mouth to try and explain all this, but Julia is already finishing her sentence. "…for Adah to still keep her beehives on the roof? We saved one colony when they swarmed during the fire and someone else has given her a gift of a new colony, along with a hive, so that she can still sell their honey and beeswax candles to make a living. She does not need much, especially with Cassia's deal with Marcus, but the bees bring in a little money so that she can pay her rent and buy food."

"Adah?" I am bewildered for a moment, then gather myself. "Yes, yes of course, there is…" I wave my arms about without indicating anything in particular "…plenty of space, wherever she wants…"

"Thank you, I will let her know," says Julia and she walks away before I can summon up the courage to speak.

ON THE ROOFTOP, ADAH'S BEEHIVES have been put in place as agreed, two of them, facing out over the city, allowing the bees to quickly rise into the air as they leave their home and set out on their foraging missions. They have a clear path they use, which will not bother us. Karbo watches them come and go for a while, kneeling by the hives, curious about their tiny lives. Inside our hut, I place the extra lamp I bought onto a shelf, glad of the additional light. Our sleeping mats are now placed on top of the strung beds, giving us a luxuriously soft night's sleep. There is no need for covers just now, the nights are too hot. I would like to leave the door open at night but dare not. Instead I have a lock fitted to the door. The lock opens only from the inside, and I wear the key on a string around my neck.

"But shouldn't we lock the roof hut from the outside, for when we're not here and someone might steal something?" Karbo asks. "What's the point of locking ourselves in?"

"Good point," I say. "I'll have it changed one day when I have time to arrange it." But I don't. I don't explain because I don't want to frighten Karbo. His presence at my side provides a little comfort, but he is only a child, if Rullus were to find us, he could not provide any defence and might even be assaulted himself. I lock the door with care each night once he has fallen asleep, which thankfully he does quickly, then check and re-check it. I think that I would scream if Rullus broke in, that Marcus would hear and come running, but then I think of how Rullus clamped his hand over my mouth, how I could barely breathe, let alone scream. I touch the lock, to be certain that it will hold. Then I sleep, but often I have nightmares where I see the lock turning without a key and the door opening, before I wake with a start and have to reach out to touch the door again and be certain that it is closed in the darkness that surrounds me.

THE DAUGHTERS OF THETIS

THE BATHS OF TITUS, JUST over the road from the Flavian Amphitheatre, will soon be ready for inauguration, right on schedule.

"They're not on schedule," objects Karbo. "They were supposed to open the same day the Games did. That was more than a month ago. They're late."

Marcus grins and lays a finger to his lips. "We don't say anything the Emperor puts his name to is late," he says. "We say the Emperor has chosen to inaugurate it on the same day that we put on a naumachia. Water everywhere, by his command, see? A new baths complex for the people, an astonishing water show in his family's amphitheatre to complete the one hundred days of inaugural Games."

Karbo looks unimpressed at this lesson on imperial etiquette. He peers down at the baths from the second storey of the amphitheatre, watching sweating slaves in the burning heat of August transplanting full-grown trees and bushes into the gardens surrounding the building, while others paint the outer walls, transforming them into glistening white with a smart red trim and yellow outlines for doors and windows. "Late," he mutters to himself.

I look around me. The cleaners are sweeping down the tiers,

we're nearly finished. Today's Games were less well attended. With no main awning, only the most committed plebs, or the richer audience members with slaves to fan them and hold parasols, fancied braving the heat. I'll be grateful when we get to September and the days cool off a little.

A long whistle draws our attention. We look down at the wooden flooring at the centre of the amphitheatre. A trapdoor is open, and Strabo's head is poking out, blowing his whistle to summon us. There's a cluster of bodyguards standing around a man in a toga, standing in the lower tiers where the senators usually sit.

"Cack," says Marcus. "It's the Aedile. What's he doing here at this time of day?"

The three of us hurry down the steep flights of stairs to find the Aedile and his entourage waiting for us.

"Welcome," says Marcus. "Won't you step into the shade?"

We stand in the cool stone corridor, its paintings thankfully completed, at least on this tier. The topmost corridor is still being decorated whenever we get the chance, although its ceiling is low and dark compared to the lofty elegance of the lower tiers. The important people never have to see the topmost corridor, so it is only the height of an ordinary room, not the double, almost triple, height allowed for the tiers below. The painters get an hour in the mornings if they're lucky, then perhaps an hour or two in the afternoon when everyone has gone home, so progress is slow. Not that the Aedile cares, he's never asked to see the top tier, not even for the spectacular view of Rome it would offer.

"I am here on a delicate matter," he says, waving away Karbo, who is offering a tray with cold water and cups. Karbo bows with grace and then disappears behind the nearest archway, where I know full well he is listening to every word that is said.

"I am at your service," says Marcus.

The Aedile clears his throat. "The recent… *visit* of the Jewish Queen Berenice to the Emperor has…" he clears his throat again, "possibly been, ah, *extended* beyond what might be considered…" He stops.

"Appropriate?" suggests Marcus. I can see he is trying not to smile; he is chewing on the inside of his cheek.

"Indeed," says the Aedile, looking relieved. "Appropriate, as you say." He pulls a cloth from his toga and wipes his sweating forehead with it.

Marcus and I wait.

"You are holding a naumachia in early October, I understand? A grand finale for the inaugural hundred days of Games?"

Marcus frowns at the change of topic. "Yes?"

"Excellent, excellent. I was wondering whether, as a… a… discreet *hint*, as it were, whether it might be possible to, um, stage something which would, in its, um, subject matter, ah, suggest to the Emperor the advisability of the visit and… and indeed the, er, *relationship*, being, um, concluded."

"You want to me to stage a story about a man getting rid of the woman he loves?"

The Aedile looks appalled at Marcus' blunt summary but gives a wordless nod.

Marcus sighs. "Did you have a specific story in mind?"

"Odysseus and the Sirens?"

Marcus grimaces. "Tying himself to the mast of his ship so he could see their beauty and hear their songs but not be tempted to jump into the sea and join them?"

"It seems suitable?"

Marcus gestures to me and I make a note on my tablet. "I'll

see if there's something we can do," he says. "You can leave it with me."

The relieved Aedile retreats, no doubt to lie down in a shaded garden after his diplomatic exertions.

"The stuff these people come up with," mutters Marcus. "So now we have to find sirens? What are we supposed to do, go fishing?"

MORE THAN TWO WEEKS HAVE gone by and Rullus is still at the popina.

"Haven't seen you for ages, are you avoiding me?" calls Cassia as I try to slip out one morning.

Reluctantly, I make my way over to the counter. Rullus, thankfully, is nowhere to be seen.

"I was busy," I say.

"Too busy to eat?"

I try to smile. "How is Rullus getting on?" I ask, his name leaving my mouth with difficulty. "He must be going home soon?" I can't help adding, hoping to hear the answer I want.

"Can't get rid of me that easily."

I jump. Rullus has appeared from the back of the popina, from the storeroom door.

Cassia laughs. "You startled her!" she says.

Rullus gives an easy smile. "Ah, I'm sorry Althea," he says. "I wouldn't want to frighten you. We should be friends. Any friend of Cassia's is a friend of mine." He nods to Cassia. "Just checking on the saltfish stocks, be back in a minute."

Cassia beams. "Thank you, Rullus."

I glance at his arms. The scratches are gone, healed in the weeks I have held my tongue. My only evidence against him is gone because I waited too long.

He steps back through the door and I look at Cassia, who is beaming.

"He's very helpful," she says. "I hadn't realised how much I was doing on my own, now that Father is getting on. I'm glad he's staying."

My stomach suddenly feels heavy. "Staying?"

"He said he'll stay as long as we need him and Father and I agreed we could do with the help. And he's..." she trails off slightly, a blush creeping up her neck... "A good man to have about," she finishes awkwardly.

"I have to go," I say. "I'm late."

My feet are heavy all the way to the amphitheatre. I have left it too long. If I had told everyone what happened, at once, if I had shaken Marcus awake and told him, then Rullus would have been thrown out of here, family or no family. But now the scratches are gone and he has already made himself helpful, pleasant, embraced as a family member by Cassius and Cassia, even, judging by Cassia's behaviour, a possible source of romantic interest. This last thought makes me feel sick. I am not falling for Rullus' act, for his helpfulness and bright smiles. Beneath them is a man whose eyes slide to where they are not wanted, who takes what he wants, violently and in the darkness, while smiling in the daylight.

I sit on the arena floor, loaded with sadness and fear, trying to think what to do.

"I need these Sirens sorting out, Althea, can I leave it with you?"

Marcus' head is poking out of a trapdoor.

"Yes," I say. "Marcus?"

"Got to run. Need to see Bestia about these bears he promised, he sent a note saying they'll be late, I need a replacement. You alright with the Sirens?"

"Yes," I say. When he has gone I sit for a few moments in the empty arena, the vast space blurred by my tears. Then I get to my feet.

I MAKE ENQUIRIES, WHICH LEAD me, unexpectedly, to gladiatorial owner Labeo.

"I have just the thing. The *very* best. I won't even spoil the surprise. Just visit the Baths of Nero early in the morning, ask for the swimmers and see what you think. I promise you'll be delighted." He beams, adjusting a gold chain round his neck, the latest addition to his ostentatious jewellery collection.

"I didn't know you provided show swimmers," I say.

"I provide *spectacle*," says Labeo enthusiastically. "Which is, after all, what the Games are, wouldn't you say?"

I nod. Labeo certainly knows how to put on a show, though his enthusiasm for the unusual sometimes borders on the obscene. I can only hope that's not the case in this instance.

I set off the next morning in the opposite direction to Marcus, heading north past the heavily damaged Theatre of Pompey to the Baths of Nero, which managed to escape the fire. They stand in a wasteland of construction sites and still-scorched buildings, including the Julia Saepta. The outer walls of the baths are soot-stained but they are still operational. We've used them occasionally since the fire as the Baths of Agrippa that used to be our local were ruined. I've never been to the baths at this time of the morning; it feels empty, only slaves here and there, cleaning for the day ahead.

"You want the Daughters of Thetis," says a male slave when I describe who I'm looking for. "They'll be practising in the main pool. Through there." He gets back to his work, busy mopping the changing rooms.

It's odd being fully dressed at the baths. I remove my shoes and make my way through to the main large pool.

I peer into the room. The pool is empty, the water faintly rippling, perhaps from a breeze. I am about to turn away, return to the man and tell him he was wrong, there are no women in here.

But from beneath the rippled surface, a pair of legs suddenly appear, bolt upright, as though their owner is standing on their head at the bottom of the pool. And behind them are another pair, and then another and another, until there are twelve pairs of legs, now slowly, very slowly, opening wide until they are almost level with the water level. And then, as suddenly as they appeared, all the legs fold, crumple into the depths to be replaced by twelve heads. I step back, startled. In the pool are twelve women, now making their way to the side and climbing out. They are all wearing underwear and breastbands in a vivid red. Most of the women head away, towards the changing room, but one strides towards me. Her dripping wet hair falls as far as her waist in tiny braids like the Egyptians wear, but much longer, her skin is a rich dark brown, beaded all over with glistening water, as though inset with gemstones.

"I don't have room on my team for another girl just now," she says. "I can send you to another team, if you're looking for one." She is very tall, she might almost stand eye-to-eye with Marcus.

"I'm not here to join up," I say.

"Why are you here, then?"

"I wanted to hire you," I say. "That is, your team. Labeo said I should talk to you."

"For what?"

"A naumachia at the Flavian Amphitheatre."

"We don't do fighting. I told Labeo."

"We don't want fighting for this show," I say. "We want to stage Odysseus and the Sirens."

She gives a half-snort. "We don't sing."

"You don't need to. The singers and musicians will take care of that part. What I need from your team is a display of your swimming, after which Odysseus' ship will sail in and you'll re-enact his meeting with the Sirens."

"We don't do nudity."

I look at her red costume. "So I see."

"Gives people the wrong idea when we do private events."

I nod.

She thinks for a minute. "No funny business?"

I think of Fausta. This was a phrase she used to use and there's something in the woman's fierceness that reminds me a little of her, though she's younger.

I shake my head. "No funny business from our side. You'll have to manage Labeo yourself."

"I already do that." She holds her hand out, like a man. I take it. Her grip is strong.

"My name is Althea," I say. "Althea Aquillius."

"Vita." Her lack of a family name tells me she is a slave, owned by Labeo.

"I'm pleased to meet you, Vita," I say. "Your team are extraordinary. How long can you stay under the water for?"

She gives me a wide grin, suddenly less fierce. "A lot longer than most people."

"I've never seen anyone hold their breath for more than a quick ducking," I say.

"Most people can hold their breath for the count of thirty, maybe up to seventy. After that they struggle unless they've been trained. The best of us can hold our breath for over one hundred and fifty counts."

"That sounds like a long time not to breathe," I say.

"Have you tried?"

"I can't swim."

"It's not that hard to learn," she says. "But it's easier if you've been taught as a child, like most things."

"Were you?"

"I could swim like a dog paddles as a little child," she says. "The rest I learnt after seeing a troupe perform for Nero."

"You belonged to Nero?"

"I was one of his slaves. I was only a child, but he liked me because I had a good memory and could recite poetry at his events."

"What was he like?"

"He should have been born to an acting family," she says. "He'd have been happier and better off with less power and a lot more performing in his life. He got obsessed with it. The senators were appalled."

"And you saw a troupe of swimmers?"

"Yes, they came and performed for him once. After that I used to sneak into his private bath area at night and practise holding my breath and standing on my head in the pool. When he died there was chaos in the palace. Four emperors in one year. Slaves running off and all sorts, no-one managing the place properly, barely knew how many slaves they even had. I went to the troupe and begged them to buy me. Nero wouldn't have allowed it, but when Vespasian became emperor, he said there were too many slaves hanging around the palace with nothing to do and sold a bunch of us off. I thank the gods he was a plain-living man."

"And you stayed with that troupe?"

"No. They liked to perform at private functions and then pimp any of us out to the clients, if they fancied a night with a water-nymph." Her lip curls. "I heard about Labeo, how he liked to have unusual elements in his offering, went to him when I was fifteen and suggested he buy me and I'd set up a water troupe for him, train the girls myself. He could see the attraction for his wealthier clients with their own pools, for their dinner parties. We perform as the Daughters of Thetis and Labeo pimps out some of the girls who are willing to earn a little extra, but he knows I won't behave myself with the clients, so he leaves me out of it. Makes it harder to save up for my freedom, but it's not worth it. I've been whored out enough for one lifetime."

I nod, impressed that a slave child found a way to become a skilled performer and claw her way out of prostitution, at least, by coming to some sort of arrangement with Labeo, who can't be easy to manage. "I'll see you at the amphitheatre then, so you can see the space and what we'll need from your troupe."

She nods and walks away without further niceties.

I walk slowly back towards the insula, thinking about Vita and her life. I think of the sorceress and whether Vita's certainty of buying her freedom one day meets her criteria for a desire. I imagine it does. Again, I turn over in my mind what my own desires might be and again, come up with nothing, or at least nothing that seems as important as what other people are striving for. Vita for her freedom, Fabia to be respected by the gladiators as a surgeon, like her father. Even Cassia, whose request was dismissed by the sorceress, seems to me to be clear in what she wants to do. At any rate, she is clearer than I. What do I dream of, wish for? My freedom has already been granted, and yet it has left me confused. I would like to be rid of Rullus, but I cannot think how to do that. I feel I can no longer speak about what happened, that I lost my moment, now lack the confidence to accuse him with no evidence, with the question hovering on everybody's lips; why did I not speak before now? How do free people find the courage to live their lives and make choices? Perhaps the life of a free person is confusing. A slave has no need to ponder their desires, for they will not be fulfilled. They do not have the opportunities to make choices, all choices are made on their behalf, by their owners. I could say I chose to join Marcus in running the amphitheatre, but the truth is that I was given to him, an expensive gift, like a good working mule or an obedient and successful hunting dog. A slave woman cannot even choose how to dress, for her mistress will have a say in it.

Perhaps, I think, I should start with some small decisions, I should make myself braver in small ways. If a slave woman cannot even choose how to dress, then as a freedwoman I could choose what to wear. I have one nice set of a tunic and hair wrap that Maria gifted me, as well as one more set I bought myself, still decent but plain. But I have worn both of them a lot, having little else to wear. I have two pale blue tunics, from my days as a slave, but I dislike wearing them, even though the cloth is still good. They remind me of the time before my freedom.

THE POPINA IS CLOSED UP for the night and Maria says that Cassius has taken Rullus out drinking. I tell Cassia that I want to make new clothes, half-hoping that finally having some time with her will let me know what may happen with Rullus. She takes me to her apartment to show me her own clothes, pulling them out of the chest in which she keeps them. As a beloved only child, Cassia has accumulated more clothes than most women in this neighbourhood, five long tunics as well as accessories: belts of leather and braided wool, three pairs of shoes, plenty of hair ribbons and a handful of hair wraps, not the large and heavy palla of a married woman, but lighter pieces with which to tie up her unruly curls.

"This was my mother's," she says, pulling out a golden-orange bridal veil, carefully folded away at the bottom of her chest. "Father said I should keep it for when I marry."

"It's lovely," I say, touching it. Someone, perhaps Cassia's mother or even grandmother, embroidered tiny flowers round the edge, in the same colour, so that they can only be seen as the light falls on the veil when it moves, a tiny, delicate touch.

"How good is your embroidery?" she asks me. "If it's good, you can just buy plain cloth and make it much prettier. I can show you how to weave trims and a belt too. And we can refresh the tunics from when you were a slave, then they won't remind you of that time."

"How are you getting on with Rullus?" I ask tentatively. I wonder if I should break my silence now, while the two of us are alone together.

She smiles. "Well enough. Father is happy to have a man about the place. And he's good-natured and helpful."

Hope rises in me. Perhaps my fears about a possible romance are just that. Cassia does not sound as if she is falling in love and Rullus has not attempted to come near me again. Perhaps I am safe after all, I think hopefully. He must leave soon and then I will be safe. Perhaps.

At Cassia's insistence, I take the older tunics to the fullery and have them dyed, changing one to a dark blue and one to a violet. I have money for one more tunic and Cassia steers me towards brighter colours than I would have chosen if I were alone. I find a dusky pink wool but she shakes her head briskly and points to a springlike yellow linen for the summer heat. We buy two light linen hair wraps, one in a soft green, one a stronger blue. Cassia shows me how to braid different trims out of woollen strands that can be added to the neckline and hem of my tunics.

I decorate the dark blue tunic with a woven orange wool belt. To the violet, I attach a wide woven trim in a soft green and blue design, which I wear with my leather belt. They look so different I forget they used to be my slave livery. I go to the cobbler in our insula, too. He is more used to making shoes for soldiers, but he turns out a simple pair of red leather sandals at my request, which I like immensely.

"I never knew you were such an elegant lady," teases Fabia when she sees me. "Cassia tells me you've got whole chests of clothes."

"It's been fun," I admit. "I've never been able to dress how I please, I've always worn livery until I came to Virgin's Street, and there hasn't been much time to think about clothes, this past year."

We buy tiny shells and beads to sew along the edges of hair wraps and Cassia shakes her head at my lack of embroidery skills and teaches me better and neater stitches. She does not have a lot of spare time, for the popina is open most days and most hours, but when she snatches a little rest here and there and I am about, we sit in the shady courtyard together and add decorations to our clothing, twining flowers and leaves, bringing delicacy to the plain fabrics. I have missed her company and I'm grateful to have found a way of spending time with her that keeps me away from Rullus.

"Ah, Cassia, there you are." Rullus is standing in the gateway of the insula, beaming. "Sorry to drag you away from your friend. Need your help with the customers."

Cassia smiles back. "I'll leave this with you," she says to me, dropping her sewing next to me. She hurries past Rullus, turning left out of the gate, back to the popina. I lower my eyes, not wanting to meet Rullus' gaze in case he starts talking to me, take Cassia's hair wrap into my own lap and try to pick up where she left off.

But Rullus comes closer, his voice lower when he speaks so that his words can only be heard by me, not by any random inhabitants of the insula who might be close by. "Trying to make ourselves pretty, are we?"

I don't answer. I can see the dark shape of him standing over me, but I can smell him, too, the smell that makes me want to retch.

Now he squats down in front of me, even closer and his voice is just a whisper.

"I'll look out for you wearing your new pretty clothes then, and I'll know you're wanting some attention when you do. And we'll keep it just between us, shall we? Otherwise I might have to come and visit you one night in that roof hut of yours."

He stands up and walks away. I gather up my embroidery and shells into my sewing basket, crush the hair wraps into it and make my way, shaking, up the stairs and back to my hut.

I put away all my new clothes into the chest I have for my belongings and go back to wearing my ordinary clothes. When Fabia and Cassia ask what happened to the pretty new tunics and hair wraps, I shrug and say I'm keeping them for a special occasion.

I TAKE TO LEAVING THE insula early without breakfast, arriving at work before everyone else. I go to the baths in the afternoons and linger longer than usual. I return late, although always before it gets dark. I stop at Cassia's only if I cannot see Rullus. If he is there, I eat a handful of olives with bread and cheese.

"You've lost weight," says Maria as I pass. "You look skinny."

I shrug, don't pause to gossip with her. "Too much work on."

"You still need to eat," she calls after me.

EVEN WHEN I ESCAPE THE fear of Rullus' presence in the insula, the thought of the naumachia hangs over us all at work, so that a heaviness seems to follow me no matter where I am or what I am doing. Every day that goes by is taking us closer to the day we have to flood the amphitheatre, which despite all our planning seems an impossible task, especially as we can't test it before the event. Even when I try not to think about it, small things will remind me, like the odd graffiti in the shape of a fish, etched onto a wall beside an ill-fitting door I pass every day on my way to the Forum and the amphitheatre. Most of the graffiti I see is obscene in nature, some of it is political, information about one candidate or another. Amongst it all the fish stands out: too simple in shape to be anything of a vulgar nature, no writing alongside it to explain its purpose, only two curved lines joining together to create a fish. Clearly it has some meaning, but I cannot fathom what it is, it only makes me think of water, which leads me back to the naumachia, round and round.

Marcus has gathered some of our team together, early in the morning before it gets too hot to think. Karbo sits holding one of the growing kittens, which is enjoying exploring the bright wider world beyond its dark under-arena home.

"We need more water-based stories. We've promised

Odysseus and the Sirens to help the Aedile, and Althea's already found the swimmers to perform the Sirens. Other ideas?"

"Got a brilliant idea," Carpophorus starts.

Marcus looks doubtful. Carpophorus, a walking mass of muscle, is spectacular and well-loved as a bestiarius, but his ideas are not always to Marcus' taste. "Which is?"

"Pasiphae and the bull from the sea."

Marcus' brow furrows. "The conception of the Minotaur?"

"Absolutely. I've got a trained bull."

Marcus waits a moment. "Trained in what way?"

"It'll copulate with a woman, if you put it in the right position. The carpenters can build something to put the woman at the right level, a platform or whatever."

It's the sort of thing Labeo would come up with. Marcus catches my eye and I shake my head, disgusted. I can just imagine a man like Rullus taking pleasure in such a spectacle.

"I'll get back to you on that," says Marcus, a sigh escaping him. "Anyone else?"

"Horses," says Karbo. "King Neptune arriving in his chariot through the water."

"Very nice," approves Marcus and I jot it down. "We'll visit the racing stables, see what they can do for us. The Blues might want to be involved; their livery will be a nice connection to the water theme."

"Dido and Aeneas?" I offer.

Marcus narrows his eyes. "A story about a Roman ruler bidding farewell to his lover, a foreign queen, before sailing home, leaving her to kill herself? Is that supposed to be a hint to them both?"

"Too heavy-handed?"

Marcus shrugs. "Well, Odysseus and the Sirens is probably

a bit subtle," he says. "The Aedile sounds like he wants us to hammer the message home, so perhaps we should add Dido and Aeneas. Titus liked being compared to Aeneas at the inaugural ceremony, so we can keep the theme going. It'll do for now."

WHEN VITA ARRIVES TO LOOK round, it is Marcus who sees her first and goes to meet her, I see her extend her hand in her trademark greeting, and Marcus, without hesitating, shakes it. I wonder if he, too, is reminded of Fausta. Vita nods to me as they pass; today she is dressed in a long green tunic with a strikingly bold orange geometric pattern as its trim, made up of tiny beads, something far brighter and bolder than a slave would normally wear or indeed be able to afford, but then she is one of Labeo's best performers and Labeo would never let sartorial hierarchy get in the way of putting on a good show. Vita, in her bright colours and with her eye-catching hair, is a walking advertisement for his services. Marcus spends over an hour showing her the dimensions of the floor, letting her try out various audience sightlines and finally escorting her below the arena floor so that she can see how we manage many of the Games backstage.

"Interesting," she says, emerging through one of the lift trapdoors.

"Has Marcus explained to you how it will work?"

"Yes," she says. "Broadly. But I'll have to come back soon to better understand some of the dimensions of your props. The ships are the most important thing. It depends how tall they are, whether there is space for us to dive, as well as how we get on board in the first place. Maybe concealed rope ladders."

I nod. "I'm sure it'll be very impressive," I say.

"Marcus says he wants me to play the part of Dido, too,"

she says. "Could you not get a woman who looks like the Jewish Queen?"

"Is it that obvious?"

She shrugs and laughs. "Everyone knows the Senate wants to get rid of Berenice. Stands to reason they'd ask you to throw in a few hints here and there, they've been doing the same at half the theatres in Rome. They'd be better off just saying it to his face."

NOW THAT I'M SHARING A room with Karbo, I become aware of his nightmares when I wake from mine. Barely a night goes by when I do not hear him whimper in his sleep, and sometimes he will wake, screaming. In the time I have known him, he has slept first in our courtyard, then in Fausta's room before she died. Since then, he has mostly slept in Maria's room as she had a little extra space while the baker's family took in Marcus and me, and so it is only now that I become aware of how disturbed his nights are. When he whimpers, I reach out sleepily and hold his hand. The whimpers die away into silence and I hope for his dreams to take on a more pleasant aspect. But instead he sometimes screams, his eyes open but staring into nothing as though he sees something I do not, or cannot leave his dreams behind.

"How did you become a slave?" I ask one day, when we have eaten our evening meal on the rooftop and the light is fading.

"Can't remember," he says.

"I used to be a slave," I say, hoping to entice him into confiding in me by reminding him of this fact.

"Years ago," he says, dismissively.

"No," I say, surprised that he does not know my recent history. "I was only set free a few months before I met you."

Now I have his attention. "By Marcus?"

"Yes, after Pompeii… Afterwards."

"Why?"

"We went back to Pompeii," I say slowly. It is not something I often talk about. "We went back a few days afterwards, Marcus was searching for his wife Livia and son Amantius."

"What was it like?"

"Like the entrance to Hades," I say. "Everything was grey. Everything. You could barely see the city for the ashes, but Marcus was desperate to find his home. He dug for hours, and there was nothing I could do to help him. He set me free, there, in all the ashes, amid that devastation. He wanted rid of me," I add, trying to be honest. "I think he wanted to die, and I was only a burden to him."

"You came back to Rome, though."

"That was Fausta's doing," I say and his face changes at the mention of her name, the pain of her death still fresh. "She knew it was the only way for us all to survive. Marcus had a job here, he could earn money, she and I could be his assistants and she thought if he stayed alive long enough, he wouldn't try to…"

"You didn't have to stay," says Karbo. "If he'd set you free."

"I had nowhere else to go," I say. "I didn't know anyone; I would have been alone in the world." I think for a moment. "As you were, before we found you," I add, trying to bring the conversation back round to him again.

"Before Maria caught me," he says.

I laugh. "You had no chance against her."

He grins.

"But before she caught you," I say, persevering. "Where were you living, how were you getting fed?"

"Slept anywhere quiet. Slept in the amphitheatre plenty of times, but not under the arena." He looks away. "There were some bad people down there."

"I'm sorry," I say, touching his hand. "How come Maria saw you often?"

"Found the insula, some of the street kids talked about it, Julia didn't throw us out like other people, looked the other way when we slept in the courtyard overnight, it was safer than most places. The gateway was never locked. The bakery gave out stale bread sometimes. Cassia would give you a bowl of soup if you asked. It was worth hanging around here."

"But before that?"

"I don't remember."

I think of my own childhood before I became a slave, how it comes back to me only in small snatches, perhaps all that I can bear to remember, or all that has been branded into me too deeply to forget. Tiny memories of what was once my home on the Greek island of Kefalonia, *my mother singing, washing hanging out, flapping in the breeze. The sound of the waves on the beach of my tiny island home.* Happy thoughts, yet so few of them left, so much forgotten with the years. And the memories I wish I could forget, *the red of my mother's death, my father on his knees before his new master, begging for me, too, to be enslaved, if he could only keep me by his side.* I don't want to press Karbo too far, probably his memories are like mine, tiny snatches he wishes were more, others he wishes would go away entirely, yet never will.

"Do you remember your parents?"

He shakes his head. "Not my father, don't know who he was."

"Your mother?"

"A slave."

I don't push him further. We sit in the gathering darkness and then his voice comes, his face hidden. "They said I was old enough to be sold. She screamed."

I hold his hand in mine and feel the shaking of his body come through it. "Then they brought me to Rome."

"From where?"

"I don't know. Somewhere down south? I've forgotten the name."

I know what he is thinking. He can never go back. He can never find her again, even if she is still living.

"I'm glad we found you," I say.

"I miss Fausta," he says suddenly. "I thought I'd found a new mother. And then she died."

My tears rise so fast they are spilling over my cheeks before he's even finished the sentence. "I miss her too," I say. "She taught me everything."

"I liked her being on our shrine," he says in a very small voice, and I wonder if he, too, has felt the loss of Marcus, his hero, in this new division of our homes.

"I'll ask Balbus to make us a new figurine," I say. It's not much to offer, but it's all I can think of. "And you have me," I add. "I will look after you."

"Until you get married," he says.

"What?"

"One day. When you get married. A new husband won't want some runaway child hanging around you," he says.

I swallow at how practical his voice is, how certain he is of being left alone again, one day. I want to protest, but then again, I know he's telling the truth. No doubt one day I will get married, although I can't imagine it for now. And Karbo is right, no man will allow his bride to bring some unknown street child into a new marriage, with no binding ties between them of any kind. Silently, I pat Karbo's hand, then keep holding it even after he has fallen asleep.

I don't mention our conversation again, but I listen out more carefully for his whimpers in the night and hold his hand as long as I am awake. I speak with Balbus and he makes a copy of the tiny Fausta from Marcus' shrine, which I bring to Karbo for our own. He holds the miniature doll in his hands, one fingertip touching the messy black curls, then stroking the folds of the toga that had marked her out as a prostitute. He does not say thank you, but he places the doll with loving care on our shrine and glances towards it every night before he goes to bed, seeking comfort from it.

"I feel I should be more of a mother to him," I say to Cassia and Fabia one evening at the popina. "But I don't really know how."

"Three motherless girls," says Cassia sighing. "None of us are going to have much guidance in how to be a mother, are we? I suppose making clothes, keep him clean, teach him manners? At least you can teach him to read and write."

"I try," I say. "He gets bored too easily and runs off to play. Copying out his letters over and over again is hardly his idea of fun. His numbers aren't bad, he listens when we do the accounts."

"Ah, ladies, good evening."

It's Rullus. Fabia waves a cheery hello, Cassia smiles.

"We were talking about what makes a good mother," she tells Rullus.

Rullus pats Cassia's shoulder. "This one will make an excellent mother. So kindly. One day soon, eh?"

Cassia blushes and Fabia laughs. I force a smile onto my face but my stomach turns over at the idea that Rullus does seem to be courting Cassia – and worse, that she is pleased with his comments. I should say something but who will believe me, when Rullus is endlessly pleasant to everyone?

THERE'S A PREACHER IN THE Forum as I go to work most days, calling out to passers-by and addressing the small crowd that gathers in front of him. I pause to hear what he is saying.

"He is your Shepherd, your light in the darkness, son of God, come unto Him and pledge your lives to Him, for He will guide you and care for you in spirit, until His second coming, when He will set you free from the bonds that shackle you. And it will be soon, very soon, prepare yourselves for His glory."

"What about our own gods?" asks one man from the crowd.

The preacher shakes his head. "You do not need them any longer," he says, with certainty. "There is but one God, and His son, Jesus, will be your guide."

"Jews and their mad ideas," scoffs the man, entirely unconvinced. "It's all very well, you saying I should ignore the gods I've worshipped all my life, but what happens when I turn my back on them and they take offence? Eh? I wouldn't want to be the one to insult them. I've seen what they can do when they're upset. My cousin Bassus lost an eye after he offended Jupiter by not praying to him…"

"Can't I pray to your god *and* ours?" asks a woman.

"And what about the Emperor's father?" asks a man.

The preacher shakes his head, almost sadly. "There is only one God," he repeats. "The Emperor Vespasian is no god, he was a man like you and me, as is his son Titus. And the gods you have been raised with are merely false idols, with all too human characteristics. Do you think that a truly divine being concerns themselves with sex and beauty, as you believe Venus does? Do you think that God needs a messenger such as Mercury, when He can speak directly to you through His own son?"

I walk on. If the preacher is not careful, he will be arrested and charged with high treason for suggesting that Titus is not the son of a god, since Vespasian was deified after his death. Not to mention for blasphemy in speaking against the gods of Rome and for spreading dissent by encouraging the crowd to follow his lead and change their ways. And if he is arrested, he will end up in the amphitheatre, probably facing wild animals, crucifixion or a gladiatorial bout he has no chance of winning, should we need to stage a battle scene and not wish to lose a professional fighter. He would do better to keep his mouth shut and worship whomever he pleases, without drawing attention to himself or his religion. The justice system in Rome is mostly lenient in such matters, for Rome is full of people from all over the Empire, worshipping all manner of gods. So long as they publicly bow their heads and make some small effort at worshipping the gods of Rome, any other shortcomings of faith are generally overlooked. But deliberately public displays of blasphemy and treason are another matter.

I ASK ONE OF THE scenery painters for a favour, and he agrees, for Karbo is a favourite amongst the amphitheatre's crew. He spends a day off site, and I only shrug when Marcus asks where he is. I send Karbo on several errands that afternoon, delaying his return to the roof hut, and when he does come back, I tell him that we're having dinner with Julia to buy time.

"Carry this lamp," I say, when it's almost dark and time for bed.

"I don't need a lamp to get into bed," he says. "I can see enough to get upstairs."

"Just carry the lamp," I insist, picking up one of my own.

"What are you, an empress, that needs this many lamps to get to bed?" he asks, stomping noisily up the stairs ahead of me.

But when he opens the door of the hut there is a satisfying gasp and I giggle.

"You never told me!" he says, eyes wide over his shoulder, before turning back to look at the walls.

The scenery painter has done a good job. Despite the small scale of the room, I could be back in Lucius' villa in Pompeii, with freshly painted frescoes on the walls, one racing team on each. Wheel spokes and the long legs of the horses appear to move in the flickering light of our lamps, the drivers' faces grimacing at the effort of guiding their teams to victory. The Blues, Karbo's favourite team, take up the largest image, on the wall right next to his bed, and as I doze off to sleep, I have to remind him to blow out the lamp and stop staring at it, afraid his passion will lead to another fire. The next day the scenery painter receives one of Karbo's enthusiastic hugs, nearly knocking him over.

"You made him very happy," I say. "Thank you."

"Anything for that one," says the man, pleased with the reaction to his work. "He'd make a good apprentice, if he had the paperwork. I suppose he's a slave, but you can't prove it either way, can you?"

I shake my head. He's right of course, it is something that I hadn't had time to think about before. If Karbo ran away from a slave trader, then legally he is still a slave, even though no one has come looking for him. And being a slave will shackle him forever to an inferior life, unable to make his own choices or even pursue chances such as apprenticeships, should anyone be willing to offer him one. I wonder what Fausta would do in my shoes, and wish she were here to guide me. I remember the day she insisted that Marcus repeat his manumission of me in front of a lawyer, so that I would have the paperwork to prove I was no longer a slave, the little freedwoman's cap in a fresh green wool she had ready for him to give me. She knew full well the importance of these actions, the difference they would make in my life and the choices I would have as a result. I take down her tiny figurine from our shrine and turn it in my hands. Fausta would have known what to do. For starters, she would have punched Rullus in the face. A few tears fall onto the black curls that top her little head. That night I stay awake long after Karbo has fallen asleep.

FOLLOWING CASSIA'S ADVICE, IN THE quiet moments before or after shows I try to groom Karbo a little. His hair was clipped short earlier in the year to keep him cool, but it's grown quickly, and he won't let me cut it again. I use the comb Myrtis gave me before she died, with her name carved into it, but his hair is impossible to comb through; every day it seems to have more tangles, despite my best efforts. If I can pin him down for long enough, it stands out like a lion's mane around his head, before swiftly tangling again as soon as he sleeps. It is Vita who comes to my rescue, watching me one day when I am trying and failing to manage it, the two of us sitting in the shade of one of the corridors after the crowds have left. She and two other members of her team have come to inspect the model ships, built half to three-quarter size for the naumachia. One has been wheeled out onto the sand so we can see how it will look, the other lies in sections in the darkness under the arena floor.

"When it grows long, you twist it into strands," she says, looking at Karbo, who is wriggling in my hands like an eel.

"Braids?" I ask, looking at her own hair.

She shakes her head. "His hair will just naturally take on the shape," she says. "Try it, you'll see."

I choose small sections and twist the hair under her guidance and sure enough, it quickly and easily forms little locks, which look like braids in the Egyptian style from a distance, it is only up close you can see they are not plaited at all but simply hold together by themselves. Karbo grows vain about them, I catch him twisting them ever tighter so that they will fall just so, quickly reaching his shoulders. The other children in our block try to imitate him, but their own curls are too loose to hold the shape. A few of the girls have their hair plaited into tiny plaits like Vita for a while, pleased with the novelty of it. I find them drawing sooty fingers across their eyelids, trying to complete the Egyptian look, although they give the impression they have been in a fight and received a black eye rather than achieving the exotic elegance they were trying to emulate.

THE SHOW-SHIPS ARE COMING TOGETHER, made by the same carpenters who make real ships. Flat-bottomed and half the usual size, they are still impressive. Once they have been built, our painters descend on them, painting them a bold red and adding extra touches such as shining copper fittings and symbols on the prows such as giant eyes. These are not practical ships that must face storms, they must glitter and shine in sunlight and torchlight, draw the attention of the crowd and leave plenty of room for the men on board to do battle across the gap between two ships. Even their sails are impressive, not just plain white but painted with motifs of warriors to remind the audience of the Trojan War that Odysseus has just left behind him. The only practical element is the wheels fitted onto them, so that they can be pushed around like carts when there is no water on which to float. When we go to inspect them, Karbo spends his time down at the docks jumping off and on them, calling out naval orders to an invisible team of sailors, until I drag him home.

"Will they really float?" he asks.

"They had better do," I say. "If anything about this show doesn't work, it'll be our team that gets in trouble."

NEPTUNE'S CHARIOT

I**T'S THE END OF AUGUST** and as promised, now that the insula has been refurbished, Julia has an apartment available for Fabia and her father, Fabius, on the middle floor. I am pleased to have Fabia's company more often. But Fabia moving in has an unexpected effect, which is that I see Marcus even less. We no longer share a roof hut, but we had often eaten our morning and evening meals together, as well as spending the days at the amphitheatre, working closely together. But the amphitheatre team has grown larger, meaning that Marcus is often somewhere else in the vast building, or, if he is briefing the team on what the next day's spectacle will hold, we are a big group, and much of my time is taken up making notes or checking lists, even though Marcus always listens to what I have to say. Now that his old friend Fabius has moved into our building, Marcus has a companion for his evenings, and the two of them often take their meals together, either at Cassia's or further afield. The nights when they go out, I am nervous. I touch my hut's lock more than once and listen out for footsteps. When they return, they will often have an evening drink or two in our courtyard, and I hear them late into the night telling old stories of their time in the army together, or friends they had in common. At least then I know he is nearby. I still see Marcus in the mornings, for breakfast, but he is not a naturally gregarious person when he has just awoken, and frequently all I hear from him is the odd grunt in reply to anything one of us might ask or comment on.

"I miss talking to Marcus," I venture one day in an unguarded moment to Maria, when I have joined her in the courtyard. "I spent so much time with him this past year and now I barely see him."

"Men prefer talking to other men," says Maria unsympathetically. "They don't understand womenfolk."

I don't argue with her, for she has stubborn views on such things, but I disagree. I had grown close to Marcus, I felt as though the two of us were a partnership within the wider amphitheatre backstage team, especially after we lost Fausta and we were the only survivors from Pompeii of our acquaintance, the only two who had been back there, and seen what had become of it. It was a shared bond, and now it has gone. Sometimes, I hear a Pompeiian accent in the street and my head turns fast, seeking out the familiar physiognomy of the city's inhabitants. Sometimes I find myself smiling at complete strangers, who look back at me in surprise, not knowing that I was there, in the lost city, days before its demise. Once or twice, I have spoken with such people, and their eyes fill with tears when they think of it, in grief at having lost many of their friends and family members, but also with guilt at having, somehow, survived, only by the merest of chances, a fishing trip, a visit to family elsewhere, service in the army away from home. Some loudly and frequently give thanks to the gods for having saved them, others only mumble something about how other, better people than they should have been saved. All of them have haunted eyes when they speak of Pompeii, nothing I nor anyone else can say will ever take away that look.

"We should eat together one evening," I say to Marcus, trying to secure his company. He agrees, but somehow one evening and then another is not suitable, for Fabia likes to chat with me and Fabius wants to explore more of Rome. Having not been here for many years, he has old friends to visit, many of whom also know Marcus, and so the days and weeks drift by and I see Marcus less and less. Karbo misses him too, he trails around after Marcus more than usual at work, eager for his attention, though mostly this only results in extra errands, which he undertakes at speed, returning to Marcus' side as soon as possible.

MARCUS SPENDS A GREAT DEAL of time cross-questioning Merula, still concerned about the flooding and whether the pitch coating will suffice. There is no true way of testing the idea beforehand, but he has a tiny amphitheatre built in wood by one of our carpenters, coats it in pitch and then spends time pouring water into it and timing how long it takes to drain out. When he stops messing with it Karbo takes it as his own, dragging it all the way home. He pours sand into the arena, then makes little gladiators out of sticks and puts on miniature Games of his own with the other children in our insula. Merula seems confident enough in his plans, though, so I leave Marcus to worry about it and instead, after much nagging from Karbo, agree to go to the racing stables with Celer as our guide, to try and convince some of the racing teams to take part in our naumachia. The stables are to the north-west of Virgin's Street, laid out close to the Tiber. There are four teams, each beloved to the brink of obsession by their fans, all of whom pledge a lifetime's loyalty to their own faction.

"Celer used to drive for the Blues," gabbles Karbo, so overexcited by the visit that it is all he can do to stay quiet.

"Who would you drive for, Althea, if you could drive for one of the teams?"

"I'm not a man," I say.

"Well, who do you support then? The Blues? Reds? Whites? Greens?"

"I'm not really sure," I say, distracted by the vast stable yard into which we have just entered. The colour blue is everywhere, leaving no doubt as to which team is based here. Horses poke their heads out from their stable doors, their names written in bold blue above each doorway, each name known to their supporters as though they were members of their own family.

"How can you not *know*? Blues forever!" yelps Karbo and several of the horses, startled, jerk their heads up.

"Shush now, or you'll frighten them," says Celer gently, his own voice kept low and steady. "Most of them are very highly strung, one loud noise and they'll be off. Speak softly when you're around the stables."

"Sorry," Karbo whispers. "Can I touch them?"

"Certainly, but remember to approach them slowly, speak softly, and watch out for the dappled one, he bites."

"What's his name?" asks Karbo, instantly drawn to the troublemaker.

"Swiftfoot. And he is. One of the best horses in years, but there isn't a stable hand without a scar from him in this yard. They only put up with him because he's so fast. Stay well away."

Karbo chooses the horse right next to Swiftfoot, a black beast, who accepts his caresses in a pleasant enough manner. Karbo strokes it absentmindedly, his eyes fixed on Swiftfoot, who rolls his eyes and stamps his feet in a menacing manner, disliking the smell of unfamiliar visitors.

"He's so beautiful," says Karbo dreamily.

"Not when you're bleeding," says Celer. "Now let's find someone in charge."

We find the stables manager, who agrees he will speak with the owner of the Blues and ask for one of their best quadriga chariots and its driver, along with four fine horses, to take part in the naumachia.

"Will the horses run through water?" I ask.

"Don't know about that," says the stables manager, considering. "Might need a bit of training first. They're used to water being thrown at them to cool them down, so they wouldn't mind that, but they're not much used to their hooves and legs being in water. Are you having the other teams?"

"We thought your livery would go better with the water," I say. "So we were going to use you for the main event, dress up your driver as King Neptune, that kind of thing. But we might end on a small race, nothing serious, one chariot from each team, just showing you all off as the water disappears and we turn the arena back to land."

"A race is never not serious," says the stables manager grinning. "The people are too besotted with their favourite faction to let it be anything but serious."

"I'll bear it in mind," I say. "No managing a win for a particular team then, just for the sake of storytelling?"

"Not if you want to live."

"Point taken."

"Any particular colours of the horses you want?"

"Not really, I'll leave that to you."

"Can we have Swiftfoot? *Please?*" Karbo, standing by my elbow, has his best pleading face on, all wide eyes and parted lips.

"You don't want him, he's vicious. We're only keeping him

because he's the fastest. You'd never see his top speed, you don't have the space for it, so it would be a waste."

"He let me stroke him," says Karbo.

"You were told not to go near him!" I say, appalled.

"But he let me," says Karbo. "Watch."

"Karbo! Come back here!"

But he has already hurried back to Swiftfoot, who stamps his feet again but, astonishingly, does indeed allow Karbo to touch him, stroking down the front of his face, ending on his upper lip, while I cringe in fear that Karbo is about to be bitten.

"Impressive," says the manager, looking surprised. "Never seen anyone stroke him. Perhaps the lad has an affinity for horses. Worked with them before?"

"Get back here," I hiss, and to my relief Karbo makes his way back over to me. "*Have* you ever worked with horses before?" I ask, but Karbo only shakes his head. "Well you're not about to work with that horse now," I finish. "We'll take whichever horses are most amenable to being trained to something new," I say. "I can't have them skittish around the water."

"We could take a few of them down to the river," says Celer. "Try them out in the shallows, see what they make of it if they've not been in water before, pick out the ones that seem steady."

The manager nods. "Leave that with you then," he says. "Choose a few and take them down there, test them out and let me know which four you want."

"No time like the present," says Celer, as we make our way down to the river's edge, each of us leading two horses. He's given me the most docile, but it still makes me nervous to be leading racehorses about as though they were pets, rather than highly strung beasts who will startle at the slightest noise and then bolt as though a race has begun, with no hope whatsoever of holding them back. Celer, having worked with horses all his life, is entirely at ease and so, I note, is Karbo, who is murmuring comforting noises to the two horses he is leading, leaning against one a little as though they are friends when we have to pause to let a cart roll by. Looking at him I wonder whether he ever has had dealings with horses, perhaps before he can remember, as a small child, to be so comfortable with them.

Of the six horses, only one is truly uncomfortable with the water, stepping back and flattening its ears in a worrying way. Another is cautious, but does not refuse. The rest seem happy enough, perhaps they find the water cooling on a hot day. They drink a little and then, encouraged by our confidence, trot happily enough a few paces in either direction with the water lapping as far as their knees.

"Not bad at all," says Celer happily as we lead the horses back to the Blues' stables. "Looks like we have our four and one to spare. King Neptune's chariot is ready. We can come back to choose more of them for the other chariots. The other stables might give a chariot each, if you're going to have them race."

"Goodbye, Swiftfoot," murmurs Karbo, pulling away from my restraining hand for one last caress.

"You really are the most disobedient child," I say, still relieved to have escaped a bloody incident involving horse teeth and a skinny child's arm. "Let's go and let Marcus know that we have our King Neptune."

I TRY TO SLIP PAST the popina on my way home, but Fabia is there and spots me, waves me over. I approach with reluctance. Rullus is there with Cassia, both serving customers at the busy counter.

"Never see you these days," says Cassia over her shoulder as she pours wine with one hand and stirs a stew with the other.

"You know how it is," I say vaguely.

"Too much work for a good woman," says Rullus. "You should be married and have your husband look after you, then you could stay at home more."

"Oh, is married life so easy?" asks Cassia.

"With the right husband," says Rullus, offering her a broad smile, then ducking through the door into the storeroom at the back of the popina.

Fabia laughs. "Considering it?" she asks Cassia.

I hold my breath.

Cassia shrugs. "Might do. He's a good enough man."

"Good enough? How romantic," says Fabia.

Cassia laughs. "Marriage doesn't have to be all romance," she says practically. "A man who works hard in the family business and is pleasant is a good find. Father dotes on him, Rullus barely lets him lift a finger anymore."

"I'm going indoors," I say. I want to cry at the idea that Cassia is seriously considering Rullus as a husband, that she is so level-headed about it. It makes it feel as though a marriage might really happen and then what? Rullus will settle into the insula for the rest of his life and mine? I will have to spend all of my life, if I wish to stay here, with my head down and my feet quick, always ready to run or hide from him? I'm so caught up in these thoughts I barely hear Fabia, then realise she is standing by my side, tugging at me to get my attention.

"I can't spend the evening with you like I promised. I've been called by one of the gladiators."

"Really?" I ask.

"Oh, not for himself," says Fabia wearily. "For his woman.

She's pregnant, the baby's due any day now and he's fretting. It's never the man I'm called for, I might as well resign myself to it."

"The sorceress said your moment would come," I remind her.

"I'm not sure I believe her," says Fabia and she waves me farewell, setting off towards her appointment. I watch her go and wish I could think of an excuse to go with her, to keep someone by my side at all times.

WE'VE SPENT WEEKS DISCUSSING WHETHER the water for the naumachia should gently trickle in from an unseen source or whether we should use some sort of waterfall effect, but the next morning I become aware that Merula has stopped listening to me. "Who is that?" he asks.

I look over my shoulder. Vita and her team are pacing across the sand, Vita is explaining something to Marcus, gesturing at the imperial box and the top seats, probably something about the sightlines. Her tiny braids are finished with red beads today, swaying around her waist as she strides back and forth.

"That's the swimming team from Labeo. The Daughters of Thetis, they call themselves. They're playing the Sirens in the show."

Merula is still staring. "I meant the woman next to Marcus."

"That's Vita, she's their leader."

Vita shakes her head at something Marcus has just said and grabs his hand, lifting it up in the air. I know she's trying to envision how high the ships will be above the swimmers, there's been a debate about whether they can easily climb aboard, allowing them to the dive off in spectacular fashion at the end of the sequence.

Merula's expression changes to crestfallen as he watches the exchange. "Is she Marcus'…" He trails off, his shoulders even more hunched together than usual, dark eyes sorrowful.

"Oh no," I say at once, but as I watch the two of them, I wonder whether Merula has spotted something I have not. Marcus has started laughing at something Vita has said. She shakes her head at him with a grin on her face and mock-pushes him away from her, before they both step close together again and look down at a diagram Marcus was busy drawing up last night, showing how he expects the sequence to take shape, the entrance and exit for Odysseus' ship, the point where the Sirens can appear. Their heads are almost touching. Something in me feels a little sad. Has Marcus developed fond feelings for Vita? It seems soon after losing Livia, but then he has been alone for almost a year. I like Vita, but the idea of Marcus having a woman in his life makes me feel even more distant from him.

"I am sorry," says Merula suddenly.

"What?"

"I didn't mean to suggest anything if you and Marcus…"

"Oh no," I say hastily. "There is nothing between us. Only –" and suddenly all the thoughts I have been keeping quiet in my head come spilling out. "We spent so much time together this past year and so much happened, we had become friends. And now I barely see him, what with the new roof huts and Fabius and…" I realise I was almost about to mention Rullus, whom Merula does not even know. I come to an awkward stop. "Well, anyway, it just seems as though I hardly see him, or even know what he's thinking about. I mean if he were…" I gestured awkwardly towards Marcus and Vita, "I wouldn't know. And I would have done, before."

Merula nods his head. "I wasn't sure…" He trails off, as

incoherent as I am. But his eyes stay on Vita and more than once he loses his train of thought, clearly smitten.

"Can Karbo swim?" asks Marcus, as our working day ends.

"I don't think so," I say.

"Meeting Vita made me think of it," says Marcus. "He should be taught. I'll teach him. Can you swim?"

I shake my head.

"Shall I teach you at the same time?"

"I don't – no," I say, confused by the unexpected offer.

"Well, I'll teach the boy anyway. Tell me if you change your mind," says Marcus. "I'm done for the day. See you tomorrow."

"Yes. Goodbye," I manage. I stand for a moment, uncertain whether to call after him. I'm pleased Karbo will learn to swim, it's a good skill to have. Perhaps I should have said yes, too. I open my mouth, but Marcus has already disappeared through one of the arches, heading to the baths and it's too late. I'll tell him another day. It might mean I see a bit more of him.

"Your aquarius been trying to buy my star performer, eh?"

I look up from my notes on the gladiators that I need Labeo to provide. "I don't know what you're talking about, Labeo. Merula tried to buy Alyssa?"

"Not Alyssa. Vita."

I think back to Merula's face when he saw Vita, his awkward questions about her. "And has he bought her?"

Labeo laughs. "Can't afford her. He went as high as he could, but Vita's not for sale, not at any ordinary price. She may be a nuisance, but she can perform and she can train other girls too, so she's worth a lot more than just the price of a slave girl. I mean, I can see why he wanted to buy her, that's the kind of slave you want in your bed, isn't it? Although having said that, he doesn't know what a troublemaker she is in that department." He twists a gold ring on one of his fingers, an anxious gesture.

"Alright," I say, disliking Labeo's gossiping, knowing he's going to share more salacious details than I want to hear. "I need a fight between dwarfs and giants for one of the myths we're putting on. If we use your dwarfs as ordinary men in the story, it'll make the giants look even bigger."

"Absolutely," says Labeo, distracted at the thought of hiring out a large group of his men.

WHEN I NEXT SEE VITA, though, I can't help asking about what happened. Her face turns dark with annoyance.

"He only tried to buy me so he can keep me in his bed," she all but spits, "just like they all do. I won't be someone's whore. I'd rather stay as Labeo's slave than that. At least we have an agreement. And he values what I can do, how I can train up other slaves to perform in the water."

"To be fair to him, I think Merula might have a soft spot for you," I say.

"I'm not taking that risk," she says. Her face turns thoughtful. "And anyway, there might be something else I can work towards," she adds.

"What?"

"Can't say yet."

I don't press her but when I see her talking with Marcus, heads together as though they are already the best of friends, I wonder whether Merula was right to ask if there is something between them, if his bid to buy her was a pre-emptive way of getting rid of Marcus as a possible rival. And I feel sad again that Marcus isn't confiding in me, that I have no idea whether he has an interest in Vita, whether his heart is ready to open up again after losing Livia.

"Why were you trying to buy Vita?" I ask Merula. He's kneeling in our under-arena space, measuring the flow of water in one of our drains, adding to his complex calculations. His pale skin flushes scarlet and he stands up suddenly, crossing his feet again, awkward.

"To set her free," he mumbles.

"What?"

"I wanted to set her free."

"Why?"

He swallows. "I thought if she were free..."

"Yes?"

"I might marry her."

I stare at him. "You could just have bought her as a slave and had her," I point out.

He shakes his head hurriedly. "No, I – I wanted her to be free to choose..." he trails off again.

I feel sorry for him. So confident when he talks about water, so certain and full of ideas. And then he turns into a stuttering wreck over Vita, full of fantasies that she might choose him if he were to set her free, like some sort of story from the old legends about a love affair between a poor fisherman and a water-nymph.

"Any-anyway," he says, rocking on his clumsily-placed feet. "She was beyond my means. So..."

"I'm sorry," I say, and I mean it. I can't really see the two of them as a match, but Merula is evidently a good-hearted, if hopelessly romantic, man and Vita would have had little to fear from him. I wonder whether Labeo, cunning as he is, really told Vita what Merula intended for her, or whether he implied to her that she would be kept enslaved and used for sex and nothing more, to discourage any interest on her part in encouraging Merula. Either way, it sounds as though Vita's price is too high, and so it's probably better to let the whole matter drop. Merula will just have to gaze upon Vita from afar.

THE FOUNTAIN

Now that the plasterwork and painting are finished, the new outdoor wooden staircase and balconies around the interior of our courtyard are quickly built and the carpenters finally depart. Julia is delighted, she goes about her days humming, filling new plant pots and placing them everywhere. As it's September already, many of her flowers will need to wait till next spring to bloom, still she prepares their planting grounds and places them where they will catch the most rays of sun. Maria takes up her customary place on the walkway balcony again, cushion tucked over the wooden railing, her breasts on top of her crossed arms, leaning on its softness, her place as guard dog rightfully restored.

"I've no idea what's been going on all this time," she says, ignoring the fact that she has spent all summer watching from her window or sitting in the courtyard, and can hardly have missed anything. "All sorts could be happening and no one the wiser. Has anyone even been keeping an eye on the builders? All they want to do is a quick job and finish, they've probably been cutting corners all over the place."

I laugh, look out from our spot on the new balcony overlooking the beautiful courtyard, the new fountain beneath us, almost ready for use, the bright clean paintwork everywhere.

"They've done a fine job, Maria, I'm sure you kept an eye on them even without a balcony."

"Well, somebody had to," she says righteously. "I've had to wake early every day to make sure they're not shirking while everyone's still asleep."

The courtyard is being paved over with fresh cobbles, now that the plumbing is complete. The toilets are already working, made larger by taking over an old disused storage room. They smell a great deal fresher than they used to and now have seating for eight at a time, which makes a change and stops queues forming of a morning. We look forward to the day when the cobbles are complete, the courtyard strangely smooth to walk through compared to its old uneven surface.

Julia holds off the fountain being turned on until we've all come home to witness the great moment, the aquarius in charge of it huffing with impatience, but not daring to argue with an ex-Vestal Virgin, for fear of what Vesta might do to him if he is rude to her handmaiden.

"You can turn it on now," says Julia graciously, when we are all gathered in the courtyard.

The aquarius makes some adjustments to the plumbing in a corner of the courtyard. There's a gasp of air being pushed out of the pipes and then the carved stone face of a stern Neptune spouts water into a wide basin, first in gargling fits and starts, then settling into a smooth flow. Everyone applauds and those nearest the basin splash the others, so that the celebration of the new fountain quickly turns into a water fight, the children shrieking in delight and all but climbing into the basin.

Its installation makes collecting water quick and easy for everyone in the insula. This pleases the women and children above all, as they are usually the ones who must carry heavy amphorae or jugs back to rooms and apartments. The children spend the hottest part of each day splashing each other amidst gleeful yelps, occasionally someone yells at them to be quiet if they are interrupting afternoon naps. Marcus and Celer rig up an awning and Julia leaves a couple of benches out for anyone who wishes to rest under it. The courtyard has become a haven of perfumed shade and babbling water, as Julia fills it with ever more pots of plants and flowers, a far cry from the first time I saw it when it was a crumbling ruin of a space. It still feels homely though, it has none of the stiff elegance of a villa's atrium, rather an easy comfort which is good to come home to each day. A new gate has been fitted, one which actually swings on its hinges rather than drooping from them. It has a large bolt on it, but I notice that Julia still leaves the gate unbarred at night, so that anyone without a home can find a sheltered safe place to sleep. Sometimes, if I rise very early, I'll startle someone who has spent the night under the shelter of the wooden staircase, and I direct them towards Cassia, who is always ready with a ladle of her ever-simmering weekly soup and a piece of yesterday's bread to dip into it. I used to take them there myself, but I don't want to risk meeting Rullus in the half-light of dawn.

THE HEAT OF SUMMER RECEDES, settling into balmy warm days, with a welcome breeze, cooler nights and the odd thunderstorm here and there to break the dry spell. The first grapes arrive from the southern vineyards, and everyone enjoys their rich sweetness, the marketplaces have bunches piled high at every fruit stall, both red and white varieties.

Karbo spends every spare moment that he has with Celer, begging for stories of his days as a racing driver. He wants to know every detail, from how the horses and drivers are chosen and trained, to how the chariots are constructed and the races arranged. Knowing the dangers of the racetrack and that Celer, despite being a kindly man, is only alive today because he spent all his money on women and drank so much that he became a liability and ended his racing career early, I try to drag Karbo away, but it's difficult. He will accompany me to work and do all that is required of him, but as soon as a show is over he'll slip away and I'll find him back in our courtyard, where Celer likes to sit in the shade most afternoons with a jug of wine. Karbo will be sat at his feet, one question after another tumbling from his lips.

"And if a chariot overturns?"

He knows the answer already, anyone who's been to the races knows what happens, but he wants to hear it all again, in lavish and bloodthirsty detail.

Celer shakes his head sadly. "You have to cut yourself free of the reins that are tied to your waist," he says. "Or you'll be dragged behind the horses along the ground. They won't stop, they've been trained to keep going. If you don't cut yourself free quickly, you'll be dead in moments, no-one can withstand being pulled along the ground at that speed. Every driver carries a sharp knife and they have it blessed in the temple as often as possible."

"Did it ever happen to you?" asks Karbo, eyes wide.

Celer pulls up one side of his tunic, revealing scars running all the way down his thigh and calf. "Those scars run the length of my body," he says seriously. "And I was lucky it was only the once."

"What's the knife like?"

"I still have mine," says Celer. He takes a knife out of a fold in his tunic, turns it so Karbo can look at it, but pulls it away when he reaches out to touch it. "Too sharp, little one," he says. "I keep it sharp even to this day, out of respect. It can cut through a rope in one swipe. It saved my life. It never leaves my side, even now I no longer race."

"How long did it take to heal?"

"Many months. The skin is still tight, it pains me sometimes. I raced for one more year after that, but my fight was gone."

"Gone?"

"When you've been badly hurt, you stop thinking you are immortal. The young drivers who've never had a bad fall, they think they are gods, they think they will live forever and ever, that is why they can drive the horses at such speed. Once they have a bad fall, as I did, they realise they are not immortal after all. And the men who have families, you see them grow afraid too, scared to leave their wife and babies alone. They don't drive so fast anymore. It's a young man's game."

"Did you stop racing because you were afraid?"

"I started drinking too much to help soften the pain of healing, and then when I recovered and went back to the track, I drank more to numb the fear before a race, but you can't drive when you're drunk, you make mistakes. I lost too many races, made too many mistakes. My days were over and I had to stop before I died on the racetrack."

"You still drink too much," says Karbo.

"Karbo," I say. "Don't be rude."

"He's right though," says Celer, refilling his cup. "Can't blame the boy for speaking the truth."

"Why don't you stop?" asks Karbo.

"Harder than you'd think," says Celer. "I thought I'd stop when I left the stables. But that was a long time ago." He gulps from his cup. "You should get yourself an education instead of hanging around here with me listening to the old days. A chariot driver's lot is no life."

"But if you win…"

"If you win a lot of races, you'll make more money than you've ever seen in your life. Women will throw themselves at you. You'll be crowned with laurels by the Emperor himself. You'll even buy your freedom, have your own slaves, live in a villa with every luxury. And then you'll die before you're twenty-five."

"But –"

"No buts. Go and learn your letters," says Celer, pulling himself to his feet and making his way somewhat unsteadily towards the stairs.

I TRY TO TEACH KARBO his letters. I give him one of my old tablets, freshly filled with wax, then have him copy the neat examples I show him. He is reluctant, bored with the slow nature of the task.

"No-one learns to write straightaway," I tell him. "It takes time and patience and a lot of repetition."

"Too much repetition," he says. "I can write all my letters."

"Not neat enough yet," I say, looking over his work. His writing looks like that of a much younger child. "Here's a fresh sheet of wax, copy out the writing one more time for today."

"What's the point?" he asks sullenly. "What do I need to read and write for?"

"So you will know what is going on and no-one will be able to fool you," I say. "You'll know what you're putting your name to, if you make a legal agreement. And if you wish, you could be a scribe. Scribes are paid better than labourers."

"That's a boring job," he says.

"Thank you very much."

"It's all right for a girl," he says. "Girls like to stay quiet and clean. I want a more exciting job."

"Such as?" I ask. I'm hoping he doesn't say gladiator, since he watches them all the time. It's not a respectable trade and it's a dangerous one. I want to keep him safe.

"Don't know," he mumbles. I think of his excitement at the stables and wonder whether he is thinking of the racing life, although he'd never dare say so to me. The racing drivers' lives are very short, even if glorious. Most of them die before they reach thirty, their death rate is far worse than the gladiators'.

"Well, whatever you want to do, if you can read and write you'll be better off," I say firmly. "And you can practise your numbers when we do the accounts tomorrow, work out the wages for the craftsmen. So sit there and copy out that page."

"Who are you to tell me what to do?" Karbo mutters. "You're not my mother," he adds, under his breath.

"Your mother would want you to be able to read and write, I can assure you," I say, a little hurt that he has thrown this truth in my face. "Get on with it," I add, more crossly than I had intended and Karbo bows his head to the work, his face one big scowl. He copies out the words poorly, then all but flings the tablet back at me and races off down one of the amphitheatre's corridors before I can make him do them again. I look down at the tablet and sigh, the words are barely legible. It will take many more lessons at this rate before he will have even a decent script, let alone the fine work of a scribe. To be fair, he does not seem to want to be a scribe, but someone with few prospects in life needs all the skills they can learn. The next day I make him sit through all the accounts, even though he yawns and twists in his seat like an eel, bored with the endless repetitive nature of this task too.

But he makes a fair fist of copying out the numbers at least, so I praise him for that.

"I'm going to the baths," says Marcus, when we finish going through it all.

"I need to ask you for something first," I say. "Can you give me a minute? Karbo, you can head for the insula, I'll catch up with you."

Marcus raises his eyebrows when I explain my plan. "You're a woman," he says. "Even my say so as your patron and guardian won't be enough. You'd have to get permission from Titus himself."

My shoulders slump.

"You can ask," says Marcus. "Next time you see him. He liked you and he's fairly amiable."

"I hardly ever see him," I say. "I might have to wait months."

We have five days of Games that try our patience to the limits while Merula's team waterproof the under-arena floor and walls, a job that should have been done well before the inauguration, had the architect not died. Running Games on a scale that the crowd expects without any access to our usual under-stage space leads to frayed tempers and hot words. On the first day our team has to dismantle all the animal pens and clear away vital elements such as Fabius' surgical area. We end up roping off one of the corridors so that we have at least a small storage area, closing three entrances to the seating, which makes for delays and more management than usual required for the crowds when they arrive for each day's events. We try to make our lives easier by running what Marcus bills as a 'special event': three days of headline bestiarii pitted against savage beasts, using Carpophorus as our star bestiarius, who is in his element fighting tigers and suchlike.

He's brave, I'll give him that. A tiger won't listen to a gladiatorial referee nor follow any accepted rules of fighting, caring only to kill. And from our perspective, two tigers take up a lot less room than a hundred head of deer. But this special focus on one star performer comes with its own problems. Carpophorus is much beloved by the ladies of Rome, who no doubt like to daydream of having him in their bedchambers and sometimes attempt to make their daydreams come true.

"I'm sorry," I tell a veiled and silk-clad lady in a litter being carried by six well-dressed slaves on the second morning of the five days. "I cannot send Carpophorus out to you, he is about to fight."

"I'll make it worth your while," murmurs the woman, holding out a little pouch to me.

"It won't be worth my while if the Emperor finds out I didn't put on a show today," I say, backing away. "Perhaps you can arrange something yourself with him after the show?"

She obviously does, because Carpophorus is late the next morning, looking pleased with himself.

"You be late again, and I'll send you to fight the lions without your sword," spits Marcus. "I've got enough on my hands without you disappearing off with your lady friends."

"She was actually a lady, though," says Carpophorus, pulling on his armour with a grin. "If I told you whose wife she is —"

"I don't want to know," says Marcus. "And I'll deny everything if you tell me. I just want you out there on the sand. Right now."

We get by somehow and spend the fifth day frantically moving everything back into the under-stage space from dawn till dusk, while above our heads a lion hunt goes ahead using a herd of antelope we drove into the arena overnight in pens mounted on vast carts through the Gate of Triumph.

"All this for one naumachia," mutters Marcus, as we look round the under-stage space by torchlight. The smooth waterproofing layer that has been applied over the past few days is almost dry, we touch it lightly, feel a slight damp chill coming from it.

"It's done now," I comfort him. "Merula says it's all waterproofed, we're nearly there."

"Apart from coating the whole floor with pitch and sealing all the doors, you mean?"

"Well, there is that," I admit.

THANKFULLY TITUS SAVES HIS NEXT visit to the Games for after our waterproofing, so that we have our usual facilities available and can put on a spectacle worthy of his attendance. He has Berenice with him again and when I see her arrive in the imperial box, I take Karbo aside.

"Get one of the kittens and keep hold of it till I tell you."

"What for?"

"Just do as I say."

"Which one?"

"The black one."

He returns a few moments later with the smallest of the litter, a tiny creature with a little dash of white in the centre of its otherwise black forehead and huge green eyes. "Now what?"

"Follow me."

We make our way through the cool corridors to the imperial box. The Praetorian Guards regard me with suspicion.

"A small gift from the backstage team for Queen Berenice," I say.

"What is it?"

"A kitten."

They hesitate.

"She will love it," I say. "The Emperor will be pleased that she is beloved by the common people."

The guards have obviously already experienced this for themselves. One of them ducks through the drapes. I can hear muttering, then he waves us through.

Titus is watching an ongoing bout between two well-known gladiators, who are making a good show of things, but Berenice has turned to see us enter. I nudge Karbo who, having a good sense of the dramatic, promptly falls to his knees and holds out the kitten almost above his bowed head. The kitten mews, as if on cue.

"Oh!" says Berenice, "Too pretty." She's smiling, her hands already reaching out for the kitten, which Karbo, lifting his head to see better, delivers into her lap. The kitten, feeling silk for the first time in its life, nestles into the folds of her clothes and purrs.

"A small gift of welcome," I say. "Motherless, your majesty. Karbo thought you might care for it."

Karbo looks up at me questioningly, obviously thinking of the plump mother cat who is at this very moment prowling around the amphitheatre, searching for rats.

"Motherless," I repeat firmly and Karbo nods vigorously.

"Poor tiny thing," says Berenice, stroking the kitten. "And you are?" she asks me.

"Althea Aquillius, scribe to the amphitheatre's manager, majesty," I say.

"And is the boy your son?" she asks.

"Motherless, majesty," I say. "Like the kitten," I add, ramming the point home.

"Poor child," she says. "Dearest?" she adds to Titus.

Titus looks over his shoulder at us. "Ah, the scribe, I remember you," he says. "Althea?"

"Your memory is astonishing, Imperator," I say.

"I don't forget someone who beats me," he says. "Beat me at shorthand," he explains to Berenice. "Excellent scribe. Offered her a job, but as she said, who would sort out this place if I took her away?"

"The boy has brought me a kitten as a gift," says Berenice.

Titus looks at the tiny creature and then back at me, his face softening. "A kind gesture," he says. "You are good to have thought of the Queen." As I thought, given the reluctance of those around him to accept the relationship, anyone treating Berenice as his rightful companion is pleasing to him. "What was that about the boy?" he adds.

"Motherless," says Berenice with sympathy.

Titus looks down at Karbo. "Do you want him as a pet as well, eh?"

"We care for him ourselves, Imperator," I say, gesturing to Karbo to leave. When he's disappeared through the drapes I add, "But I have a request, if you would look with favour on it?"

"Speak, speak," says Titus, one eye back on the gladiators.

"Did it work?" asks Marcus when he catches me in one of the corridors as the crowds disperse.

"Yes," I say. "He promised me a scroll within a few days."

"You're a wily thing," says Marcus. "Well done."

I'm painstakingly copying out a legal document when Karbo interrupts me. I hastily cover over the scroll, but his sharp eyes miss nothing.

"Why's my name on there?"

"Oh, so you have been practising your reading. I thought you'd given up."

"I can read my name," he says. "Why have you written it down?"

"None of your business."

"If it's my name, then it's my business."

I shake my head. "You'll see it soon enough. What do you want?"

"Julia said to tell you she asked at the temple and the most auspicious day is in four days' time."

"Tell her everything will be ready."

"For what?"

"You'll see," I say.

He huffs. "Why is everyone keeping secrets?"

"Why are you so nosy? Go and find someone else to bother."

"Fine," he says and stomps away. I smile and bend back to my work, outlining his name with care.

THE CHOSEN MORNING, HALFWAY THROUGH September, dawns bright and sunny, an auspicious sign. Fabia winks at me when she spots me at the amphitheatre.

"Everything ready for this evening?"

I nod.

"Did you manage to convince the lawyer, then?" "A whole wild boar made a very convincing case," I say. "The paperwork's all done."

"Paperwork for what?" asks Karbo.

"Never you mind," says Fabia.

THE DAY'S SHOW OVER AND done with, I grab Karbo before he runs off somewhere. He still insists on washing himself in the public fountains, doing so often but not exactingly.

"I think the time has come for you to attend the baths," I say. Karbo screws up his face. "You boss me around too much."

"No arguing," I tell him. "And look," I add, trying to tempt him. "I've made you a new tunic. You can wear it once I'm satisfied you're properly clean." I rummage in my satchel and hold out a new green tunic. The green is from the same cloth of a new tunic Marcus has been wearing lately, and I can see that Karbo is swayed by this.

He trails behind me to the Baths of Nero, bare feet dragging. I force him to sit in the hottest room, although he wriggles and complains throughout. When I get out a little bottle of oil and a strigil, he screws up his nose. "I don't want all that on me."

"You don't have a choice," I say. I rub him all over with oil, then show him how to scrape it off the parts of himself that he can reach, before finishing the job for him and obliging him to take a dip in the cool pool. When he emerges, his black skin is gleaming with the treatment it has received, I have never seen it look so healthy.

"See how well you look," I say.

He shrugs as if he couldn't care less, but I catch him turning first his arm and then a leg this way and that, admiring the glow.

I add some oil to his scalp and locks, rubbing it in as much as I can before he slips away, demanding to wear his new tunic. I put it over his head and pass him a little leather belt the cobbler made up for me. He puts it on, tightening it with a manly air, imitating Marcus so closely that I have to hide a laugh.

"Now for shoes," I say and pull out a neat pair of new leather boots. Karbo all but grabs them out of my hands, then quickly puts them on, strutting up and down in front of me.

"They'll keep your feet warm and dry this winter," I say. "Just one thing missing," I add.

"What's that?"

"You'll see," I say. "Fabia has gone to collect it."

"Collect what?"

"I can't tell you that," I say. "It's a surprise."

When we reach the courtyard there's a fire built up in a brazier and the smell of roasting mutton from two whole sheep. Tables have been laid out end to end and platters of food are already laid out. Loaves of bread and cheese pastries from the bakery, dipping bowls of garum and olive oil, pickled mushrooms and olives, heaped piles of grapes and blackberries, jugs of wine and sweet wine cakes, as well as a big dish of a spiced milk pudding sweetened with honey, a rare treat and Karbo's favourite.

He stares. "What's the feast for?"

I pretend not to hear him, turning instead to Julia, who is making her way into the courtyard carrying a pot of vegetable stew. "It all looks wonderful, Julia, thank you."

Julia smiles. "It's not every day a child is named," she says.

Karbo frowns. "Who's had a baby?"

Julia rests her hand lightly on his head. "Go and call Marcus, please," she says. "He's upstairs."

Karbo mutters something and disappears into the stairwell as Cassia joins us, wearing her best tunic, a bright yellow and orange, with a red headwrap embroidered all over with tiny yellow flowers, the outfit she lent me on the opening day of the Games.

"I've closed up the popina," she says. "I'm looking forward to a night off."

The residents of the building are gathering, all in their best clothes, a bright and colourful throng. The smaller children dash about, over-excited, and the adults beam as Marcus makes his way down the wooden staircase, with Karbo behind him, the two of them in their matching green tunics and leather belts. Once they reach the courtyard, Julia moves past them and ascends a few steps, so that she can look down on us all. Cassia nudges me, smiling.

"Does he still not know?"

I grin, shaking my head.

Her eyes shine with unshed tears. "He will be so happy. May the gods bless you for doing this."

The whole insula helped me pull strings here and there after Titus gave his permission. It's taken weeks of planning to change Karbo from a runaway slave to my son. First, I drew up false documents indicating that Marcus bought Karbo just over a year ago from a slave trader based in Pompeii, who, having died in the eruption of Vesuvius since then, cannot argue to the contrary. Then Marcus gave a generous gift of a whole wild boar to a careless lawyer who certified that Karbo has now been set free and finally, a higher-class lawyer wrote and certified the legal scroll which names Karbo as my newly adopted son and the Emperor himself as having given permission. Not only will I be Karbo's new mother, but Marcus will now be his legal guardian and patron, as he is to me, since he freed both of us. A woman cannot adopt without imperial consent; the scroll from Titus allowing this is a rare concession and one now securely tucked away in my most treasured possessions.

"Today we gather in this place to witness a new beginning for a child," starts Julia, who has volunteered for the role normally reserved for a priest, since Karbo is too old for the naming ceremony which should take place when a baby is nine days old. From what I can tell, Karbo is closer to nine years old, so we have had to make up our own rite of passage. "Step forward, Karbo."

Karbo stands stock still and I have to gently push him forwards. He looks over his shoulder at me, bewildered.

"The boy Karbo has been legally documented as the slave of Marcus Aquillius Scaurus," says Julia, her clear voice ringing out.

Karbo starts and for a moment I am afraid he is going to bolt, as he used to when we first found him. To be named as a slave, when he thought he had escaped such a future, must be terrifying to him. But Maria, standing close to him, has already grabbed hold of his arm, no doubt anticipating just such a reaction.

Julia smiles down at Karbo. "On this day, the slave Karbo has been set free by his master," she says, and Maria loosens her hold. "Furthermore," Julia continues, "Althea Aquillius today offers to take the boy as her own child, adopting him as her son. Extraordinary permission has been given for this, from Emperor Titus himself, and cannot be contested. Step forward, Althea."

I step forward and stand close to Karbo. He stares up at me.

"You take this boy as your son?" asks Julia.

"I take him as my son," I say.

"Do you accept Althea as your mother and promise to obey her in all matters, as a loyal son should?" says Julia to Karbo.

Karbo gives a wordless nod, his wide eyes never leaving me.

"And what do you name him?" she asks me.

"Titus Aquillius Karbo," I say. I have given him the Emperor's name as his formal first name, since this has been made possible by him, and kept Karbo as his common-use name, which he will continue to be known as. His family name comes from Marcus, since he was supposedly set free by him, and I am pleased that it matches my own.

Julia nods and lifts her hands, palms upwards. "May Nundina

and Nona bless this boy child, now named Titus Aquillius Karbo, and give him a long life."

"Long life," echo the onlookers.

From the folds of her tunic, Fabia pulls out and passes to me a fine chain, from which dangles a little gilded amulet, the bulla given to every boy child during his naming ceremony. The lack of a bulla has, until today, marked Karbo out as a foreigner amongst his Roman peers. I slip the chain over Karbo's head, before laying a hand on his black locks in a blessing. Karbo gazes up at me, amazed. His hands, hanging by his side, are shaking. The crowd breaks into applause and blessings, naming Nundina and Nona more than once, as they would for a baby.

"Well, now you have a mother and a proper legal guardian I hope you'll be more obedient," says Maria, sniffing loudly and using her palla to wipe her eyes. "Or you'll get a good beating, I should imagine."

Cassia and I look at each other and giggle. Maria's stern words are fooling nobody. It was she who bought the extra green cloth to make Karbo's new tunic and who took up a place close to Karbo during the ceremony, who knew him well enough to stop him from running off when he was named as a slave. She might as well be his grandmother, the amount of time she spends feeding him little treats and reminding him of his manners.

Karbo throws his arms about my waist, burying his face in my tunic. I kneel down and put my arms around him in a tight embrace, which leads to cheers from the crowd. When Karbo pulls away his eyelashes are wet and I dash away my own tears that have welled up at his happiness.

"Time to eat," says Cassia and everyone moves to take up a place round the long table, embracing Karbo and me as they go. I sit next to Julia and Karbo sits between us, very upright, conscious of all the attention being lavished on him.

The meal goes on for hours, new platters of roast mutton handed round, cups refilled with wine, while olive stones and grape pips pile up on our plates and the children gulp down as much milk pudding as they can. As darkness falls, we light lamps and torches around the courtyard. Someone pulls out a flute and someone else a cithara, tambourines keep the beat and favourite songs are sung, growing louder and bawdier as more cups of wine are drunk. Karbo is now racing about the courtyard with his friends, all solemnity forgotten, excitement keeping him awake long past his usual bedtime. At some point I tell him to go to bed and Karbo, for once, obeys with alacrity, the crowd cheering on this display of motherly care and filial obedience. Cassia and I laugh, our cheeks flushed with too much wine. We hold hands with Fabia and other friends and dance through the courtyard, enjoying the chance to celebrate the joyful things in life. I very much doubt Karbo is asleep, he is probably peeping over the rooftop railing at us all, enchanted enough with his new status as my son to at least have made a pretence at obedience for the past hour or so.

I make my way to the toilets and when I emerge, Rullus is standing in the shadows, blocking my way.

"So you got the Emperor himself to grant you permission to adopt a child?" he asks, his words low and slurred.

"Yes," I say.

"Ridiculous. Can't imagine why he'd do that. Women can't just go round adopting children. Why should they be given permission to adopt some street rat? They don't even have authority over their own children, that's a man's job."

"The Emperor was kind enough to think otherwise in this

instance," I say, looking away, hoping someone in the crowd will see me and come over.

"Well, I suppose amongst your lot anything goes."

"My lot?"

"Gladiators, actors, whores, all you lot."

"I'm none of those things," I say and add, lowering my voice, "but I work with them every day and most of them are better than you."

"What did you say?"

"Nothing," I say.

"I won't have Cassia hanging about with disreputable people. You stay away from her. You, that waddling little dwarf Fabia and Marcus. He's probably got his eye on her," slurs Rullus. "But she's mine. My family, and I'm going to make her my wife. Only right. Girl shouldn't be unwed at her age. Running a popina, too. It's not decent, you get all sorts trying it on."

"I'm sure you do," I say. "If you'll excuse me." I try to walk away but he catches at my arm.

"Nothing better than a whore, that's what you are," he mutters. "And I know how to show a whore a good time."

"Althea?"

Fabia is standing close to us, frowning.

"Ah!" says Rullus, with a big smile. "Come here, little one!" With one quick movement, he picks her up and deposits her on top of the nearest table. "Dance for us!"

Fabia's face freezes. "Help me down," she says to me.

I hold out a hand and she climbs back down via the bench set below the table.

"Not dancing? Where's your sense of fun?" cries Rullus. "Cassia! You'll dance, won't you?"

He grabs at Cassia's hands, leads her away in a dance that has others joining in.

"I hate people lifting me," mutters Fabia, glowering as she watches him. "I'm not a child."

"I don't like him," I say, and even this tiny confession feels like a freedom.

"Nor do I," says Fabia. "Father said he's seen him coming home late most nights from brothels. I mean, men do go there, but every night? When he's courting Cassia?"

I sit down heavily on the bench. "Is he?"

"I think so. Laughing and joking with her all the time, making little comments about wives and mothers and suchlike. I thought he was alright at first but I'm beginning to think he's not as nice as he seems."

"He – he put his hands on me once," I say, this watered-down version all I can manage to get out of my mouth.

Fabia looks at me and her face is serious. "Have you told Cassia?"

"You're the only person I've told," I manage.

"She needs to know," says Fabia.

"Will she believe me?"

"I believe you."

Tears of relief spring to my eyes. "I'll tell her," I say. "I just have to find the right moment."

THE STARS HAVE CROSSED THE sky and the songs grown slow, children have fallen asleep and been carried back to their beds. People disperse, calling out sleepy goodnights. I help Julia blow out the lamps and torches, then, carrying a little lamp of my own, make my way up the stairs to the rooftop. I open the door of my hut and see in the flickering light that Karbo has finally fallen asleep, without even removing his new shoes or belt. I'm about to go in but then I catch sight of Marcus' silhouette across the rooftop, standing by the eastward wall, looking out over the darkness of the city, soon to grow light with the coming dawn. We are going to have to get through a whole day tomorrow on barely two hours' sleep.

I walk over to his side. He straightens at my approach, wipes a hand over his eyes. I realise he has been weeping and want to creep away again, but it is too late.

"He was pleased," Marcus says, forcing a smile.

"He was afraid of losing me one day," I say. "He wanted a mother so badly; I could not see him desire something so much and not grant it if I could convince Titus to let me adopt him. And he has your protection now, too, it will be important for him to have a legal guardian and patronage."

He nods.

I swallow. "It must bring back memories," I start awkwardly.

He gives a half-shrug as though to indicate it is nothing, but cannot complete the gesture. "Amantius…"

"I know," I say. My mind fills with the searing image of Marcus on his knees, digging with his bare hands through the ashes of Pompeii, searching for his little son and his beloved wife, knowing even as he did so that they were gone, lying to himself that he might find them alive in that hellscape. And before that, I recall Livia's soft voice and hazelnut-coloured hair as she welcomed me into her home, playing peekaboo with Amantius early one morning. I only knew them for a few hours, their faces have already grown hazy in my memory.

Marcus looks away. He clears his throat. "He should get as much education as possible," he says gruffly. "You'll teach him to read and write?"

"I will," I say. "When he has caught up with children of his own age, he can attend school with a proper tutor. I can't teach him everything."

He nods. "Good work on the bill of sale," he says, attempting some humour. "Don't let slip what you did, though, or you'll have every slave in Rome wanting forged documents. And wide-eyed kittens to offer to foreign queens."

"Karbo was going to leg it when Julia said he was your slave," I say. "Good thing Maria grabbed hold of him."

"He always was fast. Now he's got a taste for the races, he'll be disappearing off there if you let him out of your sight."

"He was good with the horses though. I've never seen him so quiet and patient."

"Just as well. They're going to need all the patience we can muster to get them running through the water when the crowd's roaring. Speaking of which, it's time to sleep or we'll be dead on our feet at the show today."

"Goodnight then," I say.

"Goodnight."

I walk back to my own hut and look back briefly, expecting Marcus to be making his own way to bed, but he is still leaning on the wall, looking out over the darkness, lost in his own thoughts. For a moment, it had felt like the old days, when we spoke about everything, but then he all but dismissed me, cutting the conversation short, while continuing to think about the past without me. Perhaps I should have spoken about Rullus, but Marcus had enough on his mind. I feel lonely again, but the sight of Karbo cheers me. I have made his desire come true even if I cannot settle on what mine is, I think, and that is a good enough start. Karbo is properly documented and has me as his mother now, and no-one will be able to separate us, come what may.

WE VISIT THE STABLES AGAIN. We will need one chariot from each racing team, for the Blues aren't about to wear another team's colours, their followers would be up in arms at the very notion. We take more horses down to the river, try them out in the water, choose those who seem least concerned. Agreements are made, team drivers chosen. We have our four chariots, four horses and a driver each. They're not the very top drivers, the stables aren't about to waste their time on a show where they won't even be able to reach their top speed, but these four are the younger drivers in the next tier down, training to become the future stars of the racetrack. They can drive plenty fast enough for our needs. Mindful that they will be performing in front of Titus in an unusual environment, the stables agree to have weekly sessions to accustom the horses to water. Celer will take on this task, and Karbo begs me to be allowed to be his assistant.

"Fine," I say in the end, exasperated with the constant nagging. "Celer, don't let any harm come to him."

Karbo comes back from the first water-training session glowing with pleasure and gabbling at great length about the names and temperaments of the various steeds. When it becomes clear he isn't going to stop any time soon, I nod along, trying to make notes on the next day's show and occasionally making appropriate noises of disbelief or praise according to what seems to be required from me. I keep trying to find a moment to pluck up my courage and tell Cassia about Rullus. Perhaps I should wait until the end of the season, I think. If I just focus on the naumachia for now, then afterwards there will be plenty of time. Fabia nods uncertainly when I tell her this. "Don't leave it too long," she says.

"I won't," I promise her. "There's only a few weeks to go. What difference can it make?"

"HE'S GOOD," SAYS CELER TO me, a week later.

"Who is?"

"Karbo, with the horses. You should come and watch one day."

I accompany them to the next week's session. We're back down by the Tiber and the horses have moved beyond tentative steps in the shallows. All of them now trot through water higher than their knees, and most of them even go willingly into deeper parts and swim. Karbo is encouraging the most reluctant one beyond the shallows. He whispers to it, he strokes its neck and flanks, all the while pacing along the shoreline, getting ever deeper into the water.

"Is it safe?" I ask, thinking about the currents.

"This part is, which is why we practise here."

The horse gets in up to its chest and Karbo, in one smooth move which tells me he's done this before, slips onto its back, pulling himself up through the water by holding the horse's mane. It jerks its head, trying to decide what to do about this strange state of affairs, but Karbo is already leaning forward, whispering into its ears again and the horse relaxes, takes a few more steps forwards, then changes its gait and begins to swim.

Celer is smiling. "He's done it with all of them," he says. "One by one. That one was the last one, didn't want to go deeper than its ankles at first and now look at the two of them. He's born to work with horses."

"Don't tell him that," I beg.

"YOU'VE GOT ONE HOUR," WARNS Marcus. "I can't have the boards still wet when the hunt's on, the venatores will be slipping all over the place."

Merula nods, his face tense. The wooden trough he's had built, held up by scaffolding to get it from Nero's old cistern to the edge of the amphitheatre, will act as a kind of mini aqueduct, channelling the water three hundred paces across the buildings and roads and to one side of the amphitheatre, far above our heads. It's been painted a sky blue to help it blend into the background of a sunny day and now we're all standing waiting at the far end of the arena, to see if the water really will pour down at the rate Merula has worked out. It will mostly fall into Diana's blue-lined hunting pool, so that Merula can measure how fast it fills, but there's bound to be splashing.

He gives a signal, repeated far away at the top of the amphitheatre's highest wall, which will be seen up at the cistern, where they will open up the water flow, allowing it to reach us in moments. We stand, waiting, craning up at the trough, see a shudder in it and then…

"It's working!" yells Karbo as water streams down from the sky, pouring into the blue pool, Merula watching its progress, nodding to himself as it quickly fills, faster than we've ever managed to fill it for shows. He gives another signal and the stream falters, then stops, dribbles a little more, and is gone. It has spilled over the sides, so fast was the flow. Karbo dabbles his toes in it even as it drips away through the cracks in the boards.

"Fast enough?" asks Marcus.

"Yes," says Merula, his confidence clear. "Yes. It did what it should do. It will fill in half an hour and empty perhaps even more quickly than that, with three of the largest trapdoors open in the centre."

Applause breaks out between us, Marcus claps Merula on the shoulder, smiling, relief showing in his face.

"Thank Neptune," he says. "Speaking of which, Althea: are the costumes ready for King Neptune's arrival?"

"Yes," I say. "All the costumes are complete."

"I keep waking up and thinking I've forgotten something," he says. "Thank all the gods this will be over soon, and I'll never have to run another naumachia again. Right, clear this space. It has one hour to dry and then I've got a beast hunt to get started."

WE TRY TO KEEP THE second-to-last day of Games simple, putting on a larger but shorter gladiatorial bout in the afternoon, consisting of the re-enactment of a battle, which allows us to show off one hundred gladiators in a much shorter space of time than the usual sessions, where more of the gladiators fight in pairs. The crowd enjoys the larger spectacle and departs earlier than usual.

The last people have barely left the building when our full team gets ready for tonight's work. We have one thousand slaves in total and for this piece of work we will be using over eight hundred of them all at one time. While the remaining two hundred sweep and wash the seating as usual, making it ready for tomorrow, we dismantle, once again, all the pens and work area below the arena, for fear that the quantity of water that will flow through it would cause damage. We leave only one lift mechanism with one prop, which we will use at the very end of the show, operated by six slaves whom we have checked can swim well in case of accident; the water even at full drainage should only come to a man's waist. We have taken out all our other lifts, breaking them down into their component parts and sending them by wagons down to the warehouses for the time being, so that we do not waste them. They can be refitted over winter. While this goes on, firepits are lit at eight points around the outside of the amphitheatre, and large cauldrons are placed over each, before the pitch starts to be added. It arrives in vast solid slabs, which have to be broken into chunks with chisels, then thrown into the cauldrons to become liquid. We have perhaps overordered, but it was hard to judge how much would be needed to fully coat the wooden boards and we did not dare run out. Three trapdoors are left open. They will act as our plugs, so they cannot be sealed shut, while the rest are fully locked into place.

The smell as the pitch begins to heat up and the solid blocks melt down into thick black liquid makes me feel slightly sick, charcoal and pine resin making for a stomach-churningly strong combination.

Marcus briefs the team. "As each cauldron of pitch becomes liquid over the fire, we use these smaller dipping metal cups, each held with a long rod handle. You dip out a cup, then quickly take it to the boards and pour it on. It'll be brushed over the floor by the sweepers to smooth it out and get an even coating. You have to walk fast, it can't cool too much, or it won't brush on, just be lumpy and sticky." Marcus shakes his head. "I can't believe we're doing this. There'll be two hundred brooms thrown out tomorrow, what a waste. To say nothing of a whole floor only good for scrap in the boatyards after this."

The smell grows thicker in the air. The first few cups of pitch are spread onto the surface of the three trapdoors, to ensure they will leak as little as possible, though we have to leave their edges and hinges undone, so that they can still open and close. Meanwhile some of the doors into antechambers around the arena are being sealed with wax. It won't hold forever, but we can't put pitch on them, it would ruin them. The wax can be removed with boiling water when there is no longer a need for the seal. Usually the antechambers are where our gladiators and other performers wait to enter the arena. The only obvious way in and out now for any performers is the Gate of Triumph. The Gate of Death has also been waxed shut. The water will continue to fall from Merula's waterfall throughout the show, to make up for any leaking that may occur, keeping the water level stable.

Now the pitch is ready in large quantities, the work begins in earnest. We start at one end of the floor and spread it, working backwards towards the other end. There are a few errors at first, the pitch cooling too quickly and being impossible to spread, until we realise we must bring one whole cauldron at a time from outside and apply it quickly, then move onto the next cauldron, setting the first to boil again with fresh chunks of the cold pitch. More than ten slaves get burnt during the exhausting hours that follow and Fabius and Fabia are kept busy seeing to them, applying a lotion of wine, myrrh and honey and administering a draught of thyme and belladonna to ease the pain of the three worst patients.

It is odd to see the familiar wooden boards slowly disappear under the thick black sea of pitch, the smell making several of us feel so sick that we have to leave the building in search of fresh air. I go outside but find little respite, for there are always seven cauldrons bubbling while one is being used, slaves taking turns to stir them with long wooden paddles, a back-breaking job as it is a thick mixture. When I return, Marcus has disappeared.

"He's gone downstairs to see what it looks like from the underside," says Fabia.

I make my way downstairs and find Marcus standing in the growing gloom, holding a flaming torch for light. Usually, a little light comes in from the fine cracks between the boards, but they are slowly being filled in, so it is darker than usual and feels larger, now that it is all empty.

"Seems to be holding," he says. "There are drips on the floor, but you can't see sunlight through the boards, so it must be filling the gaps. Let's hope the leaking is far less than the flow of water."

"I feel sick," I say. "The smell is disgusting."

"My shoes are ruined," says Marcus, looking down regretfully. They have several splatters of black on them. "That's not coming off, is it?"

"We're making good time," I say.

"It's not so much the applying it, it's the drying. Is it going to be dry enough for chariots to run over it by late morning tomorrow?"

"The gods will help us," I say.

"Neptune better be on our side, it's his realm we are representing. If we do it badly, he will not be pleased. I'll offer a prayer at his shrine tomorrow morning. Where's Merula? How are the water chambers coming along?"

"Well, I think," I say. "Shall we go and check?"

Five entryways into the arena have been left unsealed. One is entirely empty, a simple stone passageway. The other four each contain a replica ship, sitting on the stone floor, awaiting their moment to shine. Most are the length of six men, one, heavily decorated, is even longer and each can hold more than twenty men aboard.

"Will they float well enough with the weight of the crew in?"

"They're flat-bottomed, they should do. Hard to steer, but then they don't have to do much and there are no waves. So long as they stay together and the men aboard row smoothly, it'll look impressive enough. The sails will come up as soon as they move out, it'll make them look bigger."

THE WORK FINISHES AS THE sun goes down, the fires finally extinguished, one thousand slaves slowly walking back to their warehouses to eat a brief meal of bread and cheese as there has been no time to cook anything, the rest of the team left to stand in the imperial box, looking out over the now entirely black floor.

"It looks ominous," I say, shivering.

Marcus says nothing, but I notice his hand shape into the gesture against evil spirits. He is as nervous as I am, even if he is trying not to show it.

"I want everyone here at dawn tomorrow," he says. "We have to know if it's going to work."

"The horses and chariots will arrive first thing," says Karbo.

"There are guards tonight watching over the amphitheatre and the water scaffolding," says Strabo. "Just so there are no silly accidents. That floor would go up like a torch if you put a flame to it. And we can't have any idiots thinking it would be fun to climb up the scaffolding."

Marcus takes a deep breath. "I'll be sleeping here tonight," he says.

"You'll sleep so badly," I say.

"Why? Do you think I'm going to sleep well back at the insula? My dreams will be full of unending waves and fish."

I'm half-tempted to suggest that we both sleep at the amphitheatre, so that I will have the comfort of Marcus close to me, free of fears about Rullus. But such a suggestion will make Marcus ask questions and I still don't know how to tell him when I have not even told Cassia.

DIDO AND ÆNEAS

THE SUN IS JUST RISING. Marcus and I are standing on ladders poking through two of the three remaining open trapdoors, our heads just above the newly pitched wooden floor. The smell is still overwhelming. We each tentatively prod the surface. It feels very slightly tacky, but not sticky.

"Jupiter be thanked," says Marcus, huge relief in his voice. He has dark circles under his eyes. "I thought it would never dry. I checked it in the middle of the night when I woke up and it wasn't dry at all. That was the end of my night's sleep." He pulls himself up the last few steps up onto the floor itself and takes a couple of careful steps. "Not bad," he comments as I join him.

I lift a foot and examine the sole. There's a little marking from the pitch, nothing too bad.

"Can we test the chariots?" Karbo's eager face is looking up at me from the trapdoor ladder.

"Yes," I agree. "Just quickly though."

Merula joins us as Karbo disappears. "The pitch is holding," he says. "I had the slaves throw several buckets of water down on it and there were no drips on the underside, at least not for now. So it should hold for the duration of the show." He looks anxious, this is his moment after all, if the water system doesn't work as planned, the whole event will be a disaster.

We stand back as the newly arrived chariots are quickly driven round, then await the verdict.

"Bit sticky," says the lead driver. "Can feel the wheels dragging. But nothing bad. Not for what you want, anyway. No good for a real race."

"Good. Now leave," says Marcus. "The longer it has to keep drying, the better. I don't want the wheels damaging the pitch."

"More likely to be the other way round," says the driver, guiding the horses away from us.

THE TRUMPETS ARE SOUNDING.

"Right," says Marcus. "Titus has arrived. Everyone ready to start?"

Nods all round.

"Then get to your posts."

There's a final blast of trumpets and the singers burst into a chorus praising King Neptune. The Gate of Triumph opens, drawing attention to a steep ramp which leads from the arena to the gate itself, then down again into the outside world. Four blue chariots make their way up the ramp, lifting them high into the gate's vast archway, then down and into the arena. The lead one is picked out in gold amongst the blue, its driver wears a golden crown as well as magnificent blue robes and carries a trident. By his side is Karbo, dressed in a blue and green tunic. The crowd applauds the appearance of King Neptune, as the other three chariots, full of additional blue and green-dressed attendants, array themselves in a line behind the chariot as it draws to a halt in front of the point where Merula's blue-painted trough hangs above them. In the crowd, Merula gives a signal, passed on up to the very edge of the top tier, even as Neptune raises his trident.

From the sky, a glistening column of water falls at his

command, the sunlight sending dancing rainbows through it. The water hits the black floor and splashes, ripples out as the chariots move on, first at a stately speed, then gathering pace as the water pours on and on, the chariot wheels spraying up arcs of water which throw cool drops onto the first few rows of seating. And then the crowd gasps as all over the amphitheatre a fine mist is sprayed over the audience. Scented water cools and perfumes the crowd, the effect achieved by our teams pumping the usual water supply for the fountains through additional tubing installed under Merula's direction this past week, with flattened ends forcing the water to emerge as a mist rather than a flow, perfume added through the specially modified tubes. The audience applauds this delightfully refreshing touch, even as before their very eyes the water deepens, the horses, trotting happily, slowing a little as it reaches their knees. At a gesture from Marcus, Neptune salutes Titus, then directs his chariot back up the ramp, through the Gate of Triumph and out again, the water lapping further up the ramp but unable to flow out of the gate.

The water is not yet very deep. The singers break into the story of Theseus and the Minotaur, how Zeus, disguised as a bull, rose from the sea and impregnated the wife of King Minos, leading to the birth of a monstrous child, half-man, half bull. Marcus has skipped over the suggestion to have a real woman copulate with a bull, though it has been done before. Instead, he has found one of the largest bulls I've ever seen and it is driven over the ramp the chariots have used to exit. The bull stamps about, mystified by the water coming up to its knees, and suddenly finds itself face-to-face with Carpophorus, who swings over the wall and into the water on a rope, sword in hand, bare-chested. There's applause and a lot of high-pitched cries of admiration, suggesting it is the ladies in the top tiers who are most pleased to see him in action.

The bull stamps again, irritated by the glinting sword and Carpophorus' direct stare and stance, which signals aggression. It begins to approach, evidently believing the man will back down, show some signs of deference, but when it does not see them, it speeds up.

I have to admire the bravery on show. Carpophorus stands entirely still, allows the bull to all but reach him and then swipes, cutting at its jowls, an instant line of red appearing. The bull bellows in pain and rage and attacks, its black horns clanging against the sword that harmed it, then it turns to try and catch the bare chest, so vulnerable. But the glinting, glistening sword is too fast, it slices again and now the bull's shoulder bleeds, blood flowing down into the water. The bellow this time is deafening, the blade even faster, Carpophorus cuts the bull again and again until he permits it to come perilously close, its own momentum driving the sword deep down into its chest, its own attack turned against it. The beast sinks to its knees as though paying homage to the bestiarius' skill and strength, even as it slowly dies and the crowd cheers. Carpophorus turns a full circle to soak up all the praise, then pulls out the bloodied sword and washes it in the deepening water, striding away to where he's pulled up over the wall into the first row of seating. The bull is dragged away with hooked poles, put onto a wheeled cart and taken through the Gate of Triumph to be butchered.

The audience has barely finished chanting Carpophorus' name when four doors are pushed open by invisible hands and, on a rush of additional water, four beautiful ships float into the arena, each full of gloriously dressed gladiators in parade armour, who set to and hoist the sails. I can see Merula beaming.

The passageways containing the ships, empty this dawn, have been filling up for hours, so that slowly, slowly, each ship began to float. They sail in, the sudden boost of water increasing the depth considerably, so that it is now deeper than a man's waist.

The musicians play a bold military theme, then the chorus tells the story of Odysseus, of his turbulent journey across the seas after the fall of Troy, seeking to return home, yet meeting one disaster after another.

"And so he came to the Island of Sirens and bade his men to plug up their ears with wax, and bind him to the mast, that he alone amongst mortal men might hear their song and yet resist their charms, living to tell the tale."

The man playing Odysseus is bound to the mast of the main ship, the ships follow one another through the water, music playing, the singers singing, and from the water emerge Vita and her swimmers. They are dressed in short tunics, painted as though they were feathers, to show the bird-like nature of the Sirens. Vita and the other women follow the ships, draw close and stretch out their hands to Odysseus, who in turn reaches out to them, desperate to join them and yet unable to do so, as his men, immune to the song of the Sirens, row on, their faces turned away from the terrible temptation of the women below.

The ships position themselves as much out of the way as they can, each of the four in a different quarter of the vast oval, tucked against the wall as the Daughters of Thetis take centre stage. There are forty girls in all, Vita's largest team. They create a circle between them. As delicate lyres and citharas play a rippling tune, they move to the music, each one rising and falling in perfect coordination with her fellow performers. The circle becomes a trident and then an anchor, a simple straight line suddenly takes on the shape of a ship and then a star. The women move as though propelled through the water by an unseen force, barely seeming to make an effort and yet every move they make brings applause, for all the spectators watching know how impossible their shapes are, as woman after woman disappears under the water for extraordinary lengths of time, only their legs or arms visible, before they rise to the surface with joyous smiles, as though what they have done is nothing, a mere child's frolicking. The water grows deeper all the time, now comfortably the depth of a man. As the women finally complete their piece, bowing their heads to Titus, he leads the rapturous applause.

Now comes the most elaborate part of the storytelling. The swimmers make their way discreetly aboard the boats, taking their places on the rowing teams in plain tunics which make them blend in as the men take over, the ships sailing round again as, opposite the imperial box, just to one side of the Vestal Virgins' own seating, a purple and gold banner falls over the edge of the front row. Vita, swiftly re-dressed as a foreign queen, her head crowned in gold and brightly coloured robes falling about her, holds out her hand to the lead ship, which makes its way to her. Once close, a man in golden armour leaps ashore, clasping her in his arms.

The chorus reminds us that Prince Aeneas, freshly escaped from the fall of Troy, knew he was destined to be the founder of Rome and so, despite his great and enduring love for the Queen of Carthage, Dido, he chose to follow his destiny rather than his heart, leaving her behind for the good of the yet-to-be Rome.

The golden-armoured man makes his farewell to Vita, who clutches at him even as he re-joins his ship, which sails away to Titus' side, as a singer gives Dido's grief a voice, lamenting her fate and insisting that she would rather die than love another.

Vita plays Dido's tragic end well, taking up a sword and enacting her suicide, finishing the scene draped lifeless over the edge of the wall, long braids touching the water below, while a group of maidens weep over her. There is vast applause. In the imperial box, Titus puts a hand to his eyes, wiping away tears as many of the women in the top tiers are doing. It looks as though he has understood the message.

The music dies away and Marcus is about to give a signal when, without warning, Titus stands and there is a sudden silence. The audience crane their necks to see what he is about to do. Is he displeased? The crowd is well aware of the relevance of the story, they wonder if Titus has been offended. Will there be a punishment for someone? I hold my breath.

"Come, Queen Dido, sail to me," he calls out loudly across the silent amphitheatre.

There's a flurry of activity. The lead ship reverses its journey, taking Aeneas back to his swiftly revived beloved. Vita turns towards Marcus for guidance, wanting him to tell her what to do, but he is too far away and cannot do anything. The silence of sixty thousand people is deafening.

The ship reaches Vita, who steps aboard and is brought to the imperial box, her body regally upright, her face set to a stillness I am sure she is not feeling. The height of the water means that Vita is almost face-to-face with Titus when the ship reaches him.

Titus leans from the imperial box, reaches out a hand and Vita holds out hers. He takes it and leans forward, kisses it, then lets it go.

"An affecting performance," he says loudly. "It shall be rewarded. You have shown true skills in recalling our glorious history and the needful sacrifices made by those who came before us. Therefore, this is yours."

The crowd gasps, for he is holding out a wooden sword, the item ritually given to a gladiator to set them free. Vita has been given her freedom.

There is rapturous applause. Vita falls to her knees in the ship, clutching the sword, tears falling down her face as the ship departs. The four doors around the arena open and the ships return to their secret passageways.

IT'S TIME TO DRAIN THE arena. Below are six slaves, who will unbolt the three trapdoors, allowing a rush of water to pour away. Once again, I hold my breath as the Gate of Triumph opens and Neptune's entourage of chariots re-enters over the ramp, shining in their blue and gold, Neptune holding aloft his trident. This time the drivers are alone, no attendants. They drive slowly through the deep water, which comes to the horses' shoulders, so that they are a hand's depth from having to swim. But three central whirlpools have opened up; the water level is visibly lowering even as the chariots canter on. One by one, three of the chariot drivers pull away their sea-trims, the chariots now revealing the colours of Rome's four racing teams even as the water, like a divine miracle, slowly disappears, the floor losing its watery glow altogether, now becoming a racetrack. A model obelisk, our only prop, rises up from the centre of the floor, mimicking the Circus Maximus. The crowd recognises it at once, along with their favoured racing teams, and scream their approval as the horses gain speed, the water all but gone and the aquatic display now become that most earthly-bound sport, beloved of Romans everywhere, chariot racing. Our choice of drainage in the very centre works to our advantage, for the teams' route takes them in a wide oval, so that there is no danger of being caught in the gaps into which water is still pouring, disappearing into the hypogeum below.

The audience are on their feet, chanting the names of the teams.

"Reds, Reds, Reds!"

"Go the Blues!"

"Come on, the Greens!"

"Whites! Whites for the finish!"

Karbo's smile is ecstatic as he leans over the wall to watch the Blues driver, released from his gravitas as Neptune, urging his team on.

THE SHOW IS ABOUT TO end but a signal from below has summoned Marcus and me from our places in the crowd. Strabo meets us in a corridor.

"Titus has asked to see both of you," he says, worried.

"What if he's annoyed, now he's thought about it?" I whisper to Marcus as we hurry towards the imperial box.

"Too late now, we've done it," says Marcus, but he sounds nervous. It's one thing to devise a suggestive show at the Aedile's wishes, but if Titus does take offence, he'll take it out on us, not the Aedile, who will plead ignorance.

We make our way through the drapes. Titus turns to face us, smiling, though his eyes are still red-rimmed from his earlier tears. "A delightful spectacle," he says. "A perfect finale to the inaugural Games."

Marcus' shoulders drop with relief. "Imperator."

"And excellent storytelling, most... most affecting, certainly. You know your history."

"The history of how Rome rose from the actions of one Prince is a glorious reminder of its power today," says Marcus.

"You must tell me exactly how it was done. It filled so fast and drained even faster, a marvel, as though the gods themselves helped you. How was it done? Was the water the full depth of the under-arena? Surely not in so little time?"

"The floor was coated in pitch like a sailing boat, then the trapdoors used as plugs for swift drainage. We used an... old water storage tank to have it fill quickly," says Marcus, carefully avoiding any mention of Nero.

"Most impressive."

"I am glad to have pleased you, Imperator," says Marcus.

"Of course, now that we know it can be done..." begins Titus.

I see Marcus stiffen and he goes so far as to interrupt Titus in a desperate attempt to stop what he can tell is coming next. "The audience will have been delighted to have seen a once-in-a-lifetime spectacle. They will be able to say they have seen something no-one else will ever see."

"Ah but now that you know it can be done, and done so well," says Titus, "it would be an excellent thing to do to end the season each year, do you not think? And perhaps next year you could have it even deeper, to allow for creatures of the sea to be displayed. No need to fill and drain it so quickly, if a greater depth is achieved, but... crocodiles? Sharks? Perhaps a night-time show... it would be very dramatic, even frightening. A magnificent spectacle. I will leave it with you."

I can feel Marcus' horror even though I can't see his face, the stiffness of his shoulders has spread to his whole body. "Imperator," he manages, his voice somehow staying steady and polite. "We will turn our minds to what is possible."

"Excellent. I look forward to next year's naumachia to complete the season. It can become a tradition. The crowds love a tradition, as you know." He looks at me. "I saw the boy playing his part. You must be proud of your son."

"I am eternally grateful for your kindness in allowing me to adopt him," I say. "You have made us both very happy."

Titus nods. "If only happiness were so easily won in all matters," he says with a sad smile. "You may go."

We make our way out of the imperial presence, Marcus striding down the corridor so fast I have to run to keep up with him, trying to come up with something comforting to say, but I can't think of anything. Marcus has detested everything about this naumachia, it has caused him worry for months. The idea that he will now have to deliver one on an annual basis is going to put him in a foul mood. By the time we reach the entrance to the under-arena, I have a pain in my side, and I let him go. We still haven't spoken to one another. The evening should have been a celebration, marking the end of the inaugural Games, one hundred days in which we have delivered a spectacular show every single day without fail. Instead, it is a gloomy one.

Julia has a bountiful meal waiting for us, but Marcus goes drinking with Fabius, no doubt to drown out the bitterness he feels. He does not come home till very late, for I lie awake a long time and do not hear him. The next day he stays in his hut, perhaps sleeping off the wine, till past midday and then sets off for the baths, so Celer informs me. We should be celebrating our freedom: no shows to put on for many months, no more continuous Games. A whole winter where we need only plan ahead and manage the upkeep of the amphitheatre, far less work with far less pressure. But Marcus stays out of sight.

AFTER A FEW DAYS OF rest I go to inspect the amphitheatre. The water drained away quickly, as Merula promised. It's still damp, but it has plenty of time to dry out, especially once we start removing the wooden flooring, letting in more air from above. I climb up one of the ladders, stand in the deserted, still-black arena. It's strange not to have to put on a show every day. The amphitheatre is empty of life without the sounds of the Games and the screams of the crowd.

"Haven't you got the winter off?" It's Vita, standing in one of the archways. She makes her way down the steps, leans over the wall to look down at me.

"Shouldn't you be out celebrating your freedom?"

"I still can't believe it. I've come here every day since then, gone through it all again in my mind, what he said, how he looked, trying to be sure it's real." Her voice wavers a little. I've never heard her so emotional.

"What did Labeo say?"

She snorts. "He was livid. Never heard so many curses out of one mouth. But you can't argue with an emperor, can you? Now he'll have to pay me properly if he wants me to keep on doing shows for him."

"Will you?"

"For a while, I suppose. While I think what to do. We've got plenty of bookings. And lots more coming in, now I'm Titus' favourite… that's how Labeo's billing me. He's hiked up the price for us."

"Will you take Labeo's name, now you're a freedwoman?"

"I will do no such thing," she says. "The paperwork's being drawn up and I chose Vita Africanus."

"Very nice," I say.

"I want to be my own woman. Although Labeo will be my legal guardian and patron until I marry, since he was my last master."

"Do you want to marry?"

"Now I'm free to, perhaps."

"Who to?" I ask, wondering if the answer is going to be Marcus.

"Don't know. Although most men would be better than being under Labeo's thumb. You're lucky, you have Marcus."

I nod.

"He's not happy, though?"

"Titus said we have to flood it all again next year – and every year, as a finale to each season. Marcus thought it was going to be a one-off. And next time the pitch won't be enough. Titus wants the full depth, dangerous animals, a night-time show, all sorts. It'll be challenging for anyone who can't swim well."

She shrugs. "Well, the Daughters of Thetis are at your service, if you need us. I owe you my freedom."

"We only chose your part," I say. "It's you that performed it well enough to earn your freedom. Did you see what the poet Martial wrote about the day?"

"Some drivel about sea nymphs?"

I laugh. "How did you know?"

Vita rolls her eyes. "He likes to put in a divine touch when he writes about the Games, it pleases the imperial family. What did he say?"

I pull open a scroll and read from it. "A well-coached team of Nereids frisked across the calm surface, their shifting formation giving colour to the waters. The trident threatened us with straight tooth, the anchor with curved; a mast, a ship, we took for real; the star of the Spartan boys, the sailors' friend, seemed really to shine, and sails to swell in a gauzy curve. Who devised such techniques amid the limpid waters? Either Thetis taught him these ploys, or she was his pupil."

Vita laughs. "I told you. He knew perfectly well who we were, that's why he mentioned Thetis. He's seen us perform before, he's a frequent guest at some of the best villas in Rome. He just likes adding a touch of poetry to his commentary, and of course he likes to please the Emperor by suggesting no one's ever seen anything like it before."

"Do you know him?"

"Only in passing. He writes well about the Games, plenty of grovelling, you must have seen all the stuff he wrote about the opening day, praising the amphitheatre as one of the wonders of the world and suggesting the animals obey the Emperor's command when he knows perfectly well the animal trainers have spent weeks and months getting them to do their bidding. Have you read his other stuff? Much bawdier. There isn't an affair in Rome he doesn't know about, and he never keeps the gossip to himself, writes it all down and publishes it. He must be responsible for half the divorces in Rome. Mind you, people ought to know better than to tell him anything at all, they know it'll end up in writing. Maybe they just use him as their messenger boy or maybe they think if they share their secrets, he'll tell them everybody else's. In unrelenting detail."

"I'll be sure not to tell him anything I want kept secret, then."

She grins. "So how many shows will there be next year?"

"Maybe one hundred and fifty? It seems like a lot more than this year, but they won't have to be consecutive, so that gives us more flexibility. We'll probably start earlier, April or even March through to September, which gives us the odd day where we don't have to do a show. We can do things like move the flooring for the next naumachia without crazy night shifts."

"That will help. Have you tried the Baths of Titus yet?"

I shake my head.

"Not a bad size," she says. "It's mixed bathing, instead of men and women at different times of day. Looks very elegant, seeing as it's just opened. Not like the crumbling ones you use."

I laugh. "They are a bit scruffy."

"We can go together now if you like. It'll be your local baths once you start putting on shows again next year. You can fall out of work and into a nice bath, think of that."

"Fine," I say. "Let's try them."

The Baths of Titus, only a few paces away from the amphitheatre, gleam with newness. Underneath, their construction and heating may have been cobbled together from Nero's private bathing rooms to give a quick result, but they are elegant enough. Outside, the gardeners are still frantically watering all the plants and whole trees they transplanted to give the illusion of an established garden, but there is still the smell of paint close to the outer walls as we enter. Inside, brand-new mosaic floors greet us, including a vast entryway motif of a hunting scene from the Games, no doubt a nod to the amphitheatre, a reminder of all the works the Flavians have commissioned since coming to power.

We make our way to the changing room to discard our clothes. Rows of brand-new niches await, so we have no trouble finding two side-by-side to leave our tunics and shoes.

We sit in the hottest room for a while although, given the time of year, I'm more inclined to hurry through this part and get into the cooler pools. We oil each other and scrape away the accumulated dust and dead skin, then make our way to the cooler rooms. The pool here is very pretty, with fresh mosaics depicting sea-scenes. The baths I usually go to definitely feel scruffy, now that I see a newly decorated version.

The cool is delightful. I sink into the water gratefully, and Vita and I lie beside each other, she floating, I holding lightly to the edge to keep myself afloat. After a few moments she rolls her head towards me.

"I forgot, you can't swim, can you?"

"No," I say. "I must seem strange to someone like you."

"Shall I teach you?"

I think about it, then nod. "I'd like that."

"Let's start you with floating."

"We're starting now?"

"Why not?"

I shrug. "What do I do?"

"Float."

"I'm not sure I know how."

Vita shakes her head. "You float without doing anything. In fact, the less you do, the better."

"But I'll sink!"

"No, you won't. Look." She demonstrates, lying on top of the water as easily as though lying on a bed. "You just lie still, and the water will hold you up."

I try, but the water goes in my ears, and I jolt my head, my belly sinks immediately, and I end up spluttering.

Vita laughs.

"I'm sorry. You looked so startled. Try again. Trust the water. It will hold you; I swear by Thetis. Just lie down as though you are sleeping, let your arms come out a little, I will put a hand under your back until you can feel yourself floating."

I splutter several more times, my nose and ears repeatedly filling with water, but after a few attempts there is a brief moment when I feel Vita's hand come away from my lower back and the water, as she promised, really does hold me up. I lift my head to tell her so and promptly sink again.

"I felt it!" I say as I come back up and she grins. I try again and this time I remember the sensation and when it comes again I remain still, even when Vita's hand moves away from me. I keep my eyes closed, the better to concentrate, trying to steady my breathing, gaining in confidence as the water continues to hold me, even daring to move my arms and legs a tiny bit. When I open my eyes, Vita is smiling down at me.

"You're doing it! You will be one of my team in no time."

"I doubt it," I say, standing up again.

"Of course you will. Carry on floating, it's good for you to trust the water. If you remember the feeling, next time we come here it will be even easier for you. I'm going to do some practise."

She sets off to the other side of the pool, plunges under the water and her legs appear. She must be standing on her head. I can't help staring at her for a while before I lie back and, after a fumbled attempt, find my floating ability again. It's quite peaceful, the growing certainty that I will not sink, that the water does indeed hold me up.

"I see you found a swimming instructor after all."

I go under immediately, jam my feet down to the floor in a panic, come back up coughing and spitting out water, open my eyes to find Marcus standing right in front of me in the pool, amused at my performance. My hands come up without thinking to cover my breasts, but then I feel foolish and have to lower them again. We are surrounded by naked men and women, why should I be shy? My cheeks and neck feel hot, though.

"Didn't mean to interrupt your swimming lesson," says

Marcus. "Is that Vita?" he adds, looking down the pool to where her legs are going through various formations.

"Yes," I manage.

"Not bad, the baths, are they? They might become my new after-work favourites, since they're right next door."

"Yes," I say. "I mean – not bad. I like the decorations."

"Fresher than the Baths of Nero. I suppose no Flavian emperor is going to refurbish those in a hurry, are they? Not without their name on the door, so we know to whom we should be grateful."

I nod. For some reason I'm finding this conversation very difficult. I feel as though I am standing too close to Marcus, am too aware of the wet skin of his chest. I step backwards slightly, bumping into the wall of the pool.

"She's a quick learner." Vita has reached us by swimming underwater, so that she suddenly appears right next to us.

"I'll leave you to your swimming lesson, then," says Marcus. He wades to the steps at the side of the pool and climbs out. I look away, somehow embarrassed though I'm not sure why.

Vita is floating, watching me. "Do you get on well with Marcus?"

"Yes," I say. "He's a good patron," I add more formally.

"The gods know how Labeo will be. He's not yet over not being my master anymore. A patron has to be more respectful. Not like the old days when he first bought me. He tried to take me into his bed."

"What did you do?"

"Bit him," she says.

"You didn't!"

"Did so. Got whipped for it. Worth it. Warned him I'd do it again and I'd do it every time. Only solution was to pick someone else to bed or sell me. And I was worth too much to him in fees for events. So he picked someone else."

"Brave."

She shakes her head. "Stupid, really. But I knew Labeo cared more about making money than which specific slave he bedded; he had plenty of others to choose from, men or women. It was a risk worth taking."

"Well, now you're free."

She splashes backwards onto the water, floating easily. "I have to remind myself all the time. And every time I do, I smile. I've kissed that wooden sword every night before I sleep, it's getting more time in my bedroom than Labeo ever managed."

I look about me as we wander back to the changing rooms, wary of bumping into Marcus again, but there's no sign of him. I'm glad to have seen him smiling though, perhaps he has recovered from Titus' insistence on a future naumachia. Now we have a whole winter to recover before our season starts again.

WHEN I REACH THE INSULA, there is a table laid out, with jugs of wine and cakes. Most of the inhabitants of the insula have gathered, including Cassius, Cassia and Rullus, all of whom are smiling.

"Althea! Come join us!" calls Cassius. "Drink a toast to my daughter and Rullus, they are to be married!"

Cassia embraces me and Cassius pushes a cup into my hand.

"To Cassia and Rullus!"

Everyone echoes the toast. My mouth silently shapes the words, while in the crowd, Fabia meets my eye, her face serious.

WHITE WATERS

Now there are no daily Games I find myself without enough to do, without enough excuses not to be more available round the insula. Cassia will find my behaviour odd.

I arrange for the amphitheatre to be given a thorough clean in every part over several days, any repairs made good. We finally finish the paintings in the top tier corridors. The warehouses where the slaves and animals live still need plenty of work, since they were not our priority during the summer, so I set in motion a plan of works for the autumn and winter, including substantial repairs to both roofs, since they leak with the slightest drop of rain. The last few animals are killed for meat or sent back to Bestia to sell on if they're of any value. Once their warehouse is empty it is easier to clean it and complete any necessary adjustments to the building. Next season, we will have stronger and larger pens available. We're also building a permanent ramp so that carts can be rolled right inside the warehouse, loaded with cages and rolled out again, which will make the job of transporting the animals a lot easier. The place smells better now that we only have mules stabled there. They pulled our carts of animals for the Games in summer and are used for various smaller tasks the rest of the year: picking up food supplies at the markets, transporting building materials, carrying their own hay and straw for food and bedding.

"Looks like the show worked, then?" says Maria from her spot on the balcony. Karbo has already bolted his food and run off to play in the twilight with his friends, I can hear them all yelling as they chase each other round the nearby streets.

"What do you mean?"

"Titus has sent the Queen away for good."

"Really? Berenice?"

"Didn't think you had that much power, did you?"

"I'm not sure it was entirely us."

"He was crying at the show, wasn't he? That's what I heard. He knew what was being hinted at. He's not a fool."

I grimace. "I'm sorry he can't marry whom he chooses. He looked like he really did love her."

"Well, she wasn't a good choice, was she? Too much like Cleopatra. Foreign, likely to cause trouble. He could have picked some nice Roman woman, couldn't he? Not exactly short on the ground. Would have made life easier for everyone. Marry close to home, keeps things simple. Look at Cassia."

I don't answer, only make a fuss over calling Karbo back from his playtime and putting him to bed.

"I'm taking you and Fabia to the baths for a treat," says Cassia. "I hardly ever see Althea, she works too hard," she adds to Fabia. "We're going to have our nails dyed."

"Ooh," says Fabia. "I've always wanted to do that, it does look pretty."

After baths, we make our way to the beauty room, set aside for women only, filled with cosmetae and their customers, surrounded by the tools of their trade: dozens of little pots containing coloured powders and rich creams, as well as miniature mortar and pestles for combining ingredients and tiny tools that hang from hoops on their belts. Our cosmetes cuts and files our nails to an acceptable oval shape, tutting over how short they are. Then she mixes a strong-smelling green herbal paste and meticulously coats each fingernail and toenail with it, careful not to let it touch our skin.

"Stay still for one hour, until it has completely dried, like a crust," she says. "Then call me back to scrape it off. Don't let it get on your skin, or you'll spoil all my work. And don't get near water or it'll be too pale."

She makes her way to her next customer while the three of us sit and wave our hands and feet about, trying to make the squidgy paste dry faster.

"I've only ever seen it on rich ladies," says Cassia. "Mind you they've got their own personal nail slaves; they can have fancy designs and all sorts. But we deserve a treat."

The cosmetes returns to us when the green sludge has dried to an unpleasant-looking stiff crust. She pulls out a tiny spoon-like instrument and scrapes it off, revealing our nails dyed a dark glowing orange, like burning embers. We admire them all the way home, almost tripping over our own feet as we peer down at our toes.

"Very pretty," says Rullus to Cassia, who smiles and makes her way through the back door of the popina into the storerooms.

Fabia walks ahead of me into the insula and I turn to follow, but Rullus leans across the counter, looking down at my feet.

"Such pretty feet," he says, keeping his voice quiet. "I've been thinking: I'm marrying Cassia for her business but I can have you on the side for a bit of fun, eh? After all, once we're married it'll be too late, I won't have to be careful what I say and do around her, the man's the master, everyone knows that. And no-one's going to marry a whore like you, who works at the amphitheatre with the likes of gladiators. So you might as well have a taste of a real man now and then."

I back away, then all but run after Fabia.

"I'VE GOT AN AUNT IN Tibur," says Fabia soon after our trip to the baths. "She's invited us to go and stay a few days, enjoy the hot springs and celebrate Fontinalia. Will you come with Karbo? Father has already invited Marcus." She lowers her voice. "I'll ask Cassia as well, perhaps if the two of you have some time away from Rullus you could tell her before they make the betrothal legal?"

I nod, feeling my heart start to beat faster at the very idea. But being with Fabia will give me confidence, I think. Cassia needs to be told.

But it turns out that Cassia cannot come, for Rullus has other ideas.

"He says we should keep the popina open during the festival, that it will be good for our profits," she says, a little disappointed.

"Can't you say no?"

She shrugs. "He's right," she says. "Father and I always took the festival off as a holiday, but a popina that wants to do well should really be open during festivals, when people have more time to eat and drink and spend a little more enjoying themselves."

"They were getting along fine," says Fabia when she hears. "She's just trying to be loyal because she's going to marry him. But he's already showing some of his true colours, all he cares about is getting his hands on their business and making Cassia work harder. You need to tell her."

I nod. "I know," I say. "When we get back."

The Acque Albule, the White Waters, have been famous for centuries. Augustus himself used them for his aches and pains and soldiers wounded in combat are often taken there to recuperate and be cured. They're less than a day's journey outside of Rome, to the north-east.

Marcus borrows a cart from the racing stables and reclaims his two horses, who live there. They're mostly used for transport, not being anything like fast enough to compete in the races. They are treated well and stabled at no cost to Marcus, allowing him to keep the two of them, as they occasionally come in handy for such journeys. The five of us climb aboard early in the morning, well-wrapped in cloaks and with a few bed mats on board to soften the ride. Marcus strokes the horses' noses and speaks gently to them, offers each a handful of grain, before climbing up and taking the reins. Karbo watches him as though memorising every move.

"Can we gallop?" he can't help asking, knowing full well Marcus will refuse.

"No," says Marcus. "But you can hold the reins for a while if you like, here, like this."

Karbo's face lights up with joyful responsibility. Marcus looks over his shoulder at me.

"Hold tight," he says laughing.

It's a pleasant enough day, the horses alternate trotting along good stretches of flat roads, walking on the hillier terrain or when they get tired. We stop in the morning to relieve ourselves and once more in the middle of the day to eat the food we have brought with us. As we come closer to the town of Tibur we pass several large and imposing villas. Many rich families keep a country home here, conveniently close to Rome but with all the benefits of the healing waters.

By late afternoon we reach Fabius' sister's house and are welcomed by her. Her house is not large, but we find enough space here and there for the bed mats we have brought. Sabina is a good host to us. She is a widow now, but her husband was a physician like Fabius, so she has been left well-provided for. Her children are grown and married, her son and daughter-in-law live with her and there are three grandchildren, who, being younger than Karbo, see him as an excellent source of new games. We have only been there an hour and he is already pretending to be a horse, carrying them on his back in turns, neighing and rearing to their obvious delight. We are well fed and spend an enjoyable evening cracking new-season nuts and telling stories.

The next morning we make our way to the hot springs, eager for a day of bathing. The strong smell of sulphur reminds me briefly of the smell in Pompeii's ruins after Vesuvius erupted, and I look to Marcus, whose face is tight. He turns to Fabius, who is making some joke, and manages a smile. I feel a little less awkward around Marcus this time; it helps that we are part of a group, but also the water covers us better than at the baths. It's an odd greenish white, hence the name White Waters. The colour is a little off-putting at first, especially when combined with the strong smell, but once we get in, the gentle warmth is relaxing. I float alongside Fabia while Karbo splashes about, practising his underwater swimming as well as diving, popping up here and there, often unexpectedly. Marcus joins us after a while and leads Karbo off to a quieter area to practise, so that we won't get splashed so much. Fabius joins us and lies back in the water.

"I wish I could send all my injured gladiators here," he says. "It does wonders for wounds and muscle pains. Marcus was a different man after he'd been here."

"Marcus has been here before?"

"Oh yes, after his injury."

"I didn't know that."

"I insisted on it. He was a good soldier and my friend. Once I saw the wound was healing I sent him home to Rome from Egypt with strict instructions to come to my mother's house, stay with her for a month and bathe in the waters every day. I came home myself a little while later and he was so much better."

"How did he get injured?"

"Oh, some thug with grand ideas about Egypt being free of the Romans. An attack from behind, cowardly. They wouldn't have had a chance if they'd fought him face-to-face. Shame though, one stroke of the sword and it ruined his leg, he's limped ever since."

"And after he'd recovered?"

"He had found Julia's by then, was living there but getting restless, wondering what to do with his life."

"Was that when he went back to Pompeii?"

"Yes. They were just about to re-open the amphitheatre after the ban and wanted someone to run it. He thought he had nothing to lose, so he applied for the job and they were delighted to get an ex-army man still in his prime. And he did a good job of it."

"Did you keep in touch all these years?"

"Oh yes. Marcus isn't a bad letter writer. He'd send me stories of gladiators and beasts and all sorts. People looked down on him for having that kind of job, dealing with the sort of people you get in that world, but he didn't care about stuff like that. He'd had people whispering about his grandfather's gambling for years, so perhaps he saw anyone can rise or fall. When he told me his right hand for the amphitheatre wasn't just a woman but a prostitute, I confess I was a bit shocked. But I met Fausta once, she was a formidable woman."

"She was," I agree. "I still miss her."

"And when he met Livia, well, that prompted a lot of letters, I can tell you. I could tell he was smitten from the very first one. All these details about the colour of her hair in the sunshine." Fabius laughs. "And then of course they had Amantius so then there were fewer letters, he was too busy."

I think of hazelnut-haired Livia and Amantius, a tiny copy of Marcus. "The anniversary's coming up," I say.

"I know."

"I thought recently, maybe, he was…"

Fabius raises his eyebrows. "What?"

"Thinking of… moving on?"

Fabius shakes his head almost immediately. "Doubt it. He doesn't drink much, but if he ever gets tipsy, all he talks about is Livia." He shrugs. "I mean, we've visited the odd she-wolves' den of an evening, but mostly at my suggestion, not his. Marcus is a man who doesn't forget easily."

"How's your swimming coming along?" Marcus is wading over, the water swirling around his hips, addressing me.

"Nothing like as good as Karbo's," I say, wondering if he heard Fabius mentioning visits to prostitutes.

"Want a lesson, while we're here?"

I follow him through the water to where he had been teaching Karbo, a quieter section of the pool.

"Let's see you float, then."

I lie back in the water, but I am finding it hard to relax and so my middle keeps dipping down, as though seeking to hide under the milky waters.

"You need more lessons," he says, putting one hand under my back, his touch gentle but sure, holding me upwards. "Right, do some strokes."

I turn over and begin swimming, a clumsy movement.

"Smoother," says Marcus. "Your legs and arms need to coordinate."

"I'm trying!" I protest.

"Try harder."

"My turn again," says Karbo, suddenly appearing out of the water.

"You've had your turn," says Marcus.

"I want to learn more!"

"You're better off teaching him," I say, "I'm nowhere near as good."

"That why you need more lessons," says Marcus, but he gives in to Karbo's pleading, taking off through the water using smooth, certain strokes, while Karbo follows enthusiastically behind him, fast but splashing water everywhere. I watch a little enviously. Vita will need to give me more lessons, I think.

ON OUR THIRD DAY AT White Waters, the thirteenth of October, it is time to celebrate Fontinalia, Festival of Springs. The guardian god of wells and springs, Fons, must be honoured and where better to do it than here? The day is a holiday, so there are crowds of people with garlands of flowers making their way round the town, some locals as well as plenty of people from Rome and even further afield. The garlands are laid on the tops of wells and floated in the waters of the hot springs. By midday, the whole of the main pool is covered with flowers, so that the water itself has all but disappeared and the bathers emerge from their dips with petals clinging to their hair and skin.

We arrive at the pools holding our own garlands, bought at the market. Fabius and Marcus murmur Fons' name and throw their garlands into the water, before following them into the warmth. Fabia and I take ours to the very edge and gently push them into the pools, watching them float off for a while. Karbo, meanwhile, is scattering petals wildly.

"Perhaps Fons would like his garland still whole?" I suggest.

Karbo shakes his head. "This is prettier," he says, and I leave him to it. Certainly the petals are pretty as they gently come to rest on the water, colours intertwining like elaborate mosaic pieces.

All I can see of Karbo is his toes, pointing out of the water.

"I wish he'd stop trying to hold his breath," I say. "He's seen what Vita can do and he wants to copy her, but it can't be good for him not to breathe for so long?"

Fabia giggles, watching the toes collapse and Karbo's gasping face suddenly emerge. "He's getting good at it though," she says. "I'm sure that was even longer than he managed yesterday."

"You have to gulp lots of air before you go under," says Karbo, joining us, still gasping.

"Yes," I say. "It's what keeps you alive. So don't forget to do it occasionally, will you?"

"When I get back to Rome tomorrow, Vita will see I've got better," he says, with a hint of hero worship.

BACK IN ROME SHORTLY AFTER our trip, I wake up and, remembering what day it is, feel a sinking in my stomach and a chill that has nothing to do with November being almost upon us. Today is the day that Vesuvius erupted, one year ago. I think back to the nearly built amphitheatre, to Marcus and its architect standing talking. How I looked down at my sleeve and saw ash, could not understand where it came from, did not know the horror that had already happened, did not realise the cloud of ash had drifted from Pompeii and all the other destroyed cities to Rome, the dark clouds heralding the news that would devastate so many.

"This will be a hard day for Marcus," I remind Karbo. "Leave him alone if you see him, please don't ask difficult questions or make a nuisance of yourself."

"Will we visit a temple and make sacrifices?"

"You and I will," I agree. "I don't know what Marcus will do." Privately, I hope that we can spend time together today. I know nobody else from Pompeii, certainly no-one who saw the aftermath of the eruption. The images of it come back at odd moments, at night is the worst, when I dream of ash everywhere and Marcus, digging and digging through it, finding nothing, turning to me with empty ashen hands. Even a few specks of ash from a fire often make me swallow, feel again the rush of fear as we raced back to Pompeii.

Julia and Maria both nod when they see me, solemn. Julia holds out a cage with two white doves in it.

"Take them to the temple in sacrifice," she says.

"Thank you."

She's holding three roses, the very last of her autumn blooms, delicate pink. "I'll leave them for Marcus' lararium," she says. "You said Livia used to wear flowers in her hair."

I've been keeping an eye out for Marcus, but I've not seen him anywhere today and have to conclude he doesn't want company. Karbo walks with me to the temple of Vulcan, where we hand the doves to a priest and light incense. I stand for a little while, praying for everyone I knew who died in Pompeii, hoping that despite the lack of funerary rites at the time, they somehow found their way across the River Styx and into the fields of Elysium, to dwell in peace.

On the way back, I tell Karbo about Felix the gardener, who never said much but was kind-hearted, and Myrtis the cook, my friend, who talked faster than anyone I knew and made the best honey cakes I've ever tasted.

"Let's make some to honour her," says Karbo, enthused at the idea of a treat.

"I don't have the recipe," I say. "She always said she wouldn't share it with anyone." But the idea appeals, and I tell Cassia about the little cakes, and the secret mix of spices Myrtis kept to herself.

"The popina's quiet today, Father and Rullus have gone off to the baths. Let's do a little baking. If it's spices you need to get right, I should be the one to help you, don't you think?" says Cassia. "Maybe you just need my namesake."

I nod. "Let's start with that then."

We make one small batch after another. We chatter to each other and for a while it feels like the days before Rullus came, the fun of spending lighthearted time together. We try both cassia and its sweeter cousin cinnamon, we add nutmeg, mace, cloves, ginger. We end up with some honey cakes that are barely edible, they're so heavily spiced. Only Karbo, leaning on the counter and watching with great interest, wolfs them down, willing to eat anything with honey in it. When Marcus finally appears, late in the afternoon, and we tell him what we're doing, he grimaces, having no sweet tooth at all.

"They're not right, are they?" I say.

He shakes his head. "Too much of everything," he comments through a mouthful.

My head droops. "You and I are the only people left who ate them," I say. "No-one else knows what they tasted like and Myrtis always said she'd never tell anyone. Perhaps I'll never get it right." My voice turns unsteady, and tears well up. I turn away, unwilling for him to see how much it matters to me, such a silly thing to be upset over, so insignificant compared to his loss.

"Pepper," he says.

I turn round. "What?"

"Pepper. I think she used pepper." He waves and walks away, back inside the insula.

Cassia and I try another batch and there it is at last, a hint of the taste I remember. We bake two more rounds and suddenly I really am in tears, choking on a mouthful of honey cake, back in Myrtis' tiny, smoky, gossipy kitchen in Pompeii. Cassia puts an arm around my shoulder.

"We'll make them for Saturnalia, give them to our friends, what do you say?"

I nod, swallow.

"Been baking?" Rullus is back. He stuffs a few of the cakes in his mouth. "Always said you were an excellent cook, Cassia," he says with his mouth still full.

"We're going to give them away for Saturnalia," says Cassia. She passes me the batch we made, then moves away, clattering with jugs and cups at the back of the popina.

"Wasting my profits?" says Rullus to me in a low voice. "You might have to compensate me. I'll think of what I might like in payment."

I TAKE A DOZEN OF the little cakes and walk down Sand Street, past the local urine collection point, till I reach a corner shrine to Libertas, where I offer up the tiny morsels that taste of the past, as well as a prayer for my old friends Myrtis and Felix and all those who perished in Pompeii.

When I return, thinking to try and find Marcus, I see, as I walk up the stairs, Julia's door open and inside, Marcus, sitting at her table, head down, shoulders heaving. Julia stands over him, her face solemn, one hand on his arm. She looks out at me and nods as I pull the door closed so that no-one will hear him sob.

I feel sad as I climb the stairs. Not just because of those we have lost, but that I did not manage to share that pain with Marcus, today of all days, that he went to Julia to be comforted, rather than come to me. I wonder if I have failed him as a friend, if I should have found a way to help him through the pain he is still suffering. I lie awake, wondering if I have lost him altogether as a friend, if we are now nothing more than two people who work together in a pleasant enough fashion, who once, through fate alone, shared a horror that has now faded away, as has the bond it created.

The next day Marcus seems his usual self, he says something about having chosen a day when our team can begin to dismantle the wooden floor, now made unusable with pitch, so that we will be able to rebuild it with fresh timber in the new year. I want to say something about Livia and Amantius, but I don't know where to start and it seems too late, and so I say nothing.

BETWEEN US, CASSIA AND I keep Karbo busy during Saturnalia. The streets ring out with loud seasonal greetings of, "Io, Saturnalia!" while we make batch after batch of Myrtis' honey cakes and I ignore Rullus' scowls when he thinks Cassia is not looking. We put handfuls of the cakes in small woven baskets with festive mottos and riddles written out in my best hand on tiny scrolls, then send Karbo to our many friends and acquaintances. These include the gladiator schools, the butcher who carves up our animals, the undertakers, as well as suppliers of everything from sand to the stallholders who surround the amphitheatre every day. In return, many gifts arrive, some of them overly lavish, especially those which arrive for Marcus. As manager of the amphitheatre, there are plenty of people who want to maintain his favour, hoping to continue supplying us next season, not to mention those who would like to become suppliers themselves and are angling for the opportunity to show off their wares to impress Marcus, rather than giving the traditionally un-ostentatious gifts among friends. Daily, we receive gifts of honeyed nuts, scarlet pomegranates, elaborately layered and spiced pickles, the very finest olives and bottles of garum and even more expensive gifts, such as bundles of reed pens for myself and a finely woven piece of yellow cloth dyed with expensive saffron for Marcus, which he passes to me with raised eyebrows.

"Don't you fancy dressing in yellow then?" I ask him, knowing full well that he prefers simpler colours, with a preference for blue or green.

Bestia, who must be delighted at having supplied us with almost ten thousand animals this past year, goes so far as to send us a lion cub, and although Karbo begs to keep it, embracing it with delight, Marcus shakes his head and instead regifts it to Titus, hoping that it may live out its life as an imperial pet rather than face death at the hands of a bestiarius.

Marcus gives Karbo a hunting knife and Julia some beeswax candles with a little joke about her guarding their flames. I have already given Karbo a box of marbles and I give Marcus a set of glass drinking cups decorated with moulded grapes that remind me of his family farm. Marcus gives me a delicately painted basket, which, when I open it, reveals a branch of gilded dates, still on the stem.

"They're too pretty to eat," I say.

"I'll help you," he offers.

We sit on the wooden stairs and make our way through a good half of the stem, the rich sweetness making me almost dizzy.

"You don't usually like dates," I say.

"Saturnalia," he says, spitting out a stone. "Everyone eats more than is good for them."

"How's the arena floor coming along?"

"If I never hear another hammer in my life it will be too soon. But it's getting there. We're more than halfway through ripping it up. When we rebuild it, we can make better trapdoors, to open more quickly, so that will help next year."

"And we can still move it away to deep fill it for the next naumachia?"

"I think so. We'll make it in sections, so we can lift them out more quickly. We'll have to store it all down at the warehouses. At least next time the Games won't be one hundred consecutive days, so we can have no shows for a couple of days beforehand, give us a chance to remove the floor, fill it up with water, get the animals in."

"Shall I come down one day? Can I help in some way?"

He shakes his head. "No. Have fun with your friends and when Saturnalia's over, you can start devising some shows for next season. Make a list of any well-known myths we haven't used yet; they always go down well with the crowd. And we can repeat a few of the most popular shows. Two of our musicians have resigned, one's too old and the other one's joining a theatre, so we need to replace a trumpet player and a water organist. Look into that, will you?"

"I will do. We're going to hold a Saturnalia feast for the slaves, down in the warehouse."

"I'll be there."

MARCUS PLAYS HIS PART WELL at the Saturnalian feast for the slaves. There's a big meal and Marcus and I, Strabo, Fabius and Fabia, Karbo and others in our management team, including Merula and Vita who have joined us for the fun of it, wait on the slaves, bowing and scraping as we bring them their plates of food, much to everyone's merriment. We have brought our musicians with us for the evening, and the noise of everyone talking and the loud playing is raucous. Marcus throws dice to determine who will be named the Lord of Misrule and one of the slaves who has a twisted spine is chosen. He's crowned with a golden circlet used in the parades at the Games and takes to his new role with pleasure, making Marcus serve at tables for the evening, Strabo tell riddles and jokes and Fabia and I sing a duet, which we do very badly, to much amusement.

"It's my first time on this side," says Vita, laughing after she has been told to walk on her hands, which she has done with admirable dexterity.

"Me too," I say. "We didn't really celebrate last year."

"We used to make Labeo do all sorts," says Vita. "Fighting, swimming, you name it. We chucked him in a fountain once, in someone's villa on the outskirts of Rome. He practically drowned, he's a very poor swimmer."

"What was he like as a master?" I ask.

She shrugs. "You've seen what he's like. It's all about the

spectacle, how much money he can make and he doesn't care how he gets it. He'll do anything for money."

I make a face.

"He was born into a very poor family," says Vita. "He grew up thinking money would solve everything. It doesn't. But it does make life a lot smoother. He doesn't have status, but he does have money, and it offers him some protection and peace of mind."

"Is he splitting fees with you, now you're free?"

"After a lot of arguing. He was afraid to lose me. My team brings in a lot of money, there aren't many slaves who can do what we do."

"And now a dance!" proclaims the Lord of Misrule.

Strabo and I end up clinging to each other as the music plays faster and faster, tripping over each other's feet. Meanwhile Marcus and Fabius pretend to show off elegant dance steps as though they were a couple, while the Lord of Misrule takes Fabia's hand and they dance around all the tables, urging everyone to join in. I see Merula dancing ever closer to Vita, but not daring to reach out for her hand, catch his look of disappointment when she is whirled away to a larger circle of dancers.

"This year you're learning to cook," says Cassia as the year draws to an end. "It's absurd you don't know how."

"I was a body slave to a rich girl by the time I was ten and a scribe to my next master. I lived in rich men's villas, other slaves did the cooking. I wasn't required to learn."

"Well, no time like the present. Help me make the weekly soup."

I spend a week chopping vegetables, soak beans and barley, learn to make pancakes and flatbreads and Cassia even teaches me how to make her famous saltfish fritters. I keep close to her and avoid Rullus where I can, but any time she leaves my side he makes comments under his breath.

"Waste of time, her teaching you cooking," he hisses. "Not about to get married any time soon, are you? Although I suppose you have to feed that street rat you've adopted."

"His name is Karbo," I say. "And Titus himself knows his name, so you might want to learn it."

"Don't take up too much of Cassia's time," he says. "She's as good as a married woman now, she has to think about my profits. She can stop making that ridiculous beggars' soup and teaching waifs and strays like you her skills, for a start."

"Does she know you're so uncharitable?" I ask. "Does she know what kind of man you are?"

"It'll be too late when she finds out, won't it?"

He stands a little too close when I am in the popina, brushes past me once too often when there is no need to. I'm glad when I can claim that our new season of Games will begin again in March, and that I have to prepare for them.

DIANA'S SPRING

THE NEW YEAR FEELS LIKE a threat rather than a promise. "Will you be my matron of honour?" Cassia asks me, in a quiet moment.

It's a role of huge importance. I will not only help prepare Cassia for the wedding day when it comes, I will also give her away to Rullus during the ceremony. I'm both flattered that she has asked me and sick at the idea of giving her to Rullus. "Of course," I say, embracing her tightly. "I'm honoured."

"YOU HAVE TO TELL HER," says Fabia. "You can't be her matron of honour and not tell her."

"I know," I say miserably.

"You want me to be there too?"

I shake my head. I know that Fabia has lost faith that I will tell Cassia, can see how afraid I am of what has to be done. But I need to do it alone.

"It has to be before the betrothal is made legal," insists Fabia.

"I know."

I DON'T KNOW WHY I choose that particular morning. I wake and know it must be today. After all this time, too much time, it must be today. I have waited too long and now I must find the courage to open my mouth, whatever it takes. Cassia will be unhappy for a while, I think. She will be sad that the wedding is not to be. I don't think she has fallen head over heels for Rullus, but she is a practical woman, she sees, in Rullus, a pleasant man, from her own family and therefore, to her mind, trustworthy. He has worked hard in the business and given her father a rest, he has plans for the business to do even better and has offered honourable marriage. But I cannot let her marry him.

"Of course," says Cassia, when I say I need to talk to her and could it be in her apartment. "Rullus, will you mind the stove?"

"Anything for my betrothed," he says. "Althea, look after my Cassia, now." He is all smiles, but there is a warning in his eyes, I know he does not like the idea of my speaking with her somewhere away from him, somewhere private.

Inside Cassia's apartment, she offers me wine, some little biscuits.

"No, thank you," I say. I sit down and then stand up again immediately.

"Sit," she says.

"I need to tell you something about Rullus," I say very fast. There. Now I cannot say 'nothing,' if she asks, I cannot get out of it, I have made a statement that is odd, that will be questioned.

"What is it?" She is not concerned. She cannot think of anything I could have to say that would be bad about him.

I talk about how late I was that evening, how the streets were already dark, how – how foolish I was to risk the streets of Rome at night. I talk of seeing the gateway and the dimly lit safety of the courtyard beyond it and then. And then.

"Then?"

The man's hands, how I could not scream nor hardly even breathe, how I struggled. I struggled, I fought, I scratched. That is the important part. I scratched. And his cursing and stumbling and my running running running.

"I'm so sorry," she says, kneeling close to me because I am shaking. "You should have told me."

I want to push her away because she does not understand what there is to be sorry about. "I didn't tell you, because."

"Because?"

Say it quickly. Say it and it is done. Say it. "Because it was Rullus."

"SHE WON'T TALK TO ME anymore," I tell Fabia. My stomach feels sick with the thought.

"She didn't believe you?"

"She said I was jealous that she was getting married and that I was trying to ruin her happiness. That she'd never seen Rullus behave badly and I was just making things up."

"Should I talk to her?"

"No. She needs to keep her friends about her. If she won't have me as a friend, she needs to keep you for when it all goes wrong."

THERE IS A BETROTHAL PARTY, at which Rullus gives Cassia the traditionally lucky iron ring to wear and a wedding date is set for September. June is a luckier month for weddings, but the popina is often busy that month, not least with catering for the weddings of better-off families which Rullus says they should be mindful of. September is a little quieter. Cassius insists on giving a dowry, as though Cassia came from a wealthy family, I think it makes him feel proud to offer it, so legal documents are signed agreeing it and Rullus kisses Cassia in front of the lawyer.

Cassia punishes me by naming Fabia as her matron of

honour, without explaining her change of choice, but Rullus smiles broadly at me when I hear this, no doubt he can guess what happened and now I have nothing against him, for I have not been believed and he has triumphed.

Everyone in the insula gives Cassia gifts, intended to help her set up house. Fabia and I buy her a length of good cloth for swaddling her future babies, as well as a tiny glass vial to keep perfume in. A grand wedding would have ten witnesses, but Cassia chooses the important older women in her life: Julia and Maria.

Rullus is often at the counter of the popina now, serving customers, always with a bright smile on his face and often waving away Cassius, telling him to rest, that an old man deserves to take life easy. If I catch Cassia's eye she only turns her face away and has Rullus serve me instead, so that I frequent the popina only when absolutely necessary.

"She'll come round," says Fabia, but she sounds uncertain.

We open the season in March, which will give us seven months to offer one hundred and sixty-five Games, the number agreed with the Aedile for this year. The extra days we have available this year are heartily welcome, they mean we do not have to put on a show every day, allowing us to take breaks when needed, especially before the end-of-season naumachia and any other particularly complex Games.

We get off to a good start in the first two weeks, showcasing a vicious battle of Carpophorus against a rhino, which he manages to kill using only a spear, and a huge re-enactment of the Battle of Zama where the crowd enjoys watching Roman general Scipio Africanus defeating the Carthage general Hannibal, for which we even provide elephants, one of whom kneels to Titus to show

Rome's superiority. There are tiger fights, acrobats bull-leaping as part of a story about Theseus and the Minotaur, and a display of Amazons fighting which uses Labeo's entire selection of gladiatrices and which Titus seems to find very compelling, no doubt helped by them all fighting bare-breasted.

In order to fill the year's programme, we've also looked back at the previous season and will be repeating a few of the most popular Games. One of these is our Diana deer hunt followed by a criminal execution, featuring Alyssa. Labeo is pleased when I book her.

"Still got it, hasn't she? Does well for me, that one. I thought she might be getting past it, but you can't see the wrinkles from a distance, I suppose. Plus, she helps the newbies with their training, especially on their archery skills. No-one shoots like her. Might make a good trainer when she's too old for the arena. But there's a few years still left in her, I'd say."

FABIUS IS OUT OF TOWN for a few days. His brother is unwell with a fever and he wants to see him for himself, doesn't trust the local doctor. Fabia is standing in for him. There have been two minor injuries from fights and the gladiators have sullenly submitted to her ministrations. But her stitching and dressing of their wounds has been neat and they are healing well. Both they and their managers have expressed a reluctant acknowledgement of a job well done.

"They'll give in to you in the end," I say.

She nods and gives me a smile, although I can see she is a little afraid at the weight of responsibility resting on her shoulders. She lays out her tools with great care before every show, a little stove with boiling water by her to clean her instruments, preparing for any and all eventualities. Her body tenses when Marcus gives the signal for our team to take their places before the show begins and she steps up onto a little wooden platform one of the carpenters knocked up for her, so that she will be the right height to treat any gladiator laid out on the table in front of her.

Diana's Hunt is our opening piece this morning. The hundred-odd deer are in place; we'll eat venison for a few nights. I look forward to it, it's one of my favourite meats. Our pool, symbolising the sacred spring in which our goddess will wash herself, is a sparkling blue in the bright March sunshine. The eyeless helmet with stag's antlers for the hapless criminal lies ready, the two groups of hounds are panting in their cages. I steer clear of the second pack, their taste for human flesh frightens me. Labeo is here again, arranging Alyssa's divine appearance. One naked breast, as before, is already on show.

"Bought a new head of hair," he says, running his hand through golden tresses bound into Alyssa's own darker blonde. They tumble down to her waist. He fixes a gilded circlet onto her head, ties it tightly into the hair with small strands of thread so that it cannot fall off while she is hunting. Satisfied, he steps back to survey her and nods.

"Bow," I remind him.

"Of course," he says, passing the bow. Alyssa takes it in her left hand, rolls her shoulders, checking the quiver is safely strapped to her back.

"Places," calls Marcus. The morning hunt is about to begin. The first pack of hounds are in their lifts.

"Ready?" I ask Alyssa.

She nods.

I open the door of her lift and she steps in, face impassive, her gilded shoes and jewellery gleaming in the dim light.

Marcus walks away, up the dark stairs leading to his place

in the amphitheatre's level of seating, by the imperial box, from where he will watch the Games, give signals as needed. I nod to Labeo and follow him, take my own place in the tiers, on the other side to Marcus, close to the Vestal Virgins' box. The music begins, the water organ bringing its delicate sound to the peaceful pastoral music, appropriate to the scene we have created.

Marcus' hand lifts and the drumming starts as Alyssa is lifted into view to the applause of the audience. Some have seen this show before, others heard about it last year and wished they'd had a chance to see it. Either way, the crowd like a divinity, especially a partially naked one.

The hunt is perfect. Alyssa's skill with a bow is without compare, her arrows flying faster than seems possible, one deer after another falling. When the first pack of hounds are released, the tempo of the hunt increases still further, until the floor is littered with the dead and dying herd.

There's a brief pause as the carcasses are dragged away, the hounds returned to their lifts, disappearing beneath the floor. Alyssa takes her time, slowly pacing around the perimeter of the arena, gradually disposing of first her bow, then her quiver. She pauses, looking up over her shoulder at the audience, turning round on herself as they bay for her to undress. She walks towards the blue pool, undoing her belt with care, then slipping her tunic over her head, dropping it to the floor, entirely naked except for her gilded adornments. The applause is deafening. She bends over to undo her sandals, the shouts from her admirers bordering on the obscene. Barefoot, she steps into the pool and washes herself, the water glistening on her skin as it trickles down her body.

She's a good performer. I've been caught up in her storytelling but realise, as the music changes again, that Marcus has given the signal. We are about to execute today's criminal.

A young man stumbles into the arena, pushed by hidden hands. He turns back to the door immediately, trying to open it, but it opens only from the inside, there is no escape. Turning back to Alyssa, he sees her play out the moment when Diana is seen by a mortal, her anger and the raising of her hand, cursing him to a terrible fate for having dared to glimpse the divine.

The trapdoor at the other end of the arena, behind her, opens up; the second pack of hounds is about to be released. They hunger for the man, they will tear him to pieces in moments, even as Alyssa escapes unscathed. She strides towards the criminal, the eyeless helmet surmounted by a stag's antlers in her hands, rams it down on his head as the bars fall, the hounds racing towards them across the already-bloodied sand.

But the blinded man grabs at where Alyssa was, manages to clutch at her golden hair and pulls her towards him. She should be grasping the rope dangling just out of reach, the rope which will lift her to safety, without which she will share in his gruesome fate.

I'm on my feet, Marcus is on his feet, the crowd is roaring.

Alyssa jerks away from the man's desperate clutches as the hounds reach them. Her right hand finds the rope as one of the hounds closes its jaws around her left hand. The rest of the pack have fallen on the man, his throat is already spewing blood, his entrails spilling out. The slaves above Alyssa are pulling her upwards but the hound will not let go of her, its jaws move even as it is lifted onto its back legs and Alyssa's mouth opens in a scream as her hand comes away into the hound's mouth and blood spurts from her arm.

I am running, running along the corridors, down the steep

steps to the dark space below the arena floor, screaming for Fabia to be ready, to clear everyone and everything out of the way. Just ahead of me in the dark space is Marcus, roaring for more light, for torches to be moved to where Fabia is waiting, her eyes wide, Labeo turns in horror as Alyssa is carried into the space, eyes closed, her naked body covered in slippery blood, the team members gripping onto her, their faces pale with horror. They all but throw her onto the waiting table, so eager are they for her to reach Fabia's hands.

Marcus is by her side. "Anything you need. Anything."

"More light," gasps Fabia and already she is lifting a scalpel, is cutting Alyssa's arm still further. Alyssa's eyes open and she screams.

"Hold her," says Fabia. "I have to find the blood vessels and tie them off, or she'll die. I don't have time to give her anything for the pain." Her face is pale, but her hands are steady and her voice is firm. "Talk to her, Althea," she adds, without looking at me, all her focus on the bleeding stump.

"I have to go," says Marcus to me. "The Games must continue; I can't leave the arena empty." He's gone before I can answer, dragging Labeo by the arm after him. Karbo appears in the doorway, having made his way down from the upper tier where he was sitting, and Marcus grabs his tunic and pulls him, too, with him.

Strabo and four of the men hold Alyssa down. I can't see much of her from where I am, only her head, still crowned with the gilded circlet and golden hair, purchased from some northern slave, now streaked with red, dangling down from her head to the floor. I step closer to her, look down at her face which is scrunched up in agony, an unearthly moaning coming from her mouth.

"Alyssa."

She tries to focus on me, eyes wildly moving about until she fixes on my gaze.

"You're a gladiatrix," I tell her, almost hissing into her face. "The best Labeo has. You're a warrior. There is no woman who can bear pain like you. What Fabia is doing to you, it's nothing. Nothing you haven't borne before." I don't dare to look at what Fabia is doing; I don't dare to break eye contact with Alyssa.

Alyssa's open mouth moves for a moment. Then her jaw clenches shut and silent, her eyes grow hard. I shudder. This is what it must be like to look into the eyes of a gladiator before they kill you.

"Yes," I say. "Yes. See? You are a warrior. This is nothing to you. Nothing. I could put a sword in your hand right now and you would fight on."

I keep talking. I don't know what I'm saying half the time, repeating reminders of how brave she is, how little she cares for any pain, how she has terrified every opponent who ever came near her, man or beast, because of her reputation, her fierceness, her skills. All the time I can hear the breathing of the men, of Fabia, Alyssa. Once, Alyssa's eyes roll up and I think she will faint, but she recovers and then Fabia speaks.

"I've tied off the blood vessels. I'll give her opium for the pain so I can finish." She steps away for a moment, her hands dripping red, plunges them in a basin of water, washes them, then wipes them on a clean cloth and takes up a small cup, into which she pours a mixture from a tiny bottle, then takes it to Alyssa, forces it between her lips.

It's a relief to see Alyssa slowly blink, her jaw loosen, the fierceness drift into confusion and then her eyes close altogether. Above us I can hear light-hearted music, the actors and dancers putting on a comedic show. Marcus returns briefly to see how we are doing and Fabia nods.

"I think the arm bones are safe," she says. "They are smooth. But all of the hand is lost." She is using tiny forceps and hooks now, prodding for chewed fragments of wrist bone, dropping them with a tiny clink into a bowl beside her. Her face is intent, and Marcus touches her shoulder lightly and leaves us again.

Gladiators have come and gone for their bouts before she's finished, each one glancing towards Alyssa and touching their hands to their chests in a salute to her as they pass, their other hand making a gesture against bad luck by their sides, each afraid that today may be inauspicious for their own fight. But there are no more casualties. A couple of small cuts will be taken care of back at the barracks.

"Done," says Fabia.

The men move back. Where Alyssa's hand was is now a stump, ending where the wrist once was. Fabia has cut and pulled together flaps of skin to create a covered end, criss-crossed with rows of tiny stitches. The arm has been wiped clean of blood and Fabia wipes it again with vinegar, the smell sharp overlaying the heavy scent of blood in the air.

"I'll dress it with honey," she says.

I nod.

Marcus returns with Labeo. "You saved her life," he says to Fabia.

"How is she supposed to fight like that?" asks Labeo, appalled, looking down at Alyssa.

"You'll be compensated," says Marcus.

"I want the price for her if she'd been killed. She might as well have been."

"You'll get it. Now shut your mouth and get out of here,"

says Marcus. "I'll have her brought back to your barracks as soon as Fabia is done, and I'll send a slave to look after her from our own team."

LABEO HAS FINALLY LEFT, AND the Games are over for the day. Alyssa has been taken back to the barracks on a litter by Marcus and three other men. I have made sure the crowds are gone and the cleaning team have started their work.

I come back to find Fabia putting away her instruments. She is boiling each one in the water to clean it, then lifting them out with little tongs and wrapping each in a cloth, for storage. She looks as though she's in a trance, her movements slow and her eyes unfocused.

"You were wonderful," I say.

She looks up as though she's only just become aware of anyone else in the space. "I was so scared," she says in a tiny voice and suddenly she drops the scalpel she is holding to the floor, her whole body shaking.

I kneel down and take her in my arms, feeling her small body shuddering, her teeth chattering. I wait a few moments, holding her as tightly as I can, until the shuddering slows and then I pull back to look in her face. "You were wonderful," I say again. "You saved her life."

"Her hand –"

"No-one could have saved her hand," I say. "It was on the arena floor with a dog chewing on it." I gag at the thought of it, then swallow and focus on Fabia again. "Let's go home," I say.

"My tools –"

"Leave them. There's no show tomorrow. We can come back and get everything then."

We walk home in silence, Fabia's hand in mine. Sometimes I

feel a shudder pass through her again. When we get back, I tell Julia what happened and Julia gets honey from Adah, mixes it with unwatered wine and gives it to Fabia, who first sips a little, before draining the cup.

"And now sleep," says Julia and Fabia follows her like a child back to her apartment and lies down on Julia's own bed, her eyes closing almost immediately. Julia pulls up a stool next to her.

"I'll watch over her. Do you need a cup of wine too?" she asks me.

I shake my head. "I think I need to sleep though," I say.

"Sleep. I'll tell Marcus where you are when he gets back. Where is Karbo?"

"Went with Marcus to take Alyssa back to the barracks."

I sleep as though dead, waking in the late evening. Marcus has left a plate of food for me outside the door, Karbo is asleep on the bed next to me. I sit in the dark and eat, then kneel under the stars and pray to Apollo, god of healing, and his son Aesculapius, god of medicine and physicians, that Alyssa will recover.

IT'S BEEN A MONTH SINCE Alyssa's accident.

"How is she?" I ask Labeo, on a visit to his barracks.

"Useless," he says in his usual brutal way. "Sits around with a miserable face on her. I thought she might at least train some of the other women, since she knows what she's doing, but she won't even do that. Might have to sell her. Won't get a proper sum for her though, not with her bow arm gone, now she's just a one-handed slave, and who wants one of them?"

"I meant how is the stump?"

"Oh, that's healed well enough, looks like. Fabia knew what

she was doing, saved her life I suppose. But she can't perform anymore, so what good was it?"

"I thought you said she was a favourite with the crowd?"

"Only if she can use a bow. She's no good otherwise, is she? That stump's off-putting. I could have sold her to one of her older fans, perhaps, as a bed companion for old time's sake, but no-one's going to want her looking like that."

I look out into the courtyard, where the women are being trained. Alyssa is slumped in a corner, knees drawn up, her eyes on the ground, not even watching the fighting going on right in front of her. Her right hand cradles her stump, as though holding a broken kitten. Labeo need not concern himself with selling her off. If she is as unhappy as she looks, she'll die of her own accord within the year.

Worried, I report back to Fabia, but she only smiles as though she is not concerned at all.

"The stump looks good," she says. "It is healing beautifully. I had Father inspect it and he was so proud of me." She glows with the remembered praise.

"But Alyssa seems…"

"I know. Don't worry. I have something planned. It's taking a little longer than I thought, but you'll see."

She won't tell me anything else and I worry about Alyssa for days before Fabia sends a message via Karbo, asking me to meet her at Labeo's barracks.

When I get there, Fabia is standing by Alyssa, looking at her arm.

I get closer and stare. Where the stump was, there is now a hand in the shape of a fist, made of gleaming bronze, attached to her arm with a leather brace.

"What is that?"

"Her bow hand," says Fabia grinning with pride. "I had a man make it for me. I told him about General Marcus Sergius Silus, in the Punic Wars. He lost part of his left arm and they made him an iron hand, just like this one, so he could still hold a shield. Now Alyssa can hold a bow, so she can still shoot. See, the thumb can open and close, to insert the bow and close around it. Once it's in place, she can shoot."

"As well as before?"

"Not quite as fast as she used to. But better than most people."

Alyssa opens her mouth. Her voice is softer than I expected, with a hint of a foreign accent to it, I'm not sure where from. "Labeo is keep me now: as trainer for the women." Her lips curve into something approaching a smile.

"I'm so pleased," I say. "Fabia, you're amazing."

Fabia is grinning. "Maybe the other gladiators will let me near them now," she says.

"I spoken with Labeo," says Alyssa, addressing Fabia. "Physician we use, he old now. Retire. I ask for you to be physician to our barracks. Labeo say yes, if you willing. He hire you."

Fabia's mouth hangs open.

"You don't want job?" Alyssa looks disappointed, but Fabia grabs her round the legs and hugs her and Alyssa breaks into a broad smile and bends down to hug her back, the bronze hand caught in Fabia's untameable hair.

THE PORT OF OSTIA

IT'S ONLY MAY AND ALREADY Julia is having to water her plants every morning or they will wilt by the end of the day.

"We've had no rain for a month," she says. "It's not right for this time of year. What will we do in summer if we haven't had the spring rains?"

"Good thing we have our own fountain," I say, "or you'd be traipsing back and forth to the public fountain down the road."

"We have you to thank for it."

"It was a good use of the money," I say, scooping up a handful of the gurgling water spouting from Neptune's mouth and gulping it down. It's cold and fresh. My share of Titus' reward for making the opening day of the Games a triumph has been well spent.

MARCUS SAYS HE WANTS MERULA to join us for breakfast and discuss the naumachia for this season. I go to the local market and fill a basket with breads, cheese, fruit and bring it to the amphitheatre, thus avoiding the popina. It's been months since Cassia has spoken to me, it hurts when I think of it.

We sit in the senatorial seats and share out the food. Merula's eyes are bright with enthusiasm, as they always are when he discusses anything to do with water. "The added depth will mean that you can have any water animal that you care to add to the spectacle," he says. "Even quite large animals."

Marcus' shoulders slump and he takes another gulp of wine. "Such as?"

"Crocodiles? Rays? Sharks?"

"Oh, may the gods have mercy on me. I knew it would come to crocodiles."

"I've never seen one," I say.

"I have, in Egypt. Vicious creatures. You can see them plotting to kill you, it's in their eyes. Merciless. If you could train them to fight in a battle your opponents would be wiped out in moments."

"Can they be trained?"

He snorts at the idea. "There are three ways to make an animal do your bidding. You can make it trust you so it will do what you want out of loyalty and a desire to please you, you can keep it hungry until it learns, or you can frighten it into submission. They can't be frightened, I wouldn't care to keep them hungry and they'll never trust you. I'd rather go up against a full-grown lion than a crocodile."

I shiver. "How big are they?"

"Length of a man, even the smallest ones. But they can be three times that. I've seen them take down a leopard with barely a fight."

I've seen leopards in the arena, their powerful wiry bodies, their merciless killing of prey. The idea of an animal who could dispatch one with ease is terrifying.

"Will they go for people?"

"If they're hungry they'll go for anything. Book us a meeting with Bestia, let's see what he can get hold of."

Bestia is not impressed with our latest shopping list of animals.

"I don't do water stuff," he says, coughing and then spitting phlegm. "Waste of bloody time. The transport's a pain, half of them die if you take them out of sea water, even the good bestiarii can't train the buggers. I stick to land animals. Or birds. Don't mind birds, you can train them and the big ones look impressive when they're flying. I've got some nice eagles in, good wide wingspan. One of them will rip out a man's intestines, no problem."

"You mean I have to travel to Ostia and find a new beast hunter to provide this lot?" prods Marcus, evidently hoping Bestia will change his mind at the idea of a possible rival for his business. "I have to hire a new beast hunter just for one show?"

"Jupiter's dick, do what you like, just keep me out of it," says Bestia. He has another coughing fit, doubling over and making a hacking noise that sounds none too healthy.

"Don't you die on me," says Marcus. "I've got enough to do without changing supplier for the rest of the shows."

"By the Furies, who said anything about dying?"

"Go and see a doctor then," says Marcus. "Tell him to sort out that cough."

"They're all shitting quacks," says Bestia.

"And you're a stubborn old goat," says Marcus.

"Is he alright, do you think?" I ask Marcus as we leave.

"I expect so, he's a tough old thing. Although he must be getting on by now, I've known him a long time. Send Fabius over to him, will you?"

Fabius tries, but Bestia roundly refuses any medical help and Fabius retires defeated from the attempt.

"Ostia it is, then," says Marcus. "I swear this one show is

causing me more trouble than the hundred days of Games last year. Remind me, why did we say yes?"

"Because you did such a wonderful job last time and the Emperor himself asked for it," I say.

"Oh yes, that'll be it. Neptune help me then. We'll go in June. Got to plan ahead to get the best stuff."

June brings the unwelcome anniversary of Fausta's death. Karbo and I light candles Adah has given us and put flowers near the tiny doll in her image, we visit the temple together and offer sacrifices and prayers. When we get home, Maria calls to us.

"You're eating with me," she says, more of a command than an invitation.

She has made a beautiful meal, including a dish of thin flatbreads layered with herbs and fresh curd cheese cooked in the baker's oven, along with a fresh green salad and tiny cakes topped with a sweetened cream and fresh strawberries. Julia and Marcus have joined us, and there is an unexpected guest, a woman dressed in a toga, a prostitute.

"Acca," I say, recognising the woman who used to talk to Fausta about anything the local prostitutes wanted, such as having members of their informal guild dressed as gladiatrix near the amphitheatre, to titillate the crowd as they came out of a show. It's her professional name, referencing the she-wolf or prostitute who suckled Romulus and Remus. I'm amazed that Maria, usually a pillar of propriety, has invited her here to dinner, but she had come to a reluctant respect for Fausta, during the time they knew each other, especially when she saw how Karbo treated her like a mother.

Acca lifts her chin at me by way of greeting.

"Fausta would have been glad to have you here," I say to her, as we make toasts to her memory.

She gives a brusque nod. "Me and the girls, we sacrificed for her today," she says. "Down at the temple of Venus."

"Thank you," says Marcus and he sounds moved.

When the evening is over I embrace Maria. "Thank you," I say.

She gives one of her shrugs. "Thought it was important. For Karbo," she adds. "He's got you of course, but…"

"Yes," I say. "Thank you."

This time I'm not going to let Marcus get away with not talking. I follow him to the rooftop and find him, as I expected, looking out over the city.

"I miss her," I say.

"Me too."

We stand in silence for a few moments. It feels companionable and safe. It is a long time since I stood here in darkness without feeling afraid.

"When I first started as manager of the amphitheatre in Pompeii, she used to come and sit in the stands to watch rehearsals," Marcus says after a while. "And she'd make these really loud comments about all the mistakes I was making, how the sightlines weren't good enough, how a different bestiarius was more popular with the women and ought to be given a bigger part. How one of two gladiators in a bout wasn't up to the skill of the other one and they made a poor match together, that the gambling wouldn't be any fun because you could see the outcome right away."

I start laughing. I can imagine her loud voice and raucous laugh, a younger, inexperienced Marcus struggling to cope with this strange new job and being harangued by a prostitute who knew all the ropes.

"In the end I said just shut up or come and work for me," he says. "She got up and walked out and I thought she'd buggered off for good. Next morning, there she was, in the arena before me, telling me if I was going to be late every morning she'd find it very hard to respect me as a manager."

We laugh together in the dark and when we wish each other good night Marcus touches my arm and I'm glad I followed him, that I forced him to talk about her rather than grieve alone for his best friend.

A WEEK LATER WE TRAVEL by river barge to the port of Ostia, following the Tiber down to its mouth, leaving Rome in a dark dawn and arriving in the heat of the day at the bustling harbour, where ships and barges cram into a limited space, bringing everything Rome needs from across the empire. Huge sacks of grain from Egypt and endless amphorae of olive oil from Hispania are being unloaded from big ships and loaded onto the river barges, along with noisy livestock and live fish in vast barrels of fresh or salted water. Customs officials are everywhere, scowling as they make notes on their tablets, trying to keep up with the flow of goods.

"I saw an elephant being put on board a ship once," says Marcus as we walk towards the town centre. "It hardly seemed possible the ship would hold such a beast without sinking, and it did not much wish to board the vessel, either, but they managed it in the end."

"Where was it going?"

"To take part in Games somewhere, I expect. It had been

trained a little, but it still disliked the heave and swell of the water."

"I don't blame it," I say. I am relishing the firm land under my feet myself, having felt nauseous at the motion of the barge. I am not a natural sailor.

In the centre of Ostia is the Merchants' Forum, a large paved square set all around with a portico divided up into little cubicles, their fronts shuttered or open for business. Each one is marked out on the pavement in front of it with black and white mosaics indicating their wares: sailing ships for chandlers; barrels with wheat sheaves for grain shipping, mostly from Egypt; leaping dolphins and Nereids for garum sauce and fresh or preserved fish; an olive branch for olive oil.

"Look for the elephant," says Marcus.

"Elephant?"

"Mosaic of an elephant. It's the agency of Sabratha, based on the coast of Africa. They ship wild animals for Games, I've heard they have a good beast hunter. Quality merchandise and he can get difficult items. Which is what we'll need."

We spot the elephant and the name of Sabratha picked out above it, but the cubicle is shuttered.

"He'll be back shortly," says the trader next door. "Probably gone to get something to eat."

"Not a bad idea," says Marcus. "Come on, let's get some food and come back later."

We wander down a few streets to find a local popina and purchase bread, cheese, olives and wine, then sit under an awning and watch Ostia bustle by. We hear more than one foreign language being spoken; a port town brings people from all over the empire and beyond.

I enjoy being in Marcus' company. It's been a long time

since we spent time together like this, without constantly being interrupted or worrying about work matters. I take a sip of wine and close my eyes to the sunshine, for once enjoying its warmth without fretting about something that has to be done.

"You were looking for me?"

I look up. The man speaking is tall and slender, with hair growing in the same locks as Karbo's. Both his skin and hair are a soft brown though, unlike Karbo's far darker tone, and each of his locks ends in a tiny sun-bleached golden curl. I wonder where his parents are from. His clothes are unusual. He's wearing a blue skirted loincloth, something like Egyptians wear, with a white top to his waist like a very short tunic, tied with a red sash. Attached to his loincloth, at the back, is a tiger's tail, the black and orange fur silky-bright in the sunshine. He has wide brass armbands over his upper arms and a string of small white shells around his neck. The skin on his cheeks and nose has been deliberately scarred in a pattern.

Marcus stands. "Marcus Aquillius Scaurus. How did you find us?"

The man grins. "The manager of the Flavian Amphitheatre? Every beast-hunter in Ostia has been watching you, hoping for your business. If I hadn't come to look for you, they'd have told you I was unavailable in the hopes of winning your interest for themselves." He holds out a hand. "Funis."

I note both that his nickname means rope, no doubt in reference to his hair, but also that he has omitted the rest of his name, unusual at a first meeting.

Marcus indicates me. "Althea Aquillius. My scribe and right-hand woman at the amphitheatre."

Funis turns his dark eyes on me and gives an open smile. "Althea."

I nod.

"I think you're going to regret meeting me," says Marcus. "Can I offer you a cup of wine before I make your life difficult with what I need?"

Funis takes the seat by my side. "There aren't many demands you can make of me that would prove especially difficult. The Games are my speciality."

Marcus waves to the serving girl. "More wine here."

Cups filled, Marcus raises his. "Your health."

"Health," echo Funis and I.

We raise our cups and drink. When we set the cups down Marcus takes a deep breath. "So."

Funis leans forwards expectantly. "So?"

"I have to put on a naumachia this autumn, on the last day of the Games in the Flavian Amphitheatre. We did one last year but now they want something bigger, the water has to be deeper, the events more spectacular, more dangerous. The trouble is that we've also been asked to showcase the battle between the Corcyreans and Corinthians, the one that led to the Peloponnesian War. It's dull as you like, they only want it because Augustus had it. We could have had something much more interesting. I don't know why the Aedile always has to poke his nose in, he has no idea what the crowds like or what looks good in the arena. Which means that everything else has to be even more spectacular, or everyone's going to sit there yawning. So it's down to the animals to provide the danger."

Funis laughs. "Ah, I see your difficulty. All water animals?"

"Yes. Last time, we had horses running through the water. It worked well enough, but now Titus wants more."

"Dangerous animals?"

"Yes."

Funis nods, unperturbed. "I can get them. If I have enough time."

"We have a few months. What's possible?"

"Crocodiles from Egypt are no problem, even hippos if you want them. They may look like fat cows, but they can kill a man, they've got a temper like rhinos. Sharks if the water's deep enough. Rays. Vipers, they can swim. Eels."

"The water's plenty deep," says Marcus. "It's half the problem though. It's no good if a man just gets dragged under the water and eaten without anyone seeing the struggle, it doesn't make for a spectacle."

Funis thinks. "The sharks are good, their fins stick up when they're circling, adds tension. The crocodiles kill their prey by rolling them in the water, it's pretty spectacular. Rays and vipers, if they attack, less so, but it all adds interest."

Marcus nods. "And you can provide them all?"

"Of course. It'll be expensive though. They're not just dangerous, they need transporting differently to most animals or they'll easily die."

Marcus shrugs. "What the Emperor wants, the Emperor gets."

"Do you have bestiarii to fight them?"

"Some. I don't know how used they are to water animals."

"Do you want me to send you some water-trained bestiarii to go with the animals?"

"That might be useful. Do you fight them yourself?"

"I used to. Not anymore." He pulls away one of the armbands, showing a large, scarred area, a clear bitemark where a chunk of his flesh has been bitten away. "It would happily have eaten the rest of it, if I hadn't put a spear in it."

"Crocodile?" asks Marcus.

He nods.

I shiver at the thought, and he catches my movement, laughs. "I still shiver at the thought of it myself, on dark nights. I thought my time had come. After that I decided not to tempt the gods any longer. So, no, I no longer fight in the arena. But I know a few men who are good beast hunters, no doubt they would be delighted to fight in front of Titus himself, they will brag of nothing else. If they survive, of course."

We make our way back to the Merchants' Forum, trying to stick to the shade offered by umbrella pine trees along the way. At the sign of the elephant, Funis pulls up the shutters of his trading cubicle and gets out his ledgers. He and Marcus put their heads together, discussing numbers of animals, adding a few extra in case some of them should die in transit, the prices of each. I take notes on the care of each animal, what food they must be given and how each must be kept. The sharks, in particular, must be kept in saltwater until we release them into the freshwater we will be using.

"They won't live long in freshwater," says Funis grimacing. "I've had too many die on me to risk it for long. They'll stay alive for your spectacle, but only if you keep them in seawater until just before the show starts."

I make a note.

"Keep the crocodiles hungry," he advises me.

I think of the hapless gladiators who will risk being drowned while clamped in the hungry jaws of a deathly monster.

"Quicker death than some," says Funis, watching my face. "Lions will eat you while you're still breathing."

I nod.

"Time to see some of the animals you're thinking of showcasing?"

"You have them here?"

"A few. Not all of them."

We follow him back to the docks, where he leads us to a warehouse similar to the one we have in Rome, only smaller. Inside there are three huge tanks and over twenty barrels of water, spread around the room. Funis takes us to one of the larger barrels and dips into it with a net on a pole, swiftly bringing up a pair of grey snakes, who writhe in the net, their mouths open, hissing.

"Vipers," he says. "They can swim and they are venomous." He lets them back into the water and closes the lid.

"I've got an octopus in that one," he says, pointing at a larger barrel. "Gets out all the time and tries to eat the fish if you don't catch it. No good to you though, not very dangerous."

"Who will you sell it to?"

"Oh, they make interesting additions to the pools of big villas. I sold one to a man once who liked to throw jewels into the pool for it to catch, found it amusing. And you can eat them, of course."

We walk to the first of the large tanks, built higher than my shoulder, I have to tiptoe to look in.

"Moray eels," says Funis. I can just make out rippling yellow grey through the water, but when Funis pulls one out, I step back. The eel has spotted grey skin and it opens its mouth at once, baring many long narrow teeth, like needles, at us. "Carnivorous," says Funis. "If you frighten them, they'll attack."

The second tank contains stingrays, whose tail barbs are both sharper than swords and venomous.

The final tank is the largest, taking up half of the warehouse floor space and it appears empty. There is a wooden platform halfway up the height of it and it has a heavy metal grid fitted over the top.

"Crocodiles," sighs Marcus, without even seeing the contents.

"Indeed," says Funis. From a hook close by he takes the carcass of a hare and throws it into the tank, onto the wooden platform. The carcass has barely come to rest when the water explodes and a crocodile has leapt onto the platform and snatched the hare. It lies on the platform as it crunches its prize, tail still dangling in the water. It is longer than Marcus and its yellow-green eyes watch us even as it swallows.

"Just as I remember," says Marcus. "I'm grateful it won't be me in the water with any of them but especially not those. We should be going."

I can't help but feel relieved once we've left the warehouse behind, a heavy bolt drawn across the door to keep its inhabitants from escaping.

"Thank you for your help," says Marcus. "If you wish to bring the animals yourself, you are more than welcome at the amphitheatre."

Funis smiles. "I am not overly fond of Rome," he says lightly. "Ostia suits me better. I miss the sea if I am not near it."

Marcus shakes hands with him and begins to walk away.

"Thank you," I say.

"It was my pleasure," says Funis. "I am sorry not to have the pleasure of getting to know you better, Althea," he adds, taking my hand with a smile that brings a little heat to my cheeks. "Should you ever wish to leave the amphitheatre, I am always in need of an assistant. There is no lessening in Rome's demand for animals; if anything it is growing now that the Flavians have invested in the Games so greatly."

I swallow. "I am glad to have met you," I say. "Goodbye, Funis." I catch myself. "What is your full name?"

"Ah, I am afraid it would be hard to say, it comes from my mother's country, the Kingdom of Kush. You know it as Dodekaschoinos," he adds, seeing my frown.

"I'd like to hear it."

"My given name is Arikakahtani. It was the name of a king, long before my mother's time, but she must have taken a fancy to the idea of having a son with a regal name. No-one can pronounce it here, so they have nicknamed me Funis, for my hair."

"Arikaka… Arikakahtani," I manage.

"Impressive."

"I have to remember a lot of names. You said it was your mother's country? Not your father's?"

"Too many questions for a first meeting," he says, not losing his easy smile. "You will lose sight of your companion if you do not hurry."

Marcus is already striding away towards the barge that will take us back to Rome.

"Oh, I – Goodbye."

"Goodbye," he says, and lets go of my hand.

I turn to leave and stumble over a loose paving slab, gather myself and hurry after Marcus.

SHIPWRECKS

IT'S JULY NOW, AND WE have all given up hoping for rain until the autumn thunderstorms come. Dust gathers in the streets, sticks hot and grimy on our skin, kicking up into the air if there is ever a breath of breeze, which there is less and less often. The whole city feels like an oven. I dread to think how the baker's family manages their work. Mostly they try to do all the baking by night, when the temperature drops, if only by very little. In the early dawn they mix and knead, by day they leave the dough to rise and make up for their night-time labours with sleeping in the daytime, leaving only one of them by turns to look after customers.

Next door to them, Cassia sweats through the day as she makes and serves food for her customers, though her offerings have cooled with the growing heat. Now she has cold salads of salted cheese and beans with herbs, garlic-herb curd cheese to spread on bread, boiled eggs and green beans with olive oil and pickles, fresh green salads and balls of spelt, flavoured while cooking into a thick mush and then shaped into little balls to be eaten cold, dipped in garum. Olives and fruit, fresh summer cheeses and cool wine make up the rest of her offerings. I mostly send Karbo to buy food for us now, but it makes me sad to eat Cassia's food knowing her warm smile no longer comes with it and often I send Karbo elsewhere, to local popinas whose food is not so good but at least does not come flavoured with sadness.

A RARE DAY OFF FROM the Games leaves us free for the day. Celer has invited Karbo to see the races and I have gone with him, anxious to keep him safe, anxious to avoid the insula.

"We need to get there by sunrise," says Celer the night before.

"So early?"

"One hundred and fifty thousand spectators. It takes hours to get everyone in, the entrances are not as well organised as the amphitheatre, not to mention it's almost three times as many people."

"Glad it's not mine to manage," I say.

We get there early, but still the crowd is already huge and Celer is right, it's not as well organised. There are, supposedly, lines one should queue in, but no-one is staying in their own lines and there's a lot of elbowing for the top tier seats, which are free of charge. Celer has already procured tickets for us, so we do not have to sit so far from the action, we are somewhere more mid-range. A few wealthy patrons of the races make their way through the crowd only by dint of surrounding themselves with heavyset bodyguards. There are soldiers everywhere, some of whom carry large clubs to quell the crowd in no uncertain terms should things get rowdy.

Just as we have at the amphitheatre, as well as the usual stalls of snacks, drinks and sweet treats, are other stalls selling portraits of the charioteers, as well as tiny wooden replicas of their chariots and horses, toys for the more privileged children or perhaps their fathers, the sort of thing Balbus the toymaker creates.

We struggle through the crowds, Celer being approached

more than once by she-wolves in gaudy-bright tunics pinned to allow a more than usually abundant view of cleavage, who tug at his arm and make lewd suggestions about what he can do to them for a very cheap price. He nods and grins at a few who greet him by name, but pushes onwards, Karbo and I in his wake. Occasionally I clutch at his tunic so we will not be separated. Karbo has his arms full of cushions we can use to sit on the seating area, should we ever get there, which I'm beginning to doubt.

Finally, we get out of the throng, as everyone, one way or another, finds a place to sit, we put down our cushions and try to settle ourselves. I give Karbo water and a peach pastry to eat as a belated breakfast, but he is too giddy to think of anything so prosaic as hunger. His head turns this way and that as he tries to take in everything.

"How do you bear coming here often?" I ask Celer. "I felt as if I couldn't breathe."

"Oh, I usually help out one of the stable hands when they bring the horses down here before dawn in return for watching with them from the starting gates," he says. "This a different view. Didn't Marcus want to join us? He was more than welcome."

"He's gone down south to Puteoli," I say. "With Vita," I add.

"Really? What for?"

"I'm not really sure," I say. "He said he was going to visit the manager of the amphitheatre there. But he has friends in the area, it's where his family was from before they ended up in Pompeii. He said he wanted to introduce Vita to some people there."

Celer nods. "The family farm's there, isn't it?"

"Yes." I think of Marcus taking me there, the sweet strawberry grapes we tasted, the deal he made me as we left: that I would work hard for him and be loyal, that in return he would free me one day and then return to the farm with his wife and son. They are gone now, swept away by Vulcan's wrath. I suppose the farm is still there, abandoned and waiting for its master to return. I wonder whether Marcus feels the time has come to return, whether he is ready to begin a new life, perhaps with Vita. Perhaps he is introducing her to a distant family branch, a first step towards marriage? I didn't feel I could question him before he went. Perhaps when he returns, he will explain. I am not sure how I feel about Marcus remarrying, I worry that we will drift further apart. It might lead to him leaving altogether, if he wants to go back to the family farm, and that thought makes my stomach turn over with fear of losing him altogether when he is so much a part of my life and work. He is also my protector. If he leaves, I will have no choice but to leave the insula and live elsewhere. I would be too afraid to do otherwise. If Rullus saw me without a protector nearby, he would not hesitate to do as he pleased with me. Nor did I need to ask how Merula felt about the trip, his face was a picture of misery at the idea of Vita going on a mysterious journey with Marcus.

"About time he found some happiness again," says Celer. He takes a gulp of wine he has brought with him and nods to a man currently walking through the tiers of seating, stopping to chat here and there. He has a broken-off branch of laurels stuck in his tunic and Celer gestures him over. I gather from their conversation that the man is a roving bookmaker, taking bets, illegally of course, as gambling is not strictly permitted, although it goes on everywhere and in plain sight. Celer consults with the man for a little while.

"…on the *third* race, mind you. No, nothing on the first two or the fourth, don't fancy any of them. Now, the fifth…"

For his part, the bookmaker, knowing Celer's connections, is asking a few questions, in case he should find out something interesting. "How is Golden Laurels doing, anyway? Heard he was limping, is that right? And has Sergius gotten over that girl or is he still moping? He drove like a ploughman last time I saw him, no spirit at all."

The pompa circensis is about to begin, a vast ceremonial procession heralding the opening of the races. Karbo's eyes surely can't get any larger, he leans forwards staring as the procession makes its way onto the track. First horseback riders from the very best families, followed by more young men on foot, who will join the infantry. The crowd erupts as the top charioteers appear in their four-horse chariots, followed by those less well-known or still young and working their way up the ranks in chariots drawn by two or three horses. Having finished with the bookmaker, Celer takes on the role of commentator for Karbo.

"Ah that's the dancers and musicians, along with the choir of satyrs, then behind them are servants, their jobs is to carry the statues of the gods and incense burners. Here comes the Emperor."

Titus is in full regalia for once, not his usual modest toga. He's riding in a four-horse chariot, and I'm reminded of the day I saw him, as a much younger man, riding through the centre of Rome in his celebratory Triumph over Judea, when he burnt the Temple of Jerusalem to the ground. Today he is not showing off Jewish slaves and loot from the Temple, only waving to the crowd to acknowledge their cheers. As the procession continues round the track and Titus makes his way to the imperial box, three bulls are taken to a temporarily erected altar and sacrificed. Celer is busy explaining the day to Karbo, who has never seen a full day's races, only caught little bits here and there when he lived on the streets and would try and sneak a glimpse between the tiers of seating.

"There'll be thirty races today. Used to be twenty-four, but the Flavians prefer a fuller day. Seven laps round the track. If you're fast, you can keep a tight line and the horses will run less distance, see? If you're slow and there's other people in the way, you have to go wide and your horses end up running further and getting worn out, so then you fall even further behind. Look, they're drawing lots to see who will go in which starting stall."

Karbo cranes his head to look. The chariots for the first race, painted in the bold colours of the four racing teams, red, blue, white and green, are being guided to their starting stalls, the horses already struggling against the stable hands' attempts to move them, eager to be off. They toss their heads, manes plaited to keep them from going in their eyes at the wrong moment, distracting them or obstructing their vision, either of which could spoil a race.

A sudden blast of trumpets accompanies the presiding magistrate dropping a white cloth. The stall doors open, the chariots are already halfway along the track before I've drawn a second breath. The speed down the straights is breath-taking, the tightness of the cornering has me wincing, certain that the drivers will make a mistake, that they will collide with not just each other but sections of the building. By the third lap, drivers and horses are visibly sweating and the sparsores along the racetrack are throwing water over both, as well as the chariot axles to stop them over-heating.

"What are they doing?" screams Karbo to Celer, indicating horseback riders who are galloping alongside the chariots, each dressed in the same colours of the chariot they are keeping abreast of.

"Telling them how the race is going!" yells back Celer. "They can't see behind them, and they don't always know how many laps someone's done, or who's gaining on them. The hortatores are telling them anything they need to know."

The riders Karbo has taken an interest in are leaning perilously from their horses so they can be closer to the drivers and though I cannot hear them above the roar of the crowd, I can see them yelling at the drivers, passing on information. The drivers do not look at them, only at the track ahead, but they can hear them and change their tactics accordingly.

As the seventh lap of the first race approaches its conclusion, it becomes clear the Greens will win despite the other supporters' cheers and Karbo's urgent screams of encouragement to the driver of the Blues. When the Greens driver holds up his arm to claim victory, Karbo very nearly weeps, but Celer whispers in his ear and Karbo pins his hope on the third race, which obligingly delivers a Blues win to fill both Karbo's heart and Celer's pocket.

The elite four-horse chariot races give way to those pulled by two or three horses, showcasing the younger drivers working their way to stardom. In between races, there are acrobats on horseback, or a few unusual races such as those featuring chariots pulled by ten horses, more of a demonstration of the skill required to manage such a number of steeds than a standard race.

I have to hide my face when both the eighth and fifteenth races end with crashes between chariots, where a driver has miscalculated how much room he has to manoeuvre or grown too ambitious. Two horses are led away limping, their racing lives over.

"Stud farm," says Celer to Karbo, who asks what will happen to them.

The third horse is not so lucky, a broken wheel spoke pierces its side as it falls onto it, blood spurting in a wide arc that hits some of the closest spectators. A hammer to the head finishes it, just as Charon does at the amphitheatre and men with hooked poles drag it off the racetrack as the pieces of chariot are gathered up and the track swept clean of debris for the next race, the programme and spectators' enthusiasm continuing unabated, death or no death.

Crashes in the sixteenth and twenty-second races only lead to broken chariots, the horses and men escaping damage.

"We call them shipwrecks," says Celer to Karbo, indicating the shattered remnants of chariots, their racing colours now mixed together on the tracks.

In the twenty-third race a chariot overturns and the driver must cut himself loose from the reins with his knife. He survives, but only just, carried from the track with blood pouring out of him all down one side of his body. I can only hope he will recover, that the Whites have a good physician ready and waiting for him.

"Can he race again?" asks Karbo.

"Doubt it," says Celer. "If he's had a bad injury, especially on his arm, he'll not have the strength or flexibility. And he'll have the fear. Once you have the fear in you, you can't race anymore."

THE VISIT TO THE RACES has a not wholly unexpected consequence. Karbo is now certain that he wishes to be a charioteer.

"Absolutely not," I say, thinking of the dead horse, the bleeding charioteer.

"Fabia said people should name their desire and then work hard for it, and look at her now, she is physician to one of the biggest gladiatorial schools in Rome! And my desire is to race chariots! For the Blues! And I will, no matter what you say, Althea."

"Mother," I remind him.

"You're not my real mother," pouts Karbo, though the provocative statement lacks the vehemence and volume of his initial outburst.

"I've been as good as since the day I met you," I say sternly. "And you know it. And you are my adopted son now, you owe me obedience. Titus himself made me your mother."

"When you won't let me do what I want to do?"

"My word is final," I say. "I am afraid for your safety. Charioteers die young, everyone knows that."

"Celer's still alive."

"He ruined himself with women and wine," I say. "It's all that helped him survive, he said so himself, or weren't you paying attention then, either?"

Karbo gives a wicked glance at me. "I could ruin myself with women and wine," he suggests and ducks as I swat at him.

"Dea Bona! You think talk like that will win me round?"

"Nothing will win you round. You're so stubborn."

I snort. "Says the boy who won't listen to anything but his own desires."

AUGUST IS COMING TO A close and the pleasure of having our own fountain in the insula's courtyard is dimmed by a city-wide declaration that private fountains must be turned off most of the day to avoid wasting water, due to the drought. Every day we scan the sky, hoping for a glimpse of clouds or the distant rumble of thunder that might indicate the end-of-summer storms that would break the heat and bring the much-needed rain, but each day dawns sharp-blue clear and the sky is silent. Even the city birds are too hot to sing, they huddle in the shady corners of rooftops, sheltering from the heat. The tiles on the rooftop are so hot that bare feet are impossible, I have to keep my sandals on until I reach the shade of my hut, which is also too hot after a day baking in the direct sun. I want to leave my door open at night to try and cool the roof hut and sleep better, but I daren't, instead each night I lock the door as usual, feeling as though I am locking out not just Rullus but Cassia's friendship, too.

"I'VE HAD ENOUGH OF THIS heat," says Marcus, wiping sweat off his face in the dark and smelly under-arena space after the show is over for the day. "It's ruining the water-clocks, they're all evaporating too fast. I'm going to have to bring in the clockmaker again to make some adjustments to them or the timings of the shows will be a mess, the clocks down here aren't matching my sundial in the seating upstairs at all. I'm going down to the river for a cold dip. Who's coming?"

Fabius, Karbo and Fabia are eager, three of the gladiators who have not sustained any injuries today nod agreeably to the idea. We make our way upstairs and out into the bright heat of the afternoon. Strabo lumbers along behind us, a few dozen slaves join us. After making our way through the hot back streets we clamber down a steep side of the river to a grassy bank much favoured for swimming. The water is already full of people who have had the same idea, especially young boys who take turns leaping in with a huge splash.

"Be careful to stay out of the current," I tell Karbo.

"He's a fish," says Marcus proudly. "Don't you worry about him."

"Even fish get caught in currents," I say. But Marcus is right, Karbo is turning into an excellent swimmer and soon enough he is flinging himself off the bank with the other boys, their yelps, taunts and cheers so loud that in the end we move further away to where the river slows briefly in a little curve, allowing those of us who cannot swim well to paddle safely.

The men strip off at once and dive in, Marcus amongst them. The female slaves peel off their tunics and wade in the water; a few can swim and strike out into the deeper part, others tread water and gratefully dunk their heads under the water to cool themselves, emerging dripping and smiling at the freshness they have not felt these past months.

I undress, then tentatively enter the river. It's blissfully cool and I lie back and float in the shallows, then, feeling braver, strike out a little, my swimming motion clumsy but, to my pride, keeping me above water. I smile to myself, pleased with my progress, but then, dipping one foot down, find I can no longer feel the bottom and panic, lose my rhythm, instead feeling again and again for a foothold and finding none, now paddling like a dog, but splashing more wildly, frightened the current pulling at me will drag me away without anyone seeing me or being able to help.

"Got you." Marcus has a hold of my arm, pulls me hard backwards, and suddenly my feet touch something under me and I am safe, find the riverbed under the water, stop struggling and stand up, turning to him. He's shaking his head.

"Thank you," I manage, still gasping. "I – couldn't feel –"

"The Tiber is not like a still pool at the baths," says Marcus, one hand still on my arm. "The currents can grasp at you when you least expect them. You were doing well, though. More practise and you'll be like Karbo," he adds, letting go of me and looking to where Karbo is trying to do handstands under the water, as Vita and her team do. "The boy's a natural."

"Fish and horses," I manage. "He must be beloved of Neptune, since he looks after both."

Marcus nods. "Are you alright now?"

"Yes. Thank you."

"Stay in the shallows. Lucky I was watching you."

I stay in the shallows, but I envy Marcus' comfort in the water, how he lies back in the water and allows it to carry him a little way off, before returning to shore with smooth, fast strokes through the water, his golden-brown skin glistening. Meanwhile Karbo is joyfully leaping into the water again and again, certain of his ability to return safely to dry land. I must keep practising.

"They've chosen a prisoner for us to use at the naumachia," says Marcus.

"Just one?"

"For the Hero and Leander scene," he amends, looking over some plans for the water rafts.

"Why choose this one in particular? We usually pick the most suitable one for a specific scene."

"This one's a troublemaker, they want to make a point."

"What's he done?"

"He's a Jewish preacher. Refuses to worship the gods or acknowledge Vespasian as a divinity. He's one of those followers of that preacher that died, Jesus of Nazareth. Troublemakers, the lot of them."

I nod, only half listening.

"Go and see him," says Marcus.

"What?"

"He's being held in the Tullianum."

I look up. "Why?" Most prisoners are not held for long, they are sent straight to us for their public punishment if that is what they have been condemned to. Occasionally we will hold a group over a few days to make the numbers larger at a particular Games. The Tullianum is an underground dungeon where Rome keeps some of its most dangerous enemies, usually leaders of a conquered land. It sits at the bottom of the Capitoline Hill, close to the Forum. Its walls are rumoured to be three times thicker than a man's outstretched arms. It used to be a water cistern, now used for darker purposes. It's a dark and frightening underworld to be banished to.

"They want to make an example of him, they don't want him lost in a crowd of other criminals being executed."

"And why do you want me to visit him?"

"I need to know if he can swim or not. And I don't just mean whether he's been taught. I mean whether they've broken anything. I can't have a big swimming scene with a man who can't swim, it'll look ridiculous."

"He's going to be drowned anyway," I say, swallowing at the thought of it.

"He has to at least start out swimming," says Marcus. "Check whether he's able and warn the jailors not to damage him before the event."

I nod. I don't much fancy the task, visiting the most frightening prison in Rome puts chills down my back, but if I can save the man from being tortured in advance of the Games he will appear in, I suppose it will be a kindness to him, even if he has been condemned to die.

HERO AND LEANDER

THE FINAL DAYS OF AUGUST are draining the last drops of energy from me, the heat unbearable.

"I'm so slow," I complain to Vita, as she outstrips me again and again along the length of the pool.

"You have to keep moving."

"I was moving!"

She laughs at me, lying back in the water and floating.

"Tell me what I'm doing wrong."

"Nothing. It's just practise, you'll get faster without even thinking about it."

"Easy for you to say."

I sigh and float beside her.

"You're not practising."

"I'm resting."

"I'll be glad when the autumn rains come. This whole city is drying up. They said they might even have to close some of the baths, or shorten the opening hours. Never known a drought like it. Not a drop since April. It was practically cooler down south."

"How was your trip there?" I ask. I've not worked up the courage to ask Marcus the same question, am not sure I even want to hear Vita's reply. But it seems absurd not to know whether Vita is Marcus' new chosen companion, as though I were only a minor acquaintance of his.

"Good," she says enthusiastically. "He showed me round Puteoli and the amphitheatre there, and further afield."

I think of Marcus' family farm near Puteoli, wonder whether she means he took her there, a place so full of meaning to him. I wonder whether he even suggested to her they might live there together, one day, since I know that being there is his ultimate desire. Is he ready to move back yet, to leave Rome and his role at the amphitheatre behind? What would I do if that happened? Who else would or even could run the Games?

"Did he –" I start but a woman leans over the edge of the pool and hails Vita, who swims over to answer her, greeting her like an old friend. They start chatting together, so that my opportunity to ask her anything must be abandoned and I am left to practise my slow, clumsy swimming again, passing the same part of the pool, over and over again.

THE WALK TO THE TULLIANUM in the hottest part of the day leaves me panting by the time I reach the large wooden door.

The guardroom is hardly the frightening place for which I had braced myself. Sunlight streams in from the open door. A couple of bored guards are throwing dice in a spacious if plain room, the walls raw stone, unadorned by plaster.

The guard at the doorway looks disconcerted at my visit. "Why would you want to see the prisoner?" he asks.

"I have to make sure he can swim," I say.

He looks baffled.

"The Emperor wants a naumachia," I clarify. "He's going to be in it."

"Thought there already was a naumachia," he says. "Last year, final day of the opening Games. You couldn't get tickets for love nor money."

"Titus liked it so much he wants another one," I say. "You going to let me see this prisoner or what?"

"I can't bring him up to see you," says the guard. "You have to be lowered down to where he is."

"What?"

"I have to lower you down. On a rope. There isn't a lot of room down there and we're not allowed to leave our posts, so it'll just be the two of you. I can't be held responsible if he attacks you."

I try to think of an alternative but find none. "Fine," I say, feigning a bravery I certainly don't feel. "Lower away."

He waves me in and the two other guards look up from their game, curious at my presence.

"Seeing the prisoner. For the Games. Works at the Flavian Amphitheatre," says the door guard.

They go back to their gambling, uninterested.

The opening in the middle of the floor is only as wide as my outstretched arms and below me everything is dark. There is a smell of damp. The rope is coarse between my hands. One of my feet is held in a loop at the bottom of the length, with the other I feel desperately for the floor as I am lowered ever further into the darkness below. I hope the guard will not loosen his grip on the other end of the rope.

My foot touches the floor and I tug at the loop, trying to get my foot out, afraid of falling. The room is very dark, and I blink, waiting for my eyes to adjust to the lack of light. The smell of damp is mixed with another smell: of unwashed human, not the sweat I am used to from many of our labourers and even myself on a hot day, but a smell of abandonment and despair, of uncaring, a sweetish smell that makes me nauseous.

"Who are you?"

I startle at the voice, even though I have been expecting to hear it since I know there is someone down here in the dark with me. I am still holding onto the rope, as though for safety. I peer into the dim corners of the room and see a man, huddled on the floor, his knees pulled up, bare feet resting on the cold stone floor. He has long hair and a beard. His head is up, his eyes watching me.

"My name is Althea," I say.

"Alon."

I'm still holding the rope. Slowly, I let go of it, steadying myself without it. "I work at the Flavian Amphitheatre," I start, unsure of how much he knows about his fate.

He says nothing.

"You have been condemned to the Games," I say, getting the words out quickly.

"I know."

"We are telling the story of Hero and Leander." I pause, hoping that he knows the story, that it will be obvious what his fate is.

"Tell me the story," he says.

I don't know if he is forcing me to tell the story to highlight the cruelty he will be facing, or whether he truly doesn't know it. It's a famous legend, surely everyone knows it?

"There was once a beautiful priestess of Venus named Hero, who dwelt in a tower in the city of Sestos," I begin slowly, aware that I am using the style of a storyteller, perhaps to make the story seem more distant than it will be for this man. "A man named Leander saw Hero at her duties during a festival and he fell in love with her, as she did with him. He persuaded her that Venus, being the goddess of love, would look kindly on their intimacy, and so they lay together. Leander lived on the opposite side of the strait of Hellespont, at Abydos, but the strait is very narrow there and Leander was a strong swimmer. By night, he could see Hero's tower, and she would set a light in it if it was safe for him to visit her. He would set out in the darkness, using her light as a guide, and swim to her tower, where she would meet him on the rocky coast and help him ashore. And so their lovemaking continued, all summer long."

The room is very quiet. I can hear the drip-drip of water somewhere.

"Were they found out?" Alon asks at last. "Punished?"

I swallow. "The end of summer brought a sudden storm," I say. "Hero had lit the torch at the top of the tower, but then she fell asleep and did not hear the wind rise. Leander, for his part, saw the light in Hero's tower and was so filled with love for her that he felt he could brave any storm, for had he not swum the strait many times that summer and always reached her arms safely?"

The dark room's damp has cooled my hot skin. I am shivering. "Hero awoke and realised a storm was in progress, but the high wind had blown out her torch, leaving Leander to swim without a guide, through the darkness rent only by thunder and brief flashes of lightening when he could see the tower and hope not to lose his way. Hero re-lit the torch and waited anxiously. But the rocky shore proved Leander's undoing, for, exhausted from battling the waves, he was flung against the rocks, unable to escape the sea's wrath. He died and Hero, seeing his dead body surface, climbed to the top of her tower and threw herself into the sea, to join him in death. Their bodies were washed ashore in a lovers' embrace and they were buried together, united at last."

"You're holding a naumachia?"

He has caught on quickly. "Yes."

"You are going to cast me as Leander? Drown me?"

"Yes."

"How?"

I think of Merula and Marcus, their faces concentrating over diagrams, adding notes or elements to sketches of the mechanism to be used. "It is something like a small raft that will allow you to swim at first, then drag you under the water. Once – once you have drowned, the raft will re-surface so that Hero will see you."

"Do I need to swim at all, or merely pretend?"

"The mechanism will hold you up a little, but you will need to swim at the beginning, across the arena a few times. As part of the story." It feels strange to be discussing the details of how this man will die with him, as though he were one of our team, considering how something must happen rather than whether it should happen at all. I have never discussed their death with a criminal before: they arrive in our space under the arena, we dress them according to our needs, occasionally we tell them what they are to do and whether they have a chance of saving themselves, if they fight well, for example. I have never had a conversation with one of them.

"And who is to play Hero? Another prisoner?"

"A show-swimmer."

"Ah. She is able to merely enact the part?"

"Yes."

There's a silence. Then he speaks quietly, almost as though to himself rather than to me. "So be it. As my Lord requires of me."

"You are Jewish?" I ask.

"Yes. But I also follow the teachings of Jesus."

I frown. "The Nazarene preacher? You are a Nazarene?"

"Indeed."

"Why were you sent here?"

"For refusing to worship false idols."

I think about this for a moment. I'm aware there are some followers of the Nazarene who refuse to offer even a basic show of worship to the Roman gods and the Emperor, as their leader did and that such refusal does not go down well with the Emperor nor the priests of Rome, who consider it treason, as well as blasphemy. "Surely you can worship both your own god and ours? You need only offer incense to the gods and say, 'Caesar is Lord,' and you would be released."

"Only?"

"Rather than die?"

"If I must die, then I must die."

"Why did they single you out? Plenty of your people get away with little or no public worship. What did you do to draw attention to yourself?"

He gives a very small chuckle. "Preached once too often and far too loudly in the Forum."

I take a step closer, look down into his face. "I remember you!"

"Do you?"

"Yes. I've seen you preaching in the Forum, answering questions."

"Then you know why I am here."

"I thought at the time you were pushing your luck."

"I do what is needful for the Almighty," he says.

"Your god is not being very helpful to you right now," I say. "Shouldn't you be praying for him to get you out?"

"His own son was crucified by the Romans, yet did not protest. How may I refuse what has been laid before me?"

"If he was the son of your god then he was divine," I say.

"It's hardly a fair comparison, is it? Expecting a man to do what a god does?"

"Jesus was a man," he says.

"You said he was a god."

"Both."

"You can't be both."

He smiles but doesn't answer.

"So," I say, trying to gather myself. "You didn't say whether you can swim."

"I can swim."

"Well?"

"Not as well as your show swimmers. Well enough for an ordinary man."

"More than once across the length of our arena?"

"I daresay."

"Then that's all I needed to know."

"Can I help you in any other way?"

Something has caught my eye. "You can tell me what this means," I say, indicating the rough outline of a fish, scratched onto the stone wall just by his head. "I've seen it before, on walls. And it was drawn on the ground by your feet when you were preaching."

He smiles. "The fish is a symbol for our Lord Jesus," he says. "We use it as a sign for meetings, or to show that one of us who follows Him lives in a certain place, so that we can find one another."

"Why a fish?"

"We call Him a fisher of men, since He drew believers to His side, out of the waters of our former lives."

"What were you, then, before you were drawn up into his net?"

"A potter. Nothing out of the ordinary. But I left everything when I heard His call."

"And it led you here?"

"Where He leads, I follow. Even here."

I spread my hands. "Is there anything I can do for you before the show?"

"Before killing me?"

"You might as well not suffer any more than you have to."

He thinks for a moment. "Paul asked one of his friends to send his cloak," he says at last. "Perhaps I, too, might make such a request without failing in my service?"

"Who is Paul?"

"One of the Lord's followers, who took leadership upon himself after His death. A great man. Wise. Dead now, he died after the Great Fire, it's hard to believe it is almost twenty years back now."

"And he wanted a cloak here in Rome?"

Alon smiles. "Here in the Tullianum. He was kept here under Nero, before he was condemned to decapitation. A quicker death than the one I have been promised, it seems."

"I think your lives as followers of this preacher would be a lot easier if you would only agree to worship Roman gods alongside him," I say.

"They would," he agrees with a smile.

I sigh. "I'll send you a cloak," I say. "And I will tell the guards you are not to be harmed while in their care."

"I'm grateful to you."

"You won't be grateful come the naumachia," I say.

"I will remember your kindness in saving me from the cold and any harm caused by uncaring guards while I am kept here."

I nod, uncertain how to end this conversation. There should

be something more, but what else can I say? He has been judged a criminal, and I put criminals to death every single day in the Games. It may be the part of the job I like the least, but I do it anyway. But I have never stood in a room and spoken with a criminal like this, knowing full well what his fate will be and that it rests in large part in my hands to carry out. Usually, the criminals arrive in a group, the evening before their execution. They are put into one of the pens in the under-arena and they are fed, for I consider it unnecessary cruelty to keep them starving. Then they must find a way to sleep. And during all of this time, wild animals around them roar and grunt and screech in their own pens, waiting for the chance to kill, while other creatures huddle, bleating and whimpering, afraid of the fate that awaits them the next morning, when their known or unknown predators will make short work of them. I walk past the pens sometimes, making notes as I go, counting the occupants the better to plan their use, or directing one of our team as to how to care for them while we have the brief management of them. I do not look into the faces of the criminals or single them out. This man, Alon, has only been singled out to be made an example of. He has gone beyond simple crimes between people and instead committed treason, threatening Rome herself rather than one of her citizens. It is only this that has brought me face-to-face with him, to hear him speak.

"I must go," I say at last. "I will send you the cloak."

"Thank you," he says.

I fumble with the rope, finally getting my foot into the loop and tugging. It grows taut in my hands as I am lifted upwards and I pull my shoulders together as I pass through the hole above, rising into bright sunshine that makes me blink. Feet firmly on the ground again, I look back down into the hole, but it is so dark down there compared to the light here that I can see nothing at all.

"He is suitable for the Games," I say. "He will perform on the last night of this season, in front of Emperor Titus himself. You must take good care of him, I need him fit and healthy."

"He's not going to be very fit and healthy, staying down there till then," says the guard and the other two shake their heads dolefully.

"Feed him better and I will send him a cloak to keep him warm," I say. "Make sure he gets it. Can't you pull him up here and have him walk about under supervision?"

"Oh no," says the guard, looking shocked at this idea.

"Breach of protocol, that would be," adds another. "We'd get in a lot of trouble."

"Once they're in the Tullianum, they stay in the Tullianum until execution day. Everyone knows that," says the third.

"Fine," I say and leave the room without bidding them goodbye, the heat as I step outside almost rocking me backwards, my dampened lungs dried out within two breaths. I make my way along the street, trying to stick to the shade, confused and saddened by the encounter. When I return to the insula, I take the brown woollen cloak Livia gave me, with its little patch of darning where a hole used to be, and tell Karbo to take it to the Tullianum right away.

"Can't I go tomorrow?" he whines. "What does anyone want a hot woollen cloak for in such a hurry? I can barely wear a tunic in this heat."

"Just take it and be grateful you're not in the Tullianum yourself," I say.

He makes his way down the stairs, still grumbling, and I go to join Adah, who has just finished looking after her bees, burning cow dung to create smoke so that she can safely handle them. I keep my distance until she replaces their wicker-work cover and comes towards me, a few chunks of honeycomb in a bowl.

"Not gathered a lot today," she says. "Just a little for myself. I'll do a full harvest soon." She holds out the bowl and I break off a small piece and put it in my mouth. It is sweet and richly, intensely floral.

"It's delicious," I tell her.

"Where's Karbo? He loves honey."

"Gone to the Tullianum."

"Why?"

"There's a prisoner there. A Jew."

"What's he done?"

"He's a follower of the Nazarene preacher."

She grimaces. "Not one of ours. They let all sorts in."

"I thought they were Jews?"

"Used to be. They still follow some of our laws. But they wanted to convert people. At first they made everyone fully convert to all our laws if they wanted to follow the Nazarene's teachings. But they wanted more people and Gentiles were a lot easier to convert if they didn't have to be circumcised, or follow all of our laws. So they grew looser and looser. I wouldn't call them Jews now."

"But you both believe in the same god? And you only have one god?"

"Yes. One. The Almighty. But now they're worshipping a man they call His son. Sounds like idolatry to me. He may have been a preacher, I don't argue with that, there's been many good preachers. They said the Nazarene was a Jew, upheld all our laws, was a good man. But now all these Gentiles…" She shrugs, puts another piece of honeycomb in her mouth and offers me some more, which I take. "What did he do, anyway? Refuse to worship the Roman gods?"

"And preached about it. In the Forum."

She shakes her head. "He should have known better, if he is a Jew. We keep quiet. We don't draw attention to ourselves, it only leads to trouble."

"He won't give in."

She nods. "Then he'll die. But the Almighty will bless him for standing true to his faith, once he had spoken out. I don't agree with worshipping the Nazarene. But the Almighty is a different matter. I will pray for this man."

STRABO IS WAITING FOR ME the next morning when I arrive at the amphitheatre. "Bestia has died."

The old beast-hunter. He's provided us with thousands of animals since the amphitheatre was inaugurated, and Marcus has known him for years. He was a foul-mouthed grumpy old man, but I'd grown used to his ways. "Have you told Marcus?"

"Yes."

"I'll miss him. Never thought I'd say that when I first met him. He should have let Fabius look after him, foolish old man. So stubborn."

Marcus has gone to attend the funeral, so I run the day's Games. He arrives back at the amphitheatre late in the afternoon, when I'm supervising the cleaning.

"How was it?" I ask.

"Well-attended. Most of the bestiarii in Rome were there, many were trained by him at one time or another and they all knew the quality of his animals was good; made their work harder but they respected him for it. No-one wants a mangy old tiger limping around, makes the man fighting it look weak."

"And now?"

"I don't know. His assistant can finish what we need for this season, everything's already been ordered and dispatched, we're nearly done on the regular shows and Funis is providing everything for the naumachia."

"Could Funis become our beast-hunter?"

"He'd have to move to Rome, we need to have someone close to hand, can't be travelling to Ostia every time we have to discuss things. I got the feeling he didn't care for the big city. But it's worth asking. When all this is over, write him a letter. He'll have part of the winter to think about it before we have to look elsewhere."

"He'd be politer than Bestia, at any rate."

"That wouldn't be hard."

Vita is back at the amphitheatre; this time we have to consider how she will play the part of Hero, requiring her to seem to fall from a tower into the water below. One idea is for her to have a length of cloth wrapped around her middle, so that it unravels as she tumbles, an illusion of falling while being safely held. It's something we've seen acrobats do.

"Can Merula talk you through how it would work?" I ask. "I've got to go to the Baths of Nero, Fabia asked me to book a bridal bath for Cassia."

Vita nods. "Can't you talk me through the falling illusion? I feel awkward around Merula. He stammers all the time and there was that misunderstanding…"

"He's still in love with you," I say. "He'd marry you in an instant, if you said the word."

"I'm afraid of marriage," she says. "I got myself out of being whored around by my masters, by getting Labeo to buy me. But I was lucky."

"You were brave," I say.

"And lucky," she says. "If my former master had found out that I approached Labeo, or if I hadn't found ways to manage Labeo… a marriage can be as bad as being a slave, if you're not careful. A husband has as much power over you as a master."

"Merula's a good man," I say. "He works hard and he's kind. It wouldn't be like having a master."

She looks away to where Merula is measuring one of the ships to ensure it will fit through the passageways once they're filled with water. Her face is full of doubt, but there is a little longing there too, as though she glimpses something but does not quite trust herself to see true.

"I have to go," I say. "Merula will talk you through it."

It's the afternoon before Cassia's wedding to Rullus and most of the women of the insula are helping Julia decorate the courtyard with flowers, both her own and bought specially for the occasion. There's much chatter and giggles, occasionally everyone breaks into songs, mostly romantic, sometimes bawdy, leading to more laughter and some ribald jokes.

"Here," Julia says, passing out little basins, "fill them with water and then we can put flowers in, that way they'll keep well overnight. Otherwise, they'll die in this heat."

We do as we're told, passing basins filled with water to Julia and Maria, who are filling them with flowers, then we suspend them in knotted strands of fine rope, so that they dangle all over the courtyard, hanging above Julia's existing plants and flowers.

"Pretty," says Fabia, but her voice is flat.

I take a break from helping out and sit with her on the rooftop. "I hate that I'm her matron of honour," she confesses. "I have to give her in marriage to Rullus!"

I nod. "Is everything ready?"

Fabia shrugs. "The baker's making the unleavened bread for them to eat during the ceremony. I'm taking her for the bridal bath at dawn, while Cassius, Marcus and Fabius go with the priest to watch for omens and make the sacrifice before sunrise, so everything will be auspicious."

I snort. "How *can* it be auspicious? The minute she's bound to him, he will show what he's really like. And it will be too late."

"I know. I did try to tell her to listen to you, but she wouldn't have it and I was worried she'd stop speaking to me, too."

We sit in silence a bit longer, neither of us feeling there is much else to say, as twilight grows over the city. At last we bid each other goodnight and go to our beds, though I stay awake a long time, wondering how I can get Cassia out of this marriage. But I can't think of anything.

I'M UP BEFORE DAWN AND so is Marcus, I meet him on his way to join Cassius and the priest. Fabius appears as we go past his door.

"Morning."

"Morning."

I follow them further than necessary and touch Marcus' arm. "If there's any doubt about the omens, any at all… you will speak up?"

He looks up at me, hovering on the stairs. "Why?"

"Just… I want to be sure." I try to smile.

He nods. But he's there out of custom and tradition, it will be the priest who declares whether all is well. I think of the multicoloured doves we released to fly over the amphitheatre the day it was inaugurated to suggest an auspicious event. Perhaps if I'd told Marcus what had really happened, all those months ago, he would have put a stop to this wedding, would have thrown Rullus out with a beating. And if Cassia had still refused to listen, we could have staged something that would have indicated the marriage was doomed, but it already is doomed and it's going ahead anyway. I stand in the dark courtyard, building up my courage.

Maria appears, taking up her usual spot above the courtyard. "Big day," she says.

"Yes."

"I knew her mother."

I nod, looking up at her dark shape.

"Good-hearted. Like Cassia. A good word for everyone, helped out anyone, even strangers. And light-hearted, too. She used to sing all the time, you could hear her from here."

I never met Cassia's mother, but now I feel her taking shape through Maria's words and the idea that Cassia is marrying a man who will take away all that is good and kind about her makes my heart sink even further. I stand in silence, waiting for Maria to say something more, but she doesn't. I wonder what Cassia's mother would say if she knew what Rullus was like.

What can I do to make things better for Cassia? Nothing. She does not even want me as a friend. But she will be in need of friends if she marries Rullus.

I think of what the sorceress said about learning to be a freedwoman and wonder whether I am in fact free at all. I have lost my friendship with Cassia. I have avoided the popina for months and so have had to eat food that is not as good or plentiful as Cassia's fare. I wear my plainest clothes, walk quickly with my eyes down, even in the insula, where I should feel safe. I have been assaulted but kept my mouth shut, as though I were a slave who might well expect to be used by her master and not complain about it. I have become a slave again, my master the fear I have of Rullus.

Enough. I will not allow Rullus to take from me the thing I value the most.

I take a deep breath and go to knock on Cassia's door.

"Come."

I push open the door and see her sitting, her bridal clothes laid out, a single flickering lamp and Fabia by her side.

"What do you want?" she asks, looking up but not meeting my gaze

"To be your friend," I say. "Can I walk to the baths with you and Fabia?"

She jerks her head, not a no, not a yes.

THE THREE OF US WALK together in silence. The baths are empty, the ceremonial bridal bath has been specially booked to take place before public hours begin. She is steamed, a plucker is let loose on her, which causes her to wince but not cry out. She is rubbed down with oils and scraped by a professional, before being put into a beautifully presented bridal bath, all perfume and rose petals, then her nails and toenails are dyed. Throughout it all, the plucker and cosmetes made chattering conversation, to which all three of us answer in painful monosyllables. I feel like the dark-hooded Charon, taking a hammer to the head of any fallen gladiator who must be put out of their misery.

We walk back to the insula, the sun now risen, which means that the auguries will have been taken, the decision already made. A priest reading omens for a wedding would need a drastic sign before they put a stop to a pre-planned event such as this, where the father has already given his consent and all the legal arrangements have been made.

"Did you find out what the Fates had spun for you, then?"

The three of us startle. Standing in the middle of Sand Street, ignoring the early morning traffic, which is weaving around her, is the sorceress. Her palla embroidered with green leaves is wrapped about her and once again I'm reminded of a tree.

Cassia gestures at her loose hair and dyed fingernails. "A husband. As I requested. Though you did nothing to bring him to me."

"And will he complete you?"

"He's a good man," says Cassia defensively, but her eyes flicker.

The sorceress follows Cassia's eyes to me.

I say nothing.

The sorceress smiles. "I wish you well on your wedding day," she says.

"I don't want your wishes," says Cassia and she walks past the sorceress and towards the insula. Fabia moves after her.

"One more thing," calls the sorceress.

Cassia stops in the middle of the road, but she does not turn round. "What?"

"There is a beggarwoman waiting at your popina for a bowl of soup. I told her the popina is likely to be shut today, but she said she'd heard you never turned anyone away."

Cassia looks round at the sorceress, her eyes a little wary, but then she nods.

"She's getting married," says Fabia. "She can't be looking out for beggars today, she has to be dressed for the wedding."

Cassia shakes her head. "Will you go and feed her, Althea?"

she asks me. "I've never let a beggar go hungry yet. It wouldn't be right on my wedding day. The soup will be cold, but there's bread and cheese and fruit."

It's the most she's spoken to me for months and I give an eager nod, glad to feel I am doing something for her.

Cassia and Fabia walk onwards, turning into Virgin's Street and disappearing through the gateway of our insula.

I stand, facing the sorceress.

"Did you find your desire?" she asks me, smiling.

"Right now, my desire is to get Cassia out of this marriage," I say. "The man she is marrying is not a good man. But I don't suppose you can help with that." I'm speaking more rudely than I normally would, but the sorceress is annoying, the way she is smiling and still speaking in riddles when a bad thing is happening, right now, in our lives, not some far-off legend.

"The right thing will happen for her," she says. "Trust me."

"Why should I trust you?"

"I've known Cassia all of her life," says the sorceress. "I know everyone around here. I see what the Fates wove for her, even if she does not."

"And was it this marriage?" I ask.

She shakes her head.

"What then? Go and tell her, if you know! Or tell me and I'll tell her!"

She shakes her head. "She must see it for herself."

"She's about to get married! Time has run out for seeing what Rullus is like!"

She shakes her head. "The Fates wove their story for her. And no mere mortal can warp their threads."

"You speak in riddles," I say, angry now. "You're just making fun of people, teasing and saying things no-one understands.

Like oracles that led to tragedies in the legends because no-one would speak clearly. I spoke up about what happened and I lost a good friend. I should have spoken sooner, she might have believed me then. When she marries this man, I may have to go and live elsewhere, just to escape him. But she will be stuck with him."

She takes hold of my arm and brings her face very close to mine. "Go back to the insula," she says.

I pull away from her hold. "That's what I'm doing."

"Do what your friend asked of you. And stay alone while you do it."

"You leave us alone," I say and push past her, hurry back to the insula and through the gateway.

I expect Cassia and Fabia to have already gone to get dressed, but instead they are standing in the courtyard with Rullus. He's dressed in a toga, as befits the occasion, but it does not look elegant, only hangs poorly on him, crumpled and bulky. Fabia is standing with her back against the wall, Cassia is face-to-face to Rullus. They seem to be arguing.

"I always feed beggars," Cassia is saying. She looks shocked, eyes wide.

"I know. And that stops today. Wasting my profits."

"*Your* profits?"

"Mine. As are you, from today. And you'll do as I say."

I glance at Fabia, who gives a tiny shake of her head, a warning to stay out of it. I step back a little, press myself against the wall as Fabia has done, keeping a wary eye on Cassia and Rullus.

"I will be your wife," says Cassia slowly. "But that does not mean I will stop doing what is right. What I have always done, and my mother before me. The beggars will be fed."

"Get to your room and get dressed," says Rullus. "Before I make you."

Cassia stands still for a moment, and I think she is going to argue, but then she looks to Fabia. "Come with me," she says.

Rullus follows them to the apartment, closing the door with a slam. I am left alone.

I feel tears spill onto my cheeks. Here it is, Cassia's future, played out in front of me. Rullus showing his true colours, knowing full well it is too late for the marriage to be revoked, Cassia realising she is beaten, her good heart about to be broken. I want to go and cry in my hut on the roof, but I have a task to do. Cassia asked me to feed the beggarwoman, and I will do it, even if it is the last beggar she will ever feed.

I use the courtyard door which leads into the popina's storeroom, from where there is a door leading into the popina itself. It is all empty, and very dark, for the dawn light is still weak. I fumble my way through the room, then undo and lift one of the shutters, allowing light to come in. I find bread and cheese as well as a couple of ripe plums and a plate to put them on. I look this way and that but I cannot see a beggarwoman on the street. I pull the shutter back down and carry the plate back towards the courtyard through the storeroom, thinking that at least I can have the plate ready if the woman comes into the insula gateway to ask for food.

"Going against my word?"

Rullus, blocking the doorway into the courtyard. I feel my breath start to come short at the sight of him, my escape route barred in both directions. I wish I had left the shutter of the popina up, so that I could have run from him into the open street. Why did I think I would be safe?

"I'm feeding the beggarwoman for Cassia," I say.

"When I told her there'd be no more of that nonsense?"

"I am not yours to command," I say, but my voice comes out too high, like a scared child.

"We'll see about that, shall we?"

I step back as he advances, one step after another, further and further into the darkness of the storeroom.

He's still fast. A lunge, the plate of food shattering on the floor at my feet, his hands on my body, his face pressed close to mine although this time I have time to scream before his hand covers my mouth. My tunic pulled up, his hand rough on my thighs.

"One more move and you'll feel this across your backside!"

Cassia is standing in the doorway. Dressed in her bridal attire; a white tunic with an elaborately tied knotted belt, her black curls covered over with her mother's flame-coloured bridal veil, floating down her back. In her hands she is holding the thick stick Cassius keeps to use on anyone who thinks they can take liberties with his daughter. Behind her is Cassius, also wearing a toga, which I've never seen him in before. Both of them look shocked and angry.

"Cassia – Cassius," stammers Rullus. He lets go of me, tries to rearrange his toga as though nothing has occurred.

"Get out here," says Cassia, her voice low.

"I –"

"Out!" she yells.

Cassius and Cassia walk backwards, Rullus slowly following them into the courtyard. When he is well clear of the door I follow. Fabia is just outside, she grabs at my legs and I squat down with my back to the courtyard wall, shaking, tears trickling down my face. She stands by my side, her short arms wrapped as far as she can round me, cheek pressed to mine.

Curious about the noise, the inhabitants of the insula begin to appear from the courtyard windows and doors, in their best clothes or half-dressed, some coming out into the courtyard or onto the balconies, others poking their heads out from upper windows. I see Karbo's face appear over the rooftop railing, followed by Marcus.

Cassia grips the stick in her hands and lifts it up high. I don't think she will do it, but she does. The full weight comes down on Rullus' left shoulder, he buckles under the blow.

"Have you gone mad?" he shouts at her, staggering back to his feet.

"No! I have come to my senses!" yells back Cassia. "I'm not marrying you."

"Just because I said Althea couldn't feed that beggar a bowl of soup?"

"Because you assaulted Althea for a second time, while showing a sweet face to father and me so you could get your greedy hands on the business. Father and I, we look out for people round here. I feed people who are hungry, I look after my friends who are loyal to me even when they've been poorly treated by my own family. I won't lower myself to marry a pig like you. Not today, not ever!"

"You can't do that!" yells Rullus. "What will happen when your father dies and you're still unmarried, eh?"

"What makes you think I'll never get married?"

"You're refusing to marry me!"

"And why would that be, do you suppose?" shouts Cassia. "Oh, I know! Because you're a mean-hearted letch of a man, who only wants a wife who can work all the hours of the day and night for him while he goes drinking and whoring and gambling! You don't care for me! You don't care about the popina or the people I feed every day. These are my people. I grew up in this insula, I know everyone who lives here and all our neighbours. I look out for them, and they look out for me. More fool me for wanting a husband, any husband, when I will always be safe and loved, whether I marry or not. Because here we care for each other, and we are good people. My friend tried to tell me the truth about you, and may Venus and Juno forgive me, I didn't listen, because I wanted to be married and I thought you were a good enough man. And you're not. You're not worthy to marry me. Go back to the miserable little village you came from and leave me alone. Leave us alone. You don't belong here."

There's a long silence and then, clapping. Everyone looks up. Maria, perilously leaning over her balcony to get a really good view, is applauding. Grins start to spread and slowly, one by one, the rest of the inhabitants begin to clap too, until the courtyard is full of loud applause from all levels. Cassia, her cheeks pink, looks at me, her eyes filling up with tears, although her mouth has widened into a smile.

"That's all very well," blusters Rullus, awkward now that the crowd has turned against him. "But your father has given his permission to this marriage. And you are subject to your father's rule. So you will be marrying me today, whether you like it or not. And when we are married, you will be subject to *my* rule. And I will go about teaching you some manners, my girl. With the aid of that stick you're holding. None of this giving food away, or consorting with people who are no better than whores."

The crowd, silent now, looks towards Cassius.

"No, Rullus," he says quietly. "You will not be marrying my daughter. Not today, not ever. You will leave us now, and return to your own town. You are no longer welcome here."

There's an approving murmur from the crowd.

"You gave your permission!"

"I withdraw it. I won't have my daughter marry a man who dishonours her friends, who threatens to beat her for showing kindness, who just wants the profits of a business we have worked hard to keep going all these years. I thought that you cared for her happiness. I only wanted to know she would be cared for after I was gone."

"And who will care for her, old man?" shouts Rullus. "When you are dead, which can't be long now. Eh?"

Cassius ignores the jibe. Instead, he spreads his hands like an orator, taking in all of us gathered in the courtyard, from Marcus and Karbo on the rooftop, past Adah and Maria, down to Julia, standing at the foot of the stairs. "They will," he says quietly. "Come, now, Cassia."

Cassia hesitates before she moves towards him, the stick still clutched in her hands. When she reaches him, he looks at her for a long moment, reaches up and lifts away the bridal veil from her head. He looks down at it in his hands, then meets Cassia's gaze and smiles. "You will be married one day, a happier day," he says. "To a better man."

Cassia gives a little sob and leans against her father, loosening her grip on the stick, so that it falls to the ground with a heavy clatter, lost in loud applause and cheers from us all. We fall silent only when Julia steps past Rullus as if he doesn't exist and makes her way to Cassius. She puts a hand on Cassia's shoulder and nods to Cassius.

"You are a good man," she says.

Cassius swallows, but nods in return. He looks tired, an old man shaken by what has happened.

I join Fabia in hugging Cassia, who is crying. Over her shoulder I see Rullus, his face sullen and crimson with humiliation, making his way out of the courtyard and through the gateway. I suspect I will not see him again.

"I'm sorry," says Cassia into my hair. "I was a fool not to believe you."

I shake my head. "You believe the best of people," I say, tears falling. "I should have told you at once, before he had a chance to worm his way into your lives."

I MAKE WAY FOR OTHER people to embrace Cassia and find myself face-to-face with Marcus, his face serious.

"Why didn't you tell me?"

I shake my head and swallow. "I didn't… there was never a moment and then it was too late…" I trail off.

"You should have told me!" says Karbo, bouncing indignantly at Marcus' side. "I would have made him sorry. Marcus, go after him and beat him up!" he adds, enthusiastically. "Make him sorry for what he did to Althea."

"I am not sure he deserves a man's beating," says Marcus. "Cassia delivered all the humiliation he was worthy of." But his face is still serious. "Althea, you should not have held such a burden in your heart, nor ever thought it was too late to tell me. And I will not forgive myself for not seeing that something bad had happened to you, for not realising that you were not safe in your own home."

I try to say something but my tears only fall faster and I find myself held tightly in Marcus' arms, Karbo joining our embrace till I have gathered myself a little.

The rest of the day is a strange one. We sit in our best clothes in the decorated courtyard and eat the wedding feast as though it were a picnic, we tell stories of brave deeds overcoming the dark things of the world. There is laughter and more hugs to reassure us all that we are safe here, amongst our friends and neighbours.

Two days later Cassia tells me that Cassius paid Rullus off to dissolve the marriage contract, that he packed his bags and left. Her last sight of him was as he trudged away, shoulders hunched, his bag slung over his shoulder.

"He can go and find some other wife," she says. "And I hope for her sake she's got a big stick somewhere."

"You were brave," I say. "I was afraid you'd be lost to a horrible marriage for the rest of your life and there was nothing anyone could do."

She shakes her head. "It was when he said I couldn't feed the beggar, that I had to stop making my soup," she says. "And I knew. I knew right then I couldn't marry him, that the soup was what I do, what I am. That I look out for people. That it was what the Fates wove for me. And it might only be a pot of soup to anyone else, it might not be important or grand, no-one will remember my name, but it is the thing I am certain of, it is what completes me. Then I came looking for him, to tell him I couldn't marry him, and I found him with you. And then I knew I'd been a fool not to believe you. That he was a bad man in every way."

I laugh, although I'm wiping tears off my face at the same time. "Every mouth you feed will remember your name, Cassia," I say.

"I owe the sorceress a thank you," she adds. "She saved me."

"Saved you?"

Cassia smiles. "Did you see a beggarwoman that day? Anywhere near the popina?"

I stare at her, thinking back. "No," I say. "No, there was no-one there."

"I'm taking her this," she says with a grin, reaching under the counter and pulling out a little roll of cloth. Inside, a sturdy wooden stick, delicately crafted in silver miniature.

TITUS' TEARS

IT'S DAWN ON THE TWELFTH day of September and it's already too hot, even a long night has not done anything to cool the city. We keep hearing the rumbling of thunder, but the sky is clear. I dread to think how hot the stone seating will be by the time we start the show tonight, when the sun will have blazed down on the amphitheatre for hours. Despite the oppressive heat I feel light, a burden lifted away from me with Rullus' departure as well as the truth being told about what he did to me, the comfort of Cassia's arms about me, our friendship renewed. Last night I unbolted my door and let what little breeze there was enter and it felt like a breath of freedom.

"I could do with being in that water right now," says Vita longingly. We're standing together in the top tier, looking down. The arena is an impressive sight from here, full of water so deep it has a rich blue-green colour and looks very inviting.

"If you want a dip, you better have it now," I say. "It won't be much fun once we put the animals in."

Vita raises a hand to shield her eyes from the glittering water.

"I'll have my chance when we do the show-swimming. Although that's less relaxing. Can't just float about and have fun. And then we have to get out sharpish, so you can get the animals in. Eels, vipers and crocodiles?"

"With rays and sharks. They don't like fresh water, so the less time they spend in it the better. The barrels they're in now may be a tight fit, but at least it's sea water. The plan is to put them in the fresh water just before we start, so that they'll still be lively."

"I wouldn't want to be the bestiarii today."

I shake my head. "Me neither. Most of the time you won't even be able to see these creatures coming towards you, at least on dry land you see the lions and other animals before they attack. Anyway, let's get back downstairs. We've got one section of a corridor cordoned off, that's where all the barrels are and where the prisoner will be kept."

We start walking down through the seating, then make our way into one of the cooler corridors.

"You're really just having one prisoner executed?"

"They want to make a spectacle of him, so they're keeping him as their star."

We reach the ground floor corridor, where an area has been roped off for our use, since we have lost our usual space below the arena. Cages and barrels are crammed together. We've sent costumes out to the gladiator barracks so they can dress there before arriving.

"What time will he be brought here?"

I hold up my small sundial. "Two hours?"

"That's early."

"We have to know we have everything and everyone in place. He'll be under guard until the performance starts."

I SPEND THE NEXT TWO hours checking everything is ready, making notes on scroll after scroll of lists. I catch Karbo loitering near the crocodile pens. They lie in their cages, glinting eyes half-closed, watching us as we move, remaining absolutely still themselves.

"Get away from that cage," I tell Karbo for the third time. He's squatting down next to the cage which holds the largest animal, a beast longer than a man.

"What is it thinking?" he asks.

"How nice you would taste if it could sink its teeth into you," I say. "Get *away*."

I hear the marching of feet and turn as four guards enter. Between them, they hold up Alon.

I grimace. He looks pale and wasted, tired even from the short walk here. How is he supposed to convince the audience he is the bold lover Leander, strong enough to brave the strait's waves to meet his beloved Hero?

"We meet again," he says.

"Are you well?"

"Well enough to drown?"

"Well enough to play your part?"

He nods.

"One of you needs to stay," I tell the guards. "He must remain under guard until he's taken into the arena. I don't have a pen to lock him into, they've all been dismantled for the naumachia."

"I'll stay," says one, younger than the others.

"Fine," I say. "There's a barrel of clean water there, a tunic and shoes, a belt. He needs to look like a brave, confident man. I've got a barber waiting: have him trimmed, shaved, washed and dressed. He looks like a prisoner, and I need him to look heroic."

I leave them to it, go and inspect the ships, waiting in their passageways. The water level is almost at their doors, as they sail out it will rise that little more, bringing it to its full depth. The ships look good, a little smaller than last time, but more of them: eight, four for each side. These ones are not flat-bottomed, which means they can steer better, making the fighting easier and more realistic. We have borrowed some sailors from the navy who will take care of managing their smooth movements on the water, leaving the actual fighting to today's gladiators, whose ceremonial armour is already laid out for the parade, which will take place on the water just before the battle proper begins.

I PASS CELER IN ONE of the corridors. He doesn't usually attend the Games, even though we often invite him to join us in watching from the side-lines.

"Come to watch the show?"

He smiles. "Karbo said I had to see the crocodiles. They're all he's talked about."

"I swear, he's going to end up with an arm missing, if he gets too close to their cages."

"I'll try and keep him away."

"Thanks."

ROUNDS DONE, I MAKE MY way out into the seating, looking down on the water. The sun has sunk, it will be twilight soon. I can hear a babble from outside, growing in volume. The crowds are waiting to enter, held back only by the ropes leading to each entrance and our staff manning each archway. Marcus is standing in the imperial box to my side, his usual final inspection point. It won't be long till Titus' servants arrive to set up refreshments and final touches such as silken cushions for the seats, brought directly from his own dwelling.

"All good?"

I nod. "Just need our audience and we're ready to start. The musicians, singers and actors are about to take their places."

Marcus nods back. "Good. I'll tell the staff to let the audience in, might as well get them all settled before Titus arrives and we have to start." He ducks out of sight behind the draped exit, I hear a muffled shout and then the noise of the crowd escalates. People begin to stream into the corridors on the ground floor, making their way up the higher tiers.

Marcus reappears. "We better get out of the way," he says. "You're standing in front of some senator's seat."

"Marcus. Marcus! Althea!" Strabo is leaning out of one of the corridors above us, his usually placid face panicked.

"What?"

He hesitates, looking about him for listening ears. "The man's gone."

"Man? What man? What are you talking about?"

"The – the drowning man." He opens his eyes wide, trying to tell us without speaking.

I gape. "He can't have done. There was a guard with him."

"The guard's been knocked out."

We make our way with difficulty through the corridors, fighting against the tide of the crowds entering the amphitheatre. Finally, we reach the ground floor and the section we've kept roped off. The stacked barrels are all in place, but the guard we left with Alon is sitting slumped on the ground, cautiously feeling his head.

Marcus yanks him to his feet. "Where's the prisoner?"

"I don't know," whimpers the man. "He attacked me and ran off."

Marcus looks as if he's about to punch him. "Ran *off*?"

I step in. "We need to organise people to look for him," I tell Marcus. "We still have over two hours of the show to get through before it's his part, even once it starts."

Marcus and Strabo set off at a run, Marcus blowing on his whistle to summon staff.

"So the prisoner just attacked you?" I ask the guard.

"Yes," he says. "Punched me." But his eyes flicker to one side and I know something is not right. I think back to my conversation with Alon in the dark and damp of the Tullianum, his strange acceptance of his fate, his quietness and calm. I stand closer to the guard, look at his face, which seems undamaged, and then into his eyes, but he will not meet my gaze.

"You're lying to me," I say softly. "He did not attack you. He was willing to follow whatever fate brought to him. You let him go. Why?"

"I don't know what you mean, I swear on Jupiter, by Mars, I –"

"Be careful," I say. "The gods do not like those who use their names for false oaths."

"I swear by –".

"Be quiet. Or I'll let Marcus get his hands on you."

He falls silent. I think about his flurry of oaths and a certainty comes over me. "You have converted to his religion," I say and watch his face change. "You didn't care about swearing false oaths," I add. "You don't care about our gods or their wrath."

"They are nothing but false idols," he mutters.

"You converted," I say. "He converted you and you let him go so he would not die?"

"Why should he die?" bursts out the man. "He speaks the truth! He says the son of God came to us, here on earth, and that if we follow His word, He will come again and take us –"

"Shut up," I say, keeping my voice low. "Shut up. If anyone hears you, you're a dead man, because you'll be taking his place. The Games must go ahead tonight, and someone must be put to death in front of the Emperor. He expects it, the whole crowd expects it. What am I supposed to do, now you've let the prisoner escape?"

Marcus is back, with Strabo. "We won't find him," he says. "He could be anywhere, there's no chance. How did this happen?"

I pull him away from the guard and explain what happened.

"I'll throw him in with the crocodiles myself," says Marcus, enraged.

"We can't tell Titus we let that happen, he was under our care as much as the guard's. It'll be us in with the crocodiles if we're not careful. So we can't put the guard in instead or there'll be questions asked which we don't want to answer."

Marcus mutters something blasphemous under his breath and glowers at the guard.

"We could get another criminal?" asks Strabo.

Marcus shakes his head. "There isn't time and we used up a whole batch of them the other day, remember?"

I nod. It's the end of the season, we were given everyone left who had been condemned to death. And time is running out. If we had a day or two, there would be a way to find someone, but now? "If we tell…" I start, but Marcus is already shaking his head.

"No, you were right," he says. "If we tell what happened there's a good chance we'll be blamed and that will mean being condemned to death ourselves, both for letting a prisoner go who was treasonous *and* for trying to lie to the Emperor by covering it up."

Merula joins us. "I heard," he says. "What do we do?"

I look about me, as though a likely-looking criminal might helpfully wander in off the street and offer themselves up to us.

"If one of Vita's team were a man we could try and fake it," I start, then trail off, unconvinced.

But Marcus' eyes light up. "Yes," he says.

"Yes what? They're women, they won't look right."

"I'll do it."

I stare at him. "What?"

"I'll be Leander."

"No."

"Vita's playing Hero's death, why can't I play Leander's?"

"Because Vita has a linen ladder to 'fall' down and all she has to do is lie still at the bottom of the tower! Leander has to drown, actually drown. Under the water!" My voice is getting louder, and Marcus shakes his head at me, touches my arm. I lower my voice. "No."

"I'm a good swimmer," says Marcus. "All I have to do is swim the arena a few times, then –"

"Then you get tied to a raft that will pull you underwater and only release you to the surface when you're dead. No."

"I can hold my breath."

"I can't believe I'm having this conversation," I say. I'm having a nightmare, one of those where people say garbled things and nothing makes sense, but you know for sure things are going very, very wrong. "How long can you hold your breath for?"

He thinks. "Sixty breaths? Ninety?"

"You're just *guessing*? No."

"You keep saying no," says Marcus. "But we don't have a choice."

"Titus will know it's you."

Marcus shakes his head. "It's dark. He expects to see a prisoner, that's what he'll see."

I'm about to cry, I can feel it, the sobs pushing up in me, my voice growing shaky. I stand still for a few moments, breathing, trying to think of what it will be like, what will need to happen if we go ahead with his plan. "Show me."

"What?"

"Show me how long you can hold your breath."

"Now?"

"Yes, now."

"But –"

"But nothing. You have to swim the arena which has crocodiles and sharks in it. Then I have to give the signal to drag you under the water," I say, and my voice goes shaky again at the thought of it. "And I have to give the second signal, to pull you out of the water, when you have been convincingly drowned. Not a quick ducking. It has to be convincing. So how long do I leave you underwater with the crocodiles?"

We stare at each other, then Marcus nods. "Barrel of water, Strabo."

Strabo and Merula roll a barrel over. Strabo opens the lid, then uses a net to fish out a huge moray eel, which thrashes about violently, its mouth open, showing rows of pointed teeth. It snaps at the net as Strabo and Merula between them transfer it to another barrel.

"I have to check the crowd is seated," says Strabo, his face worried.

"Yes, go," says Marcus. "Merula, stay with us."

The three of us stand by the barrel of water.

"Don't do this," I say. "There has to be another way."

"Count," says Marcus to Merula. "Steadily." He takes a gulp of air, then leans into the barrel, submerging his whole head.

"One," says Merula. His already pale skin has gone white, one of his hands is trembling, the other is gripping the edge of the barrel, almost touching Marcus' fingers, pale underground skin against burnt brown. "Two. Three. Four. Five."

There's a sudden burst of trumpet fanfare. Titus is making his way into the imperial box.

"Twenty. Twenty-one. Twenty-two. Twenty-three."

We hear the crowd burst into applause.

"Thirty-eight. Thirty-nine. Forty. Forty-one."

The show must start in a few moments, we never keep the Emperor waiting. How many breaths will Marcus manage? Will it be enough to convince the crowd that he has drowned in that time? I look at his body, the back of his neck, his hands tightly holding on to the side of the barrel, his back tense with the effort of not breathing.

"Sixty."

Marcus said sixty breaths. But how did he know? Has he ever tried this before? Did he say sixty because it was easy, or very hard? I have no idea, I have never tried it myself, my own breathing is too fast. And is it long enough to fool a crowd? It feels like eternity to me, the steady counting in Merula's shaking voice, but is it long enough?

"Seventy. Seventy-one."

A stream of bubbles rises from the barrel and I look at Merula, our frightened eyes locked together as he keeps counting.

"Seventy-nine. Eighty. Eighty –"

Marcus' head jerks out of the barrel, water splashes on Merula and me as we step back. He gasps for air, breathes heavily for a moment, then looks to Merula.

"Eighty-one."

"Did it feel long enough for a man to drown?"

"I don't know," I say. "It felt horrible."

Marcus ignores me. "Long enough?" he asks Merula.

Merula considers. "I think so," he says at last. "You should probably move under the water, so they think you're struggling. But that may need more air than keeping still. And if you struggle, it may draw the attention of the crocodiles."

"We could feed them?" I suggest.

Marcus shakes his head. "Can't do that. People will be expecting at least one kill by a crocodile, if we feed them they won't bother going for the gladiators if they fall in. As it is the sharks might just eat the rays, easier for them, it's all underwater." He pushes back his wet hair, wipes drips from his forehead. "No choice. I'll do what I can. Count to eighty, then pull me out. I won't be able to lie completely still when I come up, though I'll try, I'll be gasping for air, so Vita has to draw attention to herself by falling from her tower and doing her dying scene. Someone needs to tell her what's happening. Then extinguish the arena-side torches, faster than we had planned, have a slave ready in front of each one, put them out all in one go rather than one by one. The less time people have to look at me, the better."

I nod. I'm full of questions, but there's no good in asking them. What if the animals we put in the water attack Marcus, when he is swimming or when he is lashed to a raft from which he cannot escape? What if we mis-time the count to eighty, or if Marcus cannot hold his breath as long after he has swum the arena several times? But none of these questions will give courage to Marcus. They are my fears to hold and no doubt he is asking himself the same questions.

"I'll go and tell Vita now, she'll be taking her place for the start of the show."

There's a tug at my arm. Strabo is at my side, his expression strained. "Titus has asked for either you or Marcus to attend him."

"Attend him?"

"He wants you to sit with him throughout the show."

I gape. "What, all of it?"

"Yes."

"But doesn't he have…"

"He's got some distant members of his family in the box tonight, not Domitian or anyone like that. He says he wants company."

"From one of us?" I look at Marcus.

"Yes. Now. There's a Praetorian Guard waiting to escort you."

I hover, uncertain. With Marcus risking taking the place of Alon, we had relied on me being available to direct the show. I can't send Marcus to Titus, nor can I explain what is going to happen, so I have no choice but to go to him myself. I look about me.

"It has to be you," says Marcus to me.

"But –"

"I'll give the signals," says Merula.

"But you –"

"I've watched enough rehearsals. I'll manage."

I think of his dark eyes watching Vita, his stammering approach to her, his crushed demeanour after her rejection. At least I know he has a vested interest in all of this working out well. "You'll look after them both?" I ask.

He nods, serious. The team moves a little closer to him, acknowledging the new leadership. Karbo looks worried and Celer puts a hand on his shoulder.

I make a move towards the corridor where I can see an impatient Praetorian Guard waiting, then turn back. "Celer?"

"Yes?"

"Keep an eye on Karbo."

"I will."

I FOLLOW THE PRAETORIAN GUARD down the dark corridors, now empty as the audience have taken their places. The opening music plays; in only a few moments the first part of our spectacle will begin. My heart's hammering at the idea that we are about to put on a show in front of Titus, a naumachia no less, without either Marcus or myself able to influence events. And as for what Marcus is planning to do…

We've reached the imperial box and the drapes are pulled aside for me. Towards the back of the box a few men and women are seated, elegantly attired but clearly not important enough to be any closer to Titus, who is sitting right at the edge of the box, where the audience will have a good view of him. A few servants hover in the background in case they are needed. A narrow table set to one side holds various platters of delicacies: exquisitely presented figs, grapes and gilded dates, little bowls of olives, roast chickpeas and pickles, tiny rose-shaped pastries piled high and scattered with pink and white rose petals, glass jugs of wine and water alongside little glass cups decorated with gladiatorial scenes.

"Ah, Althea. Come in, come in," says Titus, waving a hand towards a seat placed by his side.

I lower myself cautiously into the chair, wondering what the spectators will make of a commonly-dressed woman appearing at the Emperor's side as though I were his wife or a member of his family. I'm conscious that my hair leaves much to be desired, being in no way elegantly arranged in the fashionable Flavian curled style, only bound up in a hair wrap. "I am very sorry, Imperator," I begin, barely allowing my behind to make contact with the chair, expecting to be rapidly sent away again. "Scaurus is unable to attend you at this particular spectacle, the naumachia requires his direct supervision, it –"

"Oh, I don't mind in the least," says Titus. He winces. "I have a headache today, a ringing in my ears. It comes and goes, drives me to distraction. Sometimes I even have men with hammers come to my rooms and make a din. It eases the pain, would you believe." He sighs. "I wanted someone to talk to me, to lessen the ringing. You'll do," he adds, giving me a pained smile.

I'm surprised the roaring and cheering of the crowd isn't helping, if the sound of hammers does. But I try to settle into the chair and give what I hope is a bright smile. "Of course, Imperator. It is my honour. What would you like to speak of?"

A servant offers me a cup of wine, which I accept, although I hold it awkwardly without drinking and shake my head when I am offered the tiny pastries, afraid of choking on a crumb and inelegantly spluttering. It's strange and frightening to be the guest of the Emperor. I look over my shoulder. His other guests are staring at me with undisguised astonishment and horror.

Titus puts a hand to his head and groans. "Such pain," he says. "They seem to grow worse with time. Do you get headaches?"

"No, Imperator."

"Give thanks to the gods who have spared you such suffering."

"Yes, Imperator."

Titus gulps down his wine and holds his cup out to be refilled. He does not even look round to see if a servant has caught the gesture, simply assumes they are watching him at all times, ready to fulfil even the most subtly expressed desire. Which they are, of course. He is the Emperor. Fear ripples through me again, the strangeness of sitting here beside him as though I were one of the great matrons of Rome. If he knew that we were planning to deceive him, deceive fifty thousand people... I stroke my wrinkled tunic down over my knees with one hand, still holding my cup out as though I'd just taken it from someone's hand.

"How is the boy? What was his name again?"

"Karbo," I say. "I am – we are so grateful for your intercession –"

"Yes, yes," says Titus, waving away my protestations. "Only right the boy should have a mother. Berenice said –" He stops. "Never mind."

"Her majesty seemed very kind-hearted," I say.

Titus turns his face away a little. "She is," he says.

I wait in silence, unsure how politic it is to say anything else about the queen.

Titus clears his throat. "The flooding is very impressive. The depth must have been hard to achieve."

"We have had the power of Rome's mighty aqueducts and a very able aquarius on our side," I say.

"What beasts will be in the water?"

"Crocodiles from Egypt, eels from the south, sharks and vipers. There are rays, too, they will be easy to spot, they come to the surface frequently."

"Are they dangerous?"

"They have barbs that can kill a man, Imperator."

It's dusk. Four men carry burning torches around the front row of seating, lighting dozens and dozens more torches, taking their time, tension building as a soft glow spreads across the dark waters. It's time for the show to begin. A blast of trumpets and the doors swing open, the eight ships rushing out on a wave of water, the increase in volume lifting them all higher. The men aboard raise their weapons, and the eight ships begin to row, while the audience applauds this water-based version of the usual costumed parade.

Once they have shown off sufficiently, the eight ships pull back, siting themselves tightly against the walls, the better to draw attention to what is happening in the centre, where Vita's women have appeared. Desirability has triumphed over modesty; they are all naked, twisting through the water, creating formations which mimic not just shapes and objects like stars and the sun, but also test the strength and bravura of the team, from holding their breath for an unfeasibly long time while their legs perform above the surface, to rolling their whole bodies through the ripples, sometimes using their power to lift a performer right out of the water, allowing her to shine above her sisters. Music plays delicate songs with moments of tension, including when they manage a triple-height structure with Vita at the top, before she leaps from the human tower they have created, diving gracefully into a circle created by the other performers.

This brief interlude complete, Vita disappears under the water, followed by her team. They do not reappear, or at least, the audience supposes they have not. In fact, the sails of the eight ships, not yet hoisted, conceal their return aboard, creeping up the sides closest to the wall, pulling on dark tunics and tucking into position among the men, so that they will not be spotted, while the sails rise up the masts, drawing attention away from them.

Before the ships begin their war, the waves beneath them must be made more dangerous. An actor dressed as King Neptune announces that his army must be assembled before we mere mortals fight our own battles. He calls for the beasts of the deep and as each one is named, our team lowers pens fastened to the wall and releases their clasps. Moray eels are followed by rays, then sharks and vipers. The most frightening are saved till last. Six crocodiles remind the audience of Rome's power over Egypt and their appearance is greeted with a round of applause. They are not dropped into the water, rather their cages, complete with solid floors but open bars, are lowered close to the water's edge, allowing each animal to stay on its open raft or dive into the water, their slinking movements causing shudders in the audience. Two crocodiles instantly dive into the water, four stay on their rafts, wary of this new place. All of them are longer than Marcus, one of them is both double his length and broader than the others. It lies very still on its platform. King Neptune warns us that from this moment on, should anyone enter his realm, they take their life into their own hands.

The water now made perilous, the chorus begins the story of the sea battle we are about to observe, between the Corcyreans and Corinthians, leading to the Peloponnesian War, over five hundred years ago. It's not a tale I have much interest in, especially as I've been obliged to listen to the chorus rehearsing it over and over again until I am sick of it, but the crowd enjoys it, cheering on the battle as the ships move about the arena, coming close enough to each other that the men on board can reach out with their swords and clash weapons, the odd victim falling overboard with a satisfying scream and splash. Two, not too badly harmed, swim back to the nearest ship and climb aboard, continue fighting. One is dispatched into the dark waters and does not re-emerge, a quick glistening fin is all we see close to where he disappeared, a silent death in the dark waters. Then a man falls and out of nowhere appear open jaws, gripping the man round his belly and I watch in horror as what Funis described happens before us; the crocodile rolling the man in the water, his arms flailing, screams drowned and then re-emerging over and over until he falls silent and the crocodile swims easily into the shadows of the water to feast on its prey.

Cruelly, I am praying that more gladiators fall in, for if Marcus enters these waters before the beasts we have sent into them have been fed to satiety, his life will be at even greater risk. I shift in my seat, wishing I could leave the box, go and tell Marcus to change the plan, even if it means confessing that we have lost a prisoner, rather than risk losing his life to one of these monsters in an agonising death. I risk a sideways look at Titus, wondering if I dare ask to be excused, but he is leaning over the edge of the box, gripped by the scene.

There is a splash and then a sudden scream that has even the fighting gladiators hesitate. The man who has fallen in is twisting in the water, thrashing against an unseen foe. A crocodile slips off its raft and swims towards him. It reaches him and its jaws open wide, close over his desperately waving arm, separating it from his body in one easy bite, as though it were a soft roll of bread. There is one more scream from the man and then he is pulled down, beneath the water and gone. The crocodile swims leisurely back to its platform.

The remaining gladiators, forced to keep fighting despite the fate of their comrade, proceed with more caution now, I can see their expressions grown fearful rather than bold, faced with this unaccustomed risk.

THE SEA BATTLE IS OVER, there is applause. The ships pull into the sides, clearing the centre of the arena. They lower a large raft into the water. Onto it step two men, bestiarii sent to us by Funis. They have been equipped with the armour and swords of Roman soldiers. They are about to fight the largest crocodile, representing the Egyptian crocodile-headed god, Sobek, strongly associated with pharaonic power.

Three members of our team, using long poles, push the huge crocodile's platform towards the men's raft. The beast does not move, it stays as still as though dead, even when the two rafts bump together.

The men approach the crocodile, swords out. The crocodile stays still until one of the men slashes at it and then it opens its vast jaw, revealing a terrifying array of white teeth that has the crowd oohing in interest.

The two men proceed to taunt the beast, first one then the other stabbing at it from different sides, so that as it snaps and twists at one, so the other will gouge at its hide from another angle, blood welling up and the enraged animal turning away towards this new attack. Finally, it lurches forwards at one man, its teeth just grazing his leg and his partner, sensing real danger, plunges his sword deep into the beast's head. The crocodile gives one last writhing lunge, but it is already dying. The men, representing Rome, have triumphed over this beast, just as Rome has triumphed over Egypt and made it her vassal state. The audience is pleased by the symbolism and claps with enthusiasm as the vast creature's corpse tips over the side of the raft and has barely time to float before grey fins begin to circle. The sharks are hungry and there is blood in the water, the two bestiarii are barely pulled to safety before first one and then another set of gaping jaws open up and crunch down through the tough hide without any difficulty.

Silently, I urge the sharks on. Let them feast on the dead monster. Let their bellies be full, one less threat to Marcus. I try to count them, hoping that all of them have eaten their fill, that there are none left who are still searching for a helpless victim.

It's grown fully dark now. Above us the sky is lit up with stars. I squirm in my seat as the music changes to a romantic ballad heralding the story of Hero and Leander. The singers finish their rendition, then the chorus step forward, ready to tell the tale. It is too late now.

A banner unfolds at one end, the pointed tip of it raised into the air, the base slipping into the water near a platform piled high with scenic rocks. Painted on the banner is a tower. By its side, in the front row of seating, appears Vita, lit by the flaming torches, her delicate white dress in the Greek style billowing in the evening breeze.

"…though Hero lived across the strait, yet Leander could by night see the shining light from her tower, a beacon of love to him and he, being a strong swimmer and full of desire for her, braved the dark waters and swam to her one night…"

Vita stretches out her arms, beckoning to her beloved Leander. I swallow.

Opposite her, a naked man appears, stands a moment, then lifts his arms, hands briefly touching together, before diving gracefully into the water.

I watch as Marcus swims towards Vita, his wet arms glistening in the torchlight as they curve through the water. I scan the water for the creatures that I know are lurking there, praying with every stroke that they will not attack him. The snakes, rays and eels, I believe will not attack unless provoked. But I am afraid of the crocodiles and sharks, what if they have not eaten enough? I try to think of what Funis said about how much we should feed them and whether that is the same as having feasted on the giant crocodile and the gladiators. Is it enough? My thoughts are muddled, I am unsure. As Marcus reaches Vita's side, she helps him out of the water with the aid of a dangling rope part-hidden in the water. They embrace, Marcus first pressing his lips to hers, then bidding her farewell, before plunging back into the waters. My hands are in fists, my nails digging into skin.

"He returned home safely that night, through the dark waters, yet his love was so strong that the following night he stood on the edge of the shore and looked towards her tower, before taking once again to the water."

Marcus dives again. Again, he swims the arena, again, he climbs to Vita's side, again, they embrace. One of the crocodiles shifts on its platform, but does not dive.

"Their passion forbidden, the world arrayed against them, and yet unable to stay apart, such was the depth of their love…"

I become aware of an odd gulping noise to my side. To my horror, Titus is openly weeping as Marcus returns to his own side, his strokes now slower. He is getting tired. Tears are running down Titus' face and he makes no effort to stem them, wiping them away with a fold of his toga. I try to give the impression I have not noticed, staring fixedly down, seeing nothing but Marcus' body. But Titus reaches out a hand and puts it on my arm, deliberately drawing my attention. I turn to him and affect faint surprise, as though a weeping emperor is a common sight and only to be expected.

"Imperator? Is – is something wrong?"

Titus gulps again. "Some of the demands of office are very hard," he says at last.

"I'm sure they are, Imperator," I say, uncertain of how to proceed. Do I pat his arm, as I might do with a friend? Or would that have the Praetorian Guards on duty seizing hold of me? I look around. The crowd has noticed Titus' obvious display of emotion and have started applauding him for it, enchanted by him being so caught up in the storytelling.

"Personal choices in particular," says Titus, his voice still choked. "When one's own desires must be put aside for the good of the Empire."

"No doubt the Empire recognises your sacrifices and applauds you for them, Imperator," I say, grasping at polite platitudes. He must be talking about Queen Berenice, perhaps prompted by Marcus embracing Vita again before he turns back to the water.

Vita lifts one arm, bidding Marcus a fond farewell.

"I have only made one mistake during my reign," Titus says, looking down at his hands.

I want to scream at him to be quiet. My fists are clenched with fear at what is about to happen. I need to watch Marcus and pray for him, I am afraid that if I don't watch him with all my concentration that something will go wrong, that he will die and no-one in this box will know but me. But I cannot scream. Instead I have to unclench my fists and smile, turn my head towards Titus and respond.

"Imperator?" I say, trying to give the impression I might be asking for further details if he wishes to divulge them but also that I am absolutely not asking, if that is more correct. I don't want him to talk anymore, I don't care about what minor thing he thinks he has done wrong when I am shaking with nerves at what we have done, what I agreed to.

"Ah, never mind," says Titus, raising a hand to acknowledge the crowd's applause. "I will not burden you with my woes, Althea."

I give a relieved nod, it is all I can manage by way of acknowledgement. Marcus has reached his own side again and now comes the part I have been dreading. The audience makes a low sound, half fear, half approval, as he is reached by members of our team. I watch as he is tied to the narrow raft, all but covered by his body once he is fully bound to it. Titus watches with interest, leaning over the edge of his box. I give thanks he has not seen Marcus in over a year, has met him only a few times.

If he recognises him, we are done for. We will be in the arena immediately, probably thrown to crocodiles as a punishment befitting our crime. If he does not and the performance continues, I may have to watch Marcus being attacked, probably by one of the evil-eyed crocodiles, their vast toothed jaws closing around him, his blood staining the water as the crocodile rolls him to his death. Or the raft will sink under the water and I will watch him drown. I have a sudden memory of the beast hunter Funis in Ostia, of the missing flesh on his arm after just such a crocodile attack, one from which he was lucky to escape alive. I clutch the stone ledge of the box, but there is no comfort from its cold hardness.

This time as Marcus sets off across the flooded arena, he is lying face down on the raft, his arms and legs bound, pulled across by a mechanism operated by a team of our slaves who usually operate the lifts. Almost as soon as it starts to move, it is also pulled downwards, and the water rises over his body. I can see his back lift as he takes in his last gasp of air, and then the water closes over his head. Silently, I start to count, struggling to keep to the same rhythm Merula used, while the chorus continues to tell the tragic tale of the two lovers.

One, two, three, four...

"But on one fateful night..."

Ten, eleven, twelve, thirteen...

"Little did they know, those two lovers, that a great storm was brewing..."

Twenty, twenty-one, twenty-two, am I counting too fast? Too slow?

Only a faint ripple in the water shows where the rope meets the raft, indicating where Marcus is underwater, the speed agonisingly slow.

Sixty-one, sixty-two, sixty-three, sixty-four – eighty, he said he could stay under for eighty, but can he, when he has swum the arena over and over again?

"Anxious Hero looked out across the strait for her beloved and yet could see nothing through the great storm."

Cymbals clash, drums keep a racing heart-beat going, the audience cranes forwards, silent in expectation.

Seventy-seven, he will be up soon, seventy-nine, eighty... eighty, now he will be lifted to safety...

But there is no sign of Marcus, the rope stays still. Something is wrong. The mechanism is jammed or the counting has been done wrong.

Why is he not up? Eighty-one, eighty-two, eighty-three... how long can a man not breathe and still live, how long, how long? Or has he already taken his last breath, have jaws closed around him without even a ripple, is he dead already?

One of the crocodiles slips off its platform, disappears into the water. The audience's heads swivel towards it, they gasp. But something else has caught my eye, a tiny motion on the opposite side, close to where Marcus should be now, a shadow, a darkness, slipping over the wall and into the water... Karbo? Have I just seen Karbo enter the water? It can't be, Celer would never have allowed...

Celer. Celer's sharp, sharp knife. Is Karbo trying to cut the rope holding the raft underwater?

Ninety-five, ninety-six, ninety-seven...

And the raft comes to the surface, Marcus tied to it. There is barely time to see him, for above him Vita cries out and leaps downwards, hitting the water with a splash.

And every torch is suddenly put out, the amphitheatre

plunged into darkness as we had planned. The audience erupts into cheers.

A few moments of darkness, then the torches are relit by the imperial box and the Vestal Virgins' box, followed by all the others in sequence. Vita is now lying sprawled over Marcus on the rocky shore, the two of them are lifted by gladiators onto one of the ships, which is guided carefully back into the underground passage it came from, disappearing from sight as the chorus finishes their tale.

"Buried in one grave, Hero and her beloved Leander, united in death even as they were separated in life…"

Is he dead?

Is Marcus dead?

He was lying so still – but he had to lie still, he could not cough and splutter, he was playing the part of a criminal, condemned to die in the Games. But he was so still…

Titus is talking, I think he must be commenting on the sentence that was passed for Alon. "Of course, treason must be punished harshly. I don't understand these people, insisting their god is the only god. No tolerance of other peoples and their beliefs, no sense of compromise. We don't ask much of them, they are free to worship their own gods, so long as they also worship ours… and have respect for the divine nature of the imperial role, when after all my father was deified…"

I try to nod at everything he is saying, try to look as though I understand and agree, but I can't speak, I can't even make sounds, I must not cry, must keep breathing, my head nodding, nodding, nodding.

"Well, it has been an excellent spectacle. As always. You will tell Scaurus so from me, I am sure he is busy managing everything. I shall be leaving now," says Titus, standing.

I stand up so fast I feel dizzy. The torches flicker, the darkness ripples before my eyes and I put out a hand, touch the stone edge of the box to steady myself, while Titus raises his arm in a salute to the crowd. They give him a standing ovation. He nods acknowledgement and waves for a moment, then moves away.

I move to follow him.

"You must remain in the box until the Emperor has left the building," a Praetorian Guard reminds me.

"Goodbye, Althea." Titus smiles from the doorway. "I shall not forget your kindness in keeping me company."

I manage to bob my head and say something, I don't know what, as he exits the box. As soon as he's done so, I make a move forward, but another guard holds up a hand to stop me.

"The Emperor's guests must also leave the building," he says.

"But I need to –" I start, but this is an argument I'm not going to win. I stand, shifting from one foot to the other, my hands clenched into fists at the slowness of the imperial party's departure. The ladies' delicate pallas, in shining shades of silk, have slipped here and there and must be gathered up, straightened, wrapped about them against "the night air" of the unbearably hot evening. A little chit-chat is engaged in, noting that Senator so-and-so didn't seem to have attended tonight, perhaps he had other more pressing engagements, giggles breaking out at what those engagements might or might not be, did you *read* Martial's latest? Oh, it's all in there, if you know where to look, you can tell *exactly* who it's about...

I feel as though someone is crushing my head with a mortar and pestle. Titus' headaches can be nothing compared to this.

The relatives, uncertain of what sort of status they ought to be granting me, given that I've sat next to Titus all evening as his personal guest, despite being dressed like one of their servants, finally mutter something in my general direction, uncertain half-smiles on their bemused faces, then make their way through the silken drapes, followed by the servants, leaving me alone.

RAIN

I RUN.
Through the corridors, pushing through the departing crowds, against the cleaners arriving for their shifts, down the steep steps, clutching at the bannisters for fear of falling.

I reach our holding area and see a crowd of staff gathered into a huddle, Vita, Merula and Strabo among them. In the shaky light of flaming torches, they all look stricken. In front of them, waiting for me, the last person I want to talk to. The Aedile.

"Marcus – Karbo –" I gasp. Behind the Aedile, Vita nods hastily and holds up her hands, a forced smile on her face, indicating all is well, the rest of the team too, nod fervently. I try to nod back, to believe them, but I am trembling all over and I still cannot see Marcus or Karbo, I have to see them for myself to believe they are safe.

"Your team outdid themselves," says the oblivious Aedile, beaming at me. "A magnificent spectacle."

"We're never doing a naumachia again," I say. My hands are clenched into fists, I'm shaking with shock. I keep looking over the Aedile's shoulder, straining to see the only two faces I need to see.

The Aedile blinks. "But it was so well-received –"

"Never again," I say.

"But if the Emperor should wish –"

"Then he'll have to get someone else," I say, and push past him, into the crowd of slaves, looking around for Marcus and Karbo. There is nothing behind them except barrels where the animals were kept.

"It's been a difficult day," Merula is saying to the Aedile behind me. "There were some – technical hitches – behind the scenes. The flooding and draining of such a space, not to mention managing performances within the water is very demanding, as I am sure you can appreciate."

I turn back on myself, pacing like some wild animal caught in its pen, back through the huddle.

The Aedile is nodding. "Of course, of course. But if the Emperor were to demand…" He sounds worried.

"Let's worry about that if it happens, shall we?" Vita says, stepping to Merula's side, blocking me so I can't reach the Aedile. "For now, everyone's happy. The Emperor was so pleased with the performance he was moved to tears, as everyone saw, and now he's going off to the countryside for a holiday and the Games are done for the season. Everyone can have a rest."

The Aedile seems reassured. "Yes, yes, of course," he agrees. "As you say, very technically demanding, understandably tiring for the team. Delightful spectacle!" he calls to me, looking past Merula and Vita to where I am standing, my hands twisting in fear.

I don't answer him. He waits and then nods awkwardly, before walking away.

Merula turns to me. "It's all right," he says, his voice low. He puts a hand on my shoulder, and the shaking of my body slows under his comforting touch. "Marcus is well. I saw him for myself. He spoke to me, he could walk. He has been taken back to the insula to rest."

"Karbo –"

"Karbo too. He was very brave. They have both been taken back to Julia's, I arranged a litter so that they would not exert themselves any further, after all that happened. Celer went with them. You can go back yourself, if you wish. I will manage everything here, if you tell me what to do."

I shake my head, close my eyes and take a deep breath. "You can help me, so it gets done quicker and we can all leave this place."

"I am at your service. Vita too." He looks to her and she nods, her face serious.

"Nobody suspected?" she asks me.

I shake my head. "I thought they were dead," I say, my voice coming out hoarse now that the Aedile has gone. "I thought..."

She nods, puts an arm about my shoulders. "The ropes to move the raft were stuck, Marcus had to try and get free and he could not, I could see him struggling but if I had intervened..."

I nod. "I know."

"Karbo took Celer's knife and slipped into the water, saying he would cut him free by diving underneath. Merula had the crocodile pushed in on the opposite side to create a diversion. Karbo was very brave, he risked his life for Marcus."

I shake my head, still unable to let go of my fear.

Merula takes over the story. "We tried to persuade him against it, but his small size and the colour of his skin made him less noticeable in the dark. We told him that he must not try beyond his breath, that all our lives were at risk if we were found out. But he succeeded and then Marcus played his part well, no-one knew. The Aedile asked where the body was before you arrived, we said we had already thrown it to crocodiles in pens on the other side of the building. He seemed happy enough, as you saw."

My shoulders heave as I try to breathe deeply, to let go of the fear. I feel first Vita and then Merula embrace me and then, slowly, all of our team gathers into a huddle, arms about shoulders all around us, and we weep with relief.

I STAGGER BACK THROUGH THE gateway of the insula, the stars bright above me, the sky soon to change to dawn. I've left Vita and Merula to finish the last few small tasks of the day and walked back through the Forum and the local streets with two male slaves carrying torches to keep me safe, barely seeing where my feet were placed, head still swirling, my body weak with shock.

"Julia!" calls Maria somewhere above me, from her perch. She is lit by a single wavering flame from a lamp, she must have waited all this time for my return. "Althea is back!" She looks down at me. "Don't worry about Karbo, he's in my room and asleep."

"I heard what happened," says Julia, appearing on the balcony above me. She walks down the stairs towards me, puts both hands on my shoulders, looks into my face. "All is well now. All is well. We will celebrate and give thanks that they are safe tomorrow. Marcus must rest. As must you."

"I didn't do anything," I say, "I was trapped in the imperial box, I couldn't help, I couldn't..." Tears start to fall, my hands are shaking. I try to wipe my face.

"You must rest," says Julia. "Go and see Marcus, it will set your mind at ease. He is well, only very tired after such an ordeal. Fabius visited him and gave him a strengthening tonic.

He wanted to give him a sleeping draught, but he will have no need of that, his eyes were half-closed by the time he had told me what happened."

"I don't want to wake him if he is asleep."

"He said I must send you to him as soon as you got home. He said to wake him if he was asleep."

I CLUTCH AT THE BANNISTER all the way up the stairs, it is the only thing keeping me on my feet. At Maria's apartment, I look in on Karbo, needing the sight of him. I kneel by the bed in the dim lamplight, place my hand lightly on his chest, feel him breathe for a few moments, with Maria's hand on my shoulder. When I reach the roof, it is so dark I can barely make out my hut, which is in total darkness. There is a faint light from Marcus' hut, though, and I make my way over to it, hesitate before opening the door without knocking. He must be asleep, I do not want to wake him, whatever he said.

His eyes are open, fixed on the door as I open it. "You're back."

"You're awake."

"Couldn't sleep without knowing you were well."

I stare down at him. "I was sitting on my arse in the imperial box watching a spectacle," I say at last, my voice shaking. "You were fighting for your life, and you want to know if I am well?"

He lifts himself onto one shoulder, eyes serious. "You were sitting on your arse in the imperial box, as you put it, unable to move while you watched someone you care about drown and your son die trying to save him, or so you thought, while having to make polite conversation with an emperor," he says and I sink to my knees by the bedside, shoulders heaving. He sits up, wraps his arms about me and I sob into his tunic.

"I thought you were dead. I thought Karbo…"

"I know," he keeps repeating. "I know." He rocks me and I continue to sob until in the end I have to pull away to wipe my nose inelegantly on my tunic.

"Is Karbo well?" he asks.

"He's asleep in Maria's apartment."

"He was very brave."

"I thank Neptune you taught him to swim."

"If I hadn't, he might not have risked his life trying to save me."

"Then you'd be dead."

He gives a half-snort of laughter, the sort of sound he used to make when Fausta amused him. "True. Just as well I taught him, then."

I rest my head against his chest and breathe in the smell of him, comforting and familiar. I relish the few words we have spoken, the quick banter in the face of fear that made us friends over these past two years, the certainty of the other person being in our lives. When my breathing slows, Marcus pushes me lightly away.

"You're falling asleep," he says. "Go and get in a proper bed."

"Promise you'll still be alive tomorrow," I say.

"I promise not to drown in my bed four storeys up in the air," he agrees.

I WAKE TO BRIGHT SUNLIGHT and when I squint to examine my sundial, it is halfway through the morning already, I haven't risen so late in years. Outside the bees hum about their business, calm and certain of their work, as ever.

"I've made fresh honey wine for this evening," says Adah. She's standing by one of the hives, one hand resting protectively on it. "You'll take a cup later, it will settle your nerves after the upset."

"I thought I was watching Marcus die," I say. "I thought Karbo would die too, that I would lose them both in one night."

She nods.

"I thought my world would end," I say.

"Marcus is well. I saw him this morning, he woke less than an hour ago, went to the baths. Said he needed a shave and a haircut, that he'd be back later today."

"I'll do the same," I say. "Karbo and I both need to get clean. I'm not sure I want to see a pool of water ever again, though."

"Wash the fear away," says Adah, turning to go back downstairs. "And I'll have that cup of honey wine waiting for you later today."

I STAND FOR A WHILE in the hot sun, eyes closed, face turned up to it, trying to let its bright heat take away the cold fear and dark of last night, the slithering creatures of the deep waters and the endless counting still echoing in my head. *Seventy-five... eighty-five... ninety-five... how long can a man not breathe and still live, how long, how long?*

"What time is it?" Karbo, arriving at the top of the stairs, yawning and squinting in the sun.

I grab hold of him and squeeze him to me.

"I was a hero," he says, his words muffled in my tunic. "Everyone said so. Marcus said so."

"You were."

He pulls away and looks at me, large eyes a little wary. "Aren't you going to tell me off?"

"It's not the right time for that."

"What time is it?"

"Time to get a stack of pancakes in you and go to the baths together," I say.

"Where's Marcus?"

"Already gone to the barber."

"I think I need four pancakes today," says Karbo, hopeful.

"Me too," I tell him, taking his hand in mine and leading him down the stairs. "Me too."

We wolf down almost nine pancakes between us, eating till we are heavy with date syrup and gulping down more than one cup of fresh grape juice, the sweetness upon sweetness bringing us back to life. We laugh together at a stray dog's pleading eyes, begging for our remaining pancake. We know full well it belongs to the local butcher and is hardly short of food, only as fond of pancakes as we are. Karbo feeds it the scraps bit by bit and strokes its fur with lovingly sticky fingers.

"Can I have a puppy?" he asks.

"Perhaps," I say. "But right now, you need a bath, not a pet."

We emerge hours later from the baths, my nails freshly stained orange, our skin glowing, my hair washed and his oiled. Once back in our hut, I dress him in clean clothes and have him put on his belt and boots, nod admiringly at him.

"You've grown this summer," I say. "That tunic used to go well below your knees, I know it did."

"I'll be taller than you, soon," he says proudly.

"You will."

"I'm hungry again."

"We'll be eating as soon as it's dusk, wait till then," I say. "Or you'll grow between now and tomorrow morning."

"Can I go and see Celer?"

"Before you go, I have something to tell you," I say.

"What?"

I take a deep breath. "I've made a deal with the stables."

"The stables?"

"The Blues, specifically."

"What about them?"

"You can work there, starting next month. One day a week, as a stable hand. They'll pay you."

Karbo's face lights up. "Thank you!" he bursts out, hugging me wildly.

"You'll be shovelling horse shit and polishing leather, not racing horses," I say. "Don't say I didn't warn you. It's not a glamorous job, you'll be begging me to get you out of the deal in a month."

"I'll be in the Blues stables," says Karbo, whirling round in glee and falling onto the bed. "I'll be the happiest boy in Rome."

"If horse shit makes you happy, then you most certainly will," I agree. I'm trying to sound stern, but his smile is too broad for me to do anything but smile back. "I'm glad you're happy," I finish, abandoning my attempts to dampen his enthusiasm. "You did seem to have a gift with the horses," I add.

"I love them," says Karbo, his voice almost serious. "I'll be the best stable hand there ever was and one day –"

"Yes, yes," I say hurriedly. "Never mind 'one day'. For now, you're a stable hand and we'll see what comes of it if you work hard and behave yourself. No-one is making any promises. I can only pray the gods look after you and keep you safe from harm."

"I will pray for their blessing and guidance," says Karbo, making pious eyes.

"That'll be a first," I say. "Go and tell Celer then, and say thank you. He put in a good word for you with the stable master."

Karbo scrambles over the bed and bolts for the stairs, leaving me to gaze at the bright chariot-racing scenes on our walls, hoping I've done the right thing.

I sit by the beehives for a while, where they cast a little shade.

"Here you are." Marcus is standing over me, freshly shaved and groomed.

"How are you feeling?"

"Oddly well. Perhaps I should spend more time getting half drowned."

"You've been gone all day."

"Gave thanks at a temple and went to the baths. And dropped by to see how the water was draining, it's all gone, those drains are pretty reliable. Place smells like a fish tank, though. I've asked Vita and Merula to tonight's celebrations before they run off making their own plans."

"Their own plans?"

"Vita wants to buy some of her girls out, go on a tour of the empire showing off their skills. They'll have a lot of demand."

"What's Merula got to do with it?"

"He's going to be part of the team, their own aquarius. As well as her husband, as soon as they can arrange the wedding."

"Husband?"

"You didn't know?"

"I knew he liked her. I thought she didn't care for him."

"She wanted to be his wife, not a slave girl for a bit of fun on the side."

"How do you know all this?"

"She told me. When we travelled down south."

"I thought you were…"

"What?"

"Showing her the family farm," I manage, looking away.

"Why would I want to do that?"

"That's not where you went?"

"I took her to meet the manager of the amphitheatre in Puteoli. He might do a naumachia with her as the star, in Lake Avernus. I vouched for her. I visited the farm on my own, though."

"How was it?" I ask, thinking back to the day I saw it, the sweet strawberry grapes we ate from the tumbled-down vine.

"As it was. A few more tiles have fallen off the roof." He shrugs.

"Do you want to go back there?" I ask, a little afraid of the answer.

"Not yet. I've barely had a moment to think, we seem to stumble from one problem to another. I'd like a couple of peaceful years, build up some money, know I've done all I can here. Though I might change my mind if Titus keeps insisting on sodding naumachiae."

"Did you go back to Pompeii?"

He shakes his head. "Didn't have the heart."

"I'm glad you're staying," I manage. "I…" my words trail off. "I don't feel I've seen much of you, this past year."

He laughs. "You miss me? Is that what you're saying?"

"Yes," I say.

He squats down so he's facing me directly, speaking more seriously. "I'm sorry. I should spend more time with you and Karbo. I'm your patron, I should be helping you both make your way in the world. Keep Karbo out of trouble at the stables for starters, when he's stopped being giddy with joy at the prospect of shovelling horse shit." He suddenly laughs. "And finish teaching you to swim properly. You never know when you might have to dive in and rescue me."

THE DAY TURNS TO DUSK, and I pull out my best clothes, free at last to wear them without Rullus' comments to frighten me, then go to help with the preparations for the evening celebration. Tables have been laid out, Julia has hung garlands of red and orange autumn flowers everywhere. I'm standing, admiring it all, when a little boy comes into the courtyard, carrying a bundle of brown cloth. I've not seen him before.

"I'm looking for Althea Aquillius," he says.

"That's me."

"I was told to give you this." He holds out the cloth.

I take it, let it unfold. It's my cloak, the one I sent to Alon. Something falls from it, clinks on the courtyard cobbles. I stoop and pick it up. It's a shard of old pottery. I turn it over. Scratched into it are two swooping lines, together making the simple outline of a fish.

"Who gave you this?"

"A man. He said to say thank you."

"Where was this man?"

"Near the gate to the Appian Way. He gave this to me and then climbed on a cart heading out of Rome."

I give the boy a sweet cake from the feast we're about to have and send him on his way. I put the cloak away in my hut, then consider the little terracotta fish lying in my hand. I could be angry, I suppose. Alon escaping put Marcus and Karbo in great danger. But then again it brought me closer to Marcus than I have felt this past year, it reminded him to spend more time with Karbo and me. And Alon struck me as a good man at heart, whatever his strange views on the gods. In the end, I lay the tiny shard on the rooftop wall looking out over the city. Perhaps a fish will summon rain, I think with a smile. And we could all do with the drought finally breaking.

CASSIA IS HARD AT WORK frying batches of her salted fish fritters. I sneak one from a dish and she slaps my hand.

"Out of my kitchen, you."

"I'm glad it is still *your* kitchen," I say, and she grins and waves me away.

Women from the different rooms and apartments of the insula make their way in and out of the courtyard with contributions to the meal, everything from roast pumpkin and mashed turnip fried with garlic to an aromatic herb salad served with hot freshly-made flat breads. The baker's wife hurries by with loaves of bread while her eldest daughter balances a vast basket of blackcurrant buns in one hand and a large sweet pastry overlaid with a plum preserve in the other. I help her lower both safely to the table and she follows her mother back to the bakery to fetch cheese pastries and sweet wine cakes, a staple at any celebration. I sent Karbo to fetch fruit earlier and now I arrange it on large platters: grapes, melons, early apples and pears, none of the dainty presentation of Titus' fare, but a bountiful and colourful harvest nonetheless.

Julia is standing at the entrance to her apartment. "We have been blessed," she says. "It has been a year of renewal after so many terrors." She looks me over. "And escapes from dark futures."

I nod. "It would be nice to have a peaceful year," I say.

"May the gods send us one," she agrees.

Cassia allows me to fetch and carry on the strict understanding that I'm not to help myself to any of the foods she is entrusting me with. I'm carrying a platter of venison to the table, one last meat-filled meal. We will have to rely on Cassius' smoked and salted meats over winter, but tonight we feast on the last fresh meat from this year's Games. When Karbo comes running into the courtyard and grabs at my arm, the platter rocks precariously.

"Hey!" I yelp. "You'll have this all over the courtyard!"

"Titus," he gasps.

I put the platter down on the nearest table. "What about him?" A horrible thought strikes me, and I look over my shoulder at the gateway Karbo's just pelted through. "He's not making a visit to us, is he?" That would be all I need, I think, an impromptu visit from Titus just when we were all looking forward to a relaxing evening.

"Dead," manages Karbo. He's holding his side and panting, there are beads of sweat on his face.

"Dead?" I stare at him. "What are you talking about, dead? I was just with him yesterday evening, he was fine. He's only forty-one. He went to his countryside estate for a holiday. How can he be dead?" My skin suddenly crawls. I drop my voice to a whisper. "Was he assassinated? Poisoned?"

Karbo is getting his breath back, shaking his head. "He was sick with a fever. He said his head hurt, he was clutching at it, they say. He only made it to the first staging post, he never reached the family estate."

Marcus is halfway down the wooden stairs. "What's going on?"

"Titus has died," I say.

"Titus?"

"The Emperor."

"Assassinated?"

It's worrying that both of us thought it. "Karbo says not. Sick. A fever."

Marcus' shoulders slump. "We could do without a new emperor," he says.

"Will it be Domitian?"

"I suppose so," says Marcus. "Better him than another civil war. I doubt he'll be as easy-going to serve as Titus though."

I nod, thinking of Domitian's narrow, sullen face, his stiff posture and lack of conversation. His wife Domitia, her hair arranged in impossibly stacked curls and the rest of her draped in the finest silks and jewels. She'll enjoy being Empress, I think.

THE COURTYARD IS ABUZZ WITH the news all evening. More dribs and drabs of information reach us, some of it very odd, such as Domitian immersing his dying brother in ice to make his fever abate, which may or may not be true. Titus' body is returned to Rome and some people head towards the Forum to see if they can watch the procession go by, but most of us stay put. The Games are over for another year, we can relax a little. There are toasts made and promises of sacrifices to various gods, hoping that they will bless us with peace and stability in the coming change.

Late at night news comes that Domitian left his dying brother's side, hurrying to the Praetorian Guard's barracks to ensure their loyalty, possibly with promises of payments. They in turn have sworn their allegiance to him, perhaps because there are no other firm favourites, perhaps swayed by his promises. Either way, their allegiance means that he will be Emperor, as we thought, but there's some tutting at the lack of brotherly love he displayed. There's a perfunctory toast to the new Emperor, more to show willing than anything else.

"What was the hurry?" asks Cassia. "Who else would have claimed the title?"

Her father shakes his head. "You're too young to remember how frightening the Year of Four Emperors was for all of us," he says. "You were only a child. But there could have been real trouble. Domitian will have known he needed to be declared Emperor quickly, before anyone else got any funny ideas about laying claim to the title. So be it. At least there will not be any civil war this time. He has a sturdy claim and he's made it swiftly. He doesn't seem such a bad man either."

"He has a surly face," says Cassia. "Looks like someone slapped him."

"I've heard nothing bad about him. No doubt he felt sidelined by his father and brother until now, perhaps being Emperor will put a smile on his face," says Cassius amiably.

"And on his wife's, she'll have fun being Empress," says Cassia. "I've never seen a woman who enjoys her status so much. Though her ornatrix will be hard-pressed to fit any more or higher curls on that head of hers. How many slaves' hair is she wearing, anyway?"

I giggle but it turns into a yawn against my will. "I need to sleep." I say. "We've finished the Games for the season, we have a new emperor. I'm going to sleep like the dead."

In the shadows of the courtyard, I catch a glimpse of Merula and Vita, standing very close together, her head tilted to one side as he speaks earnestly to her, before she turns back to him with a smile. Her hand reaches out to clasp his and he wraps one arm about her waist, pulling her close to him for a moment before they move further into the shadows, where I can no longer make them out.

"Who'd have thought it," murmurs Cassia, following my

gaze. "Him so shy and her so bold. I never thought he'd work up the courage to even speak to her."

"Perhaps they are learning from one another," I say.

"They certainly share an affinity for water. Their children will be part-fish."

"Here's to their future little fishes," I say, raising my cup.

"Little fishes," echoes Cassia.

"Why are we drinking toasts to fish?" asks Fabia, joining us. She's unsteady on her feet.

"You're not toasting anyone," I tell her. "You can't even walk straight."

"I'm celebrating my desire coming true," she says happily.

"I'm glad for you," I say. "What did you take to the sorceress?"

"My first wages from Labeo."

Cassia and I nod at the appropriateness of the payment.

"Time for bed, now," I say and the other two protest, but only weakly.

"You still have to find your desire," Cassia reminds me.

"Well, yours took a stick to come true and Fabia's took knives. Maybe I need a weapon of some sort. Enough of your nonsense. Goodnight."

"Goodnight," they chorus.

I start climbing the stairs but am waylaid by Adah, peeping out of her door along the walkway.

"I promised you honeyed wine. It's a good batch, the new honey is very sweet from the drought."

I don't really want to delay sleep any longer but I like to sit with Adah and so I follow her to her little room.

"You heard about Titus," I say.

She nods, murmurs something under her breath.

"You're glad he's dead," I say.

"The Almighty has punished him," she says. "He did not forget what Titus did to my people. He sent Vesuvius, the plague and the fire to Rome and now he has taken Titus." She passes me a cup of honeyed wine. "Did you hear what they found inside him?"

I take the cup, frowning. "Inside him?"

"There was an autopsy this afternoon, when they brought his body back to Rome. Inside his head they found a giant insect that had been growing in his brain ever since the Temple was destroyed at his hand."

I think of Titus clutching at his head and talking about trying to drown out sounds in his head with hammering and the roar of the crowd, his tears. "I haven't heard this anywhere else."

"It is not something the imperial family would like known. That their actions were punished by a greater deity than their own."

"How do you know about it then?"

"One of my people performed the autopsy."

"A Jew?"

She nods. "A doctor. The word spread quickly amongst us. We will be giving thanks for this sign of the Almighty's greatness."

I nod. Titus' death will give Adah and her people a sense of justice for his desecration of their holy place. But I will say a small prayer for Titus, for his kindness in allowing me to adopt Karbo and his unhappiness at not being allowed to keep Berenice by his side.

"Goodnight, Adah."

"Goodnight, child," she says.

When I reach my hut, I barely have the energy to undress, kicking at my sandals to get them off without having properly undone them, tugging at my headwrap and belt, both of which try to resist me. At last, I do as already-sleeping Karbo has done and lie down in just my tunic, pulling it up a little so my legs are mostly bare against the heat. I can hear rumbles of thunder somewhere in the distance, but I don't get excited about them. No doubt tomorrow will be just as dry and dusty as today and all this summer has been, though at least I can leave the door open to get any small breeze that might help cool the hot night. I murmur my prayer for Titus before my eyelids grow heavy, and I drift into sleep.

I WAKE AT DAWN, TO a soft pitter-pattering sound on the roof. I lie still, frowning, confused for a few moments, until I realise what the unusual sound is.

Rain.

It is raining.

The drought has finally broken.

I make my way to the door, which stands ajar, stubbing my toe on the threshold. I put out a hand to push the door and as I do so the pitter-patter turns to a heavy drumming, my arm already wet even with the door only half open. Rain. I step out into the downpour, uncaring that I am getting drenched. It is such a wonderful feeling to be rained on again, to feel the fresh cool water pouring out of the sky. I turn and walk barefoot through the rain to the very edge of the wall, looking out over Rome as the thunderous clouds split with flashes of lightning. I should be scared by it, but instead I feel elated. I catch one last sight of the tiny shard with the fish on it, just as the rain tips it over the edge of the wall, falling into the street below. The rain soaks my crumpled tunic to my body in moments and the cold chill is delightful. I peer down into Sand Street and see the dust dissolving, the dirt and grime of these past months being swept away down the street as tiny streams form, already running towards the Tiber. I find myself laughing out loud, delighted at the sight of them, then turn to go back indoors but stop abruptly.

Across the rooftop, his back to me, Marcus is standing outside his own hut, facing out across the city. He is naked. The rain pours down over his bare skin, his neck, arms and lower legs burnt brown by the sun, the rest of him untouched, pale golden. His head tips back. Face raised to the rain, he slowly stretches out his arms, palms up as though he were praying, revelling in the rain as I have been.

Standing in the rain, my hair and clothes dripping, I stare across the rooftop, my eyes drinking in the sight of him, from his broad shoulders down to the old scar that still marks his right leg. A flash of lightning flares out across the city and finally, finally, I know what will complete me, the name of my desire. My mouth opens without knowing and I allow my lips to speak its name, my voice lost in a boom of thunder.

"Marcus."

I hope you have enjoyed this story, the second book in the Colosseum series. If you have, I would really appreciate it if you would leave a rating or brief review, so that new readers can find *Beneath the Waves*. I read all reviews and am always grateful for your time in writing them and touched by your kind words.

WATER DRAINS INTO EARTH

Rome, 82AD. Domitian is the new Emperor. Below the arena floor a dark labyrinth is being built, the hypogeum of the Colosseum. Lit by burning torches, echoing with the roars of wild animals, this is a place for men, women and beasts with a taste for blood. A new beast-hunter with a secret past takes his place in the team. Will he make his way into Althea's heart before Marcus realises his own desires and takes action? Why are gladiators dying before they've even reached the arena? And can the new Emperor be trusted? Hearts beat faster as blood spills across the arena's sand.

AUTHOR'S NOTE ON HISTORY

THIS IS THE SECOND BOOK in a series that started as the simple question I asked myself: who were the people who made up the 'backstage team' for the Colosseum? There is hardly any mention whatsoever of them and yet Games on such an immense scale could not possibly have been put on without a very large and permanent team in place.

Beneath the Waves focuses on water, from naumachiae to the baths, aqueducts and running water of Rome, to hot springs and the early symbol of Christianity, the fish. The other three books in this series focus on the same team through the themes of fire (*From the Ashes*), earth (*On Bloodied Ground*) and air (*The Flight of Birds*).

From varied sources, it seems that the Colosseum hosted at least two naumachiae but possibly no more, before the building of a brick maze-like hypogeum beneath the arena floor which did not allow for any more flooding. It is possible that the second naumachia was during Domitian's time, but I have kept both events in Titus' time, mainly because the hypogeum and other related building projects were very much Domitian's.

The decoration of Cassia's popina is a direct copy of a beautiful recent find in Pompeii, I have posted a CGI video restoration on my Facebook author page. It is exactly how I imagine my fictional popina, right down to it being placed on the corner of a building for best customer footfall.

One of the only direct historical references to the backstage work that would have gone into creating Games at the Colosseum is the epigram I have quoted by Martial, in which the poet marvels at the show-swimmers taking part in the naumachiae put on in the amphitheatre, asking whether they learned their skills from the sea-nymph Thetis, or she learnt her own skills from them.

The Romans were capable of amputation and there is also evidence of prosthetics, from an Egyptian big toe 3000 years ago (so that the person could continue to wear thonged sandals) to General Marcus Sergius Silus, who had an iron hand fitted after amputation so he could hold a shield with his right hand and switched his sword to his left hand, continuing to fight and win many battles in the Punic Wars (264 to 146 BC).

There is no clear evidence of what caused Titus' death, which was officially blamed on a fever (possibly malignant malaria). There were various rumours. One was that Domitian poisoned him, which is unlikely, although he did not show a lot of brotherly concern for Titus' wellbeing, instead focusing on staking his own claim as Emperor. Jewish tradition claims that having been punished throughout his reign (with the eruption of Vesuvius followed by a 'pestilence' and a three-day fire in Rome) for destroying the Temple of Jerusalem, Titus was then killed by a gnat going up his nose by the Almighty's command and causing a growth in his brain, found during an autopsy. According to historians Dio and Suetonius, he did seem to suffer from sadness (including the recorded public weeping at the closing Games) and did not do a lot of work just before he died, so it is possible that he had a brain tumour. Apparently, his last words were that he had made only one mistake, although no-one knows what this was in reference to, possibly in relation to allowing his brother to plot to take over as the emperor.

The Kingdom of Kush was located in modern Northern Sudan and Southern Egypt.

Professor Crapper of Northumbria University wrote a very helpful article, titled 'How Roman engineers could have flooded the Colosseum,' while a 2015 NOVA production with Adriano Morabito (Director of Subterranean Rome) looked at naumachiae and how ships (of ten to fifteen metres long) could have been brought into the Colosseum from side passages pre-filled with water. Both sources considered many solutions for filling and draining the Colosseum, most of which my aquarius Merula runs through and which I have drawn on. The idea of putting pitch on the existing wooden arena floor, as the team choose to try for the first, shallow, naumachia, is mine.

The average person, without training, can hold their breath underwater for thirty to ninety seconds (the Romans did not measure time in seconds). Many of the specific Games I have written about actually happened. Those that I have invented were based on very similar approaches, such as the regular re-enacting of myths and legends of the Greeks and Romans. The poet Martial marvelled at horses and bulls behaving as normal in the water.

GLOSSARY

Aedile   A senator in charge of commissioning the gladiatorial games.

Bestiarius   Gladiator specialising in fighting animals (plural bestiarii).

Bulla   Protective amulet worn by boys. Girls wore an equivalent pendant in the form of a crescent moon.

Cithara   Roman precursor to the guitar.

Cosmetes   Beautician (plural cosmetae).

Domina   Mistress.

Dominus   Master.

Fullery   A laundry which washed, dried and also dyed garments. Human urine (collected on street corners) was used as a cleaning and bleaching aid.

Futuo   Swear word: fuck.

Garum   Fish sauce, a very popular condiment.

**Imperial
Palace**   The place indicated on the map is an approximate location of Nero's Golden House (which Titus might have continued to use for official receptions) and also, later, the building started by Domitian at the beginning of his reign and completed in 92AD. There were additional locations, both official and residential, where the emperors would have been located in Rome.

Insula   Block of apartments/individual rooms, often built around a central courtyard.

Lararium   Household shrine.

Naumachia   Water-based spectacle often featuring re-enactments of sea-battles, held on lakes or in flooded man-made structures such as the Colosseum.

Nereids   Sea-nymphs (goddesses of the sea).

Ornatrix   Hairdresser.

Palantine   One of the hills of Rome, used by many as an expression to suggest the Emperor's residence.

Palla   A large rectangular outer garment of wool or linen, worn predominantly by married women, draped around the whole body, a fold of which could be placed over the head for protection and as a sign of propriety.

Popina   Streetside café (most poor Romans did not have cooking facilities, so street food outlets were very common and popular).

Tablet   A wooden 'book' of two or three 'pages', filled with wax, on which notes could be made using a metal pen called a stylus, then erased when no longer required. More formal, permanent writing could be done with ink and a reed/quill pen onto scrolls of papyrus.

Tullianum   One of the very few prisons in Rome, used for high status prisoners or those to be made an example of, as prison sentences were not used as punishment, only as brief holding places.

Venator   Performer who hunted animals for the morning hunt (technically not gladiators as it was hunting, not combat).

THANKS

T HANK YOU TO STREETLIGHT GRAPHICS, I'm always grateful to have you with me on my writing journey.

Thank you to my beta readers for this book: Helen, Etain, Martin. Your comments and ideas are always insightful.

Thank you to my editor Debi Alper for improving my craft as well as giving my characters a harder time (and the readers a better story!).

Thank you to Matt Whelan for joining me at the proofing stage, glad to have had the loan of your eyes!

Many scholars and historians were very helpful during my research. My thanks for all their fascinating work and especially to my historical consultant for this series, Steven Cockings. I am so very grateful for your extensive knowledge and lived experience. You educate me every day with your photos and commentaries from your events and explorations of Rome, as well as the great care you put into checking my manuscripts.

Professor Donald G Kyle's considerable body of work on Roman spectacles and especially on the disposal of bodies (human and animal) from the arena, was invaluable. Professor Christopher Ellett very helpfully provided me with his work on beast-hunts and executions. Professor Kathleen Coleman of Harvard University helped me to access her research on gladiators and naval shows. Fik Meijer has written a wonderfully vivid book on chariot racing.

All errors and fictional choices are of course mine.

CURRENT AND FORTHCOMING BOOKS INCLUDE:

Historical Fiction
China
The Consorts (novella, free on Amazon)
The Fragrant Concubine
The Garden of Perfect Brightness
The Cold Palace

Morocco
The Cup (novella, free on my website)
A String of Silver Beads
None Such as She
Do Not Awaken Love

Rome
From the Ashes
Beneath the Waves
On Bloodied Ground
The Flight of Birds

Picture Books for Children
Kameko and the Monkey-King

Non-Fiction
The Storytelling Entrepreneur
Merchandise for Authors
The Happy Commuter
100 Things to Do while Breastfeeding

BIOGRAPHY

I MAINLY WRITE HISTORICAL FICTION AND have completed two series: The Moroccan Empire, set in 11th century Morocco and Spain, and The Forbidden City, set in 18th century China. My current series focuses on the 'backstage team' of the Colosseum (Flavian Amphitheatre) beginning in 80AD in Ancient Rome. For more information on me and my books, visit my website www.melissaaddey.com

I was the 2016 Leverhulme Trust Writer in Residence at the British Library and won the 2019 Novel London and Page to Podcast awards. I have a PhD in Creative Writing from the University of Surrey. I run regular workshops at the British Library and speak at various writing festivals during the year. I live in London with my husband and two children.